The Wedding Diary

The Wedding Diary

Margaret James

Published 2013 by Choc Lit Limited
Penrose House, Crawley Drive, Camberley, Surrey GU15 2AB, UK
www.choclitpublishing.com

A CIP catalogue record for this book is available
from the British Library

ISBN 978-1-78189-016-5

Printed and bound by CPI Group (UK) Ltd, Croydon, CR0 4YY

Acknowledgements

Thank you to everyone at Choc Lit for your hard work on this novel.

Thank you also to Exeter Writers for coming up with the workshop which inspired this story, to all the people in my family who have – as always – been totally supportive and encouraging, to Trisha Ashley for suggesting I should try something new, to Lulu Di Minto for allowing me to use her name, and to First Great Western, Arriva and Virgin, on whose trains I wrote a great deal of this novel and still spend so much of my life.

Saturday, 23 April

Where's the silver lining?

All chocolate is medicinal. It's a well known fact. When taken in sufficient quantities, it mends a broken heart.

As Cat lay on the sofa she and Jack had bought together – she'd chosen it, of course, while he had stood there looking bored and saying yeah, whatever – eating her way through a big block of highest-possible cocoa content, premium-grade dark chocolate, she thought, whatever happened? How did I end up like this, alone on Easter Saturday and wondering if I should get a dog?

Why does the man I love behave so badly? Or do I have something wrong with me and could I get it fixed? Do I need some therapy? Do I need to get my aura sorted?

Then the landline rang.

Maybe it was Tess? Perhaps she didn't have a date tonight and maybe she and Bex were coming round with bottles of something alcoholic and a giant pizza?

Or had Tess mentioned going to a gig?

She could have changed her mind.

Or maybe, maybe Jack—

'Hello?' she said and crossed her fingers.

'Good evening!' chirped a woman. 'May I speak to Catherine Aston, please?'

'You're speaking to her now,' said Cat. But then of course she wished she hadn't, and braced herself for the inevitable. Did she want home/contents/motor/travel/pet insurance, faster broadband, double glazing, a timeshare in Barbados, a new conservatory?

'Your mobile isn't on,' said Chirpy Woman.

'Oh, isn't it?' Cat rummaged through the rubbish at the

bottom of her bag, found her BlackBerry and saw that it was dead. 'You're right,' she said. 'I'm sorry, do I know you?'

'We haven't met, Miss Aston,' admitted Chirpy Woman. 'But I hope we will, and very soon!'

Then Chirpy Woman switched to alien-life-form-trapped-inside-a-GPS-receiver mode. 'I am delighted to announce that you, Miss Catherine Aston, are the lucky winner of the glittering first prize in our exciting national competition. You have won a luxury wedding package for up to fifty guests at the prestigious Melbury Court Hotel. You and your fiancé have been chosen from among six thousand other couples to receive—'

This is surreal, thought Cat, as Chirpy Woman burbled on. This is like the opening of a movie starring Jennifer Aniston or Sarah Whatsit Parker. This isn't like my life.

'So,' continued Chirpy Woman, segueing into human mode again, 'you have a choice of almost any date between October and next March, except for Christmas Day and Boxing Day and New Year's Eve. Well, Catherine – may I call you Catherine? – what do you think of that?'

'No one calls me Catherine. I'm always known as Cat. I don't know what I think.'

'You're probably in shock. So why don't you and Jack – it is Jack, isn't it? I don't have your entry form in front of me right now – snuggle up together and have a little private celebration. Next week, you'll be getting the official confirmation in the post. We'll send you all the brochures, menus, DVDs of wedding packages and of actual weddings at the gorgeous Melbury Court Hotel – everything you'll need to know, in fact.'

'I see.'

Although Cat could just about remember filling in the entry form in *Bridal* magazine, bought so she and Tess and Bex could have a lunchtime drool over wedding gowns and wedding favours, over wedding flowers and wedding venues, and although she vaguely recollected writing fifty words about what made a perfect wedding and sending off some photographs of herself and Jack, she was certain this must be a wind-up.

Someone must have got her details from her Facebook page, found her landline number and be having a laugh at her expense. It was – what – half past eight on Saturday night? Only mates and mothers rang up on Saturday night.

'You do wish to accept the prize?' demanded Chirpy Woman just a little bit impatiently.

'I–'

'Well, of course you do, my sweet, provided nothing's changed? Oh, don't worry, angel, that was just my little joke. Later on this month, or maybe next, when you and Jack have read the brochures and had a little think, we'll be setting up a formal meeting and a photo opportunity.'

'A photo opportunity?' repeated Cat. This is all ridiculous, she thought. Why don't I hang up now?

'Yes, we'll want lots of pix of you and Jack,' said Chirpy Woman. 'Larking around and having fun, but also being serious and soulful. Gazing adoringly into each other's eyes and looking like you're blissfully in love. We'll need a lot of that.'

'Oh – right.'

'We'll have you indoors, outdoors, formal poses, casual stuff, him kissing you, perhaps you tickling him. You know the sort of thing? We're hoping we can get you in *Hello*. We loved the shots you sent us. They were fabulous. Everyone at Supadoop Promotions is really looking forward to meeting you and your delicious Jack.'

Jack, reflected Cat.

As Chirpy Woman talked about receptions, bridesmaids, flowers and wedding gowns, she thought – meeting Jack is going to be a problem.

Last month, Jack had gone to find himself. Since then, she hadn't heard from him, his phone was never on, and there'd been no activity on Facebook or on Twitter.

He had disappeared, disapparated like flipping Harry Potter, he'd dematerialised. He'd also stabbed and slashed and shredded the canvas of her life so it was all in tatters and could never be repaired.

She was assuming he'd be doing stuff in various pubs and clubs. Open mic and stand-up, he'd be hoping for a break, that he'd be talent-scouted and on his way to stardom at long last.

Or perhaps he'd joined the Foreign Legion or the SAS?

She couldn't ask his family. Jack didn't have a family – not a single brother, sister, maiden aunt in Macclesfield or cousin in Australia. There was nobody at all. Or that was what he'd said.

As for his friends, Jack's friends were all like him.

They came, they borrowed tenners, ate the contents of your fridge, left empty beer cans in your kitchen and curry cartons underneath your sofa, then they went. No one ever heard of them again, and—

'Cat, are you still there?' demanded Chirpy Woman. She sounded somewhat irritable now. 'I said we're looking forward to meeting you and Jack. I'll be in touch. So don't forget to charge your phone.'

'Yes, of course,' said Cat. She was about to add *but there's a little problem and who are you, anyway, you didn't give your name* when she realised she was listening to the dialling tone.

Adam Lawley took one long step back and then threw overarm with all his might.

There was too much background noise of traffic, not to mention the ceaseless hum of London, for him to hear the splash, although he knew it must have hit the water. So now it was at the bottom of the Thames. This wasn't entirely good because it wasn't paid for yet.

But he still felt better – just a bit.

He sat down in the middle of a bench, loosened his tie and undid the top button of his shirt. He stared across the river, wondering how long it took to drown. People said that drowning in cold water was a peaceful death. But how did they know?

They hadn't tried it, had they?

If he did decide to drown himself, maybe he should find a more salubrious place to do it than the Thames at Millbank? It wouldn't be poetic or romantic, would it, being fished from the water with a condom in his mouth?

'You can't sit there,' said someone in a smoker's rasping growl.

'Why not?' demanded Adam, still staring straight ahead.

'S'my bench, that's why not.'

Adam glanced round and saw a stooped old man, laden down with splitting carrier bags and grubby holdalls. The brindled dog that stood beside him was looking very narked to find a stranger on his patch.

'Sorry, mate,' said Adam, standing up.

'S'all right, no harm done. You can sit at the end there, if you like.' The man sat down himself and started sorting through a very tattered plastic bag, pulling out old newspapers and bits of grubby blanket. 'You got the money for a cup of something?' he enquired. 'Some change to buy some biscuits for the dog?'

Adam shoved one hand into a trouser pocket, pulled out everything he found there. 'Here,' he said and pushed a crumpled mess of screwed-up paper at the man.

'You sure, mate?' said the tramp. He stared down at the money in astonishment. 'I mean, there must be fifty quid 'ere. No, I tell a lie, there's more'n fifty, there's seventy, eighty, ninety—'

'You're welcome to it. Go and have lunch at Claridge's, why don't you? Get some Harrods biscuits for your dog?'

'What?'

'You heard.'

'Aha, I know what's goin' on.' The man eyed Adam shrewdly. 'You've just 'ad a bust-up with some lady.'

'Yeah?'

'I'd stake my life on it. Listen to me, son – you're not yourself tonight. But you'll be better in the morning. So I'll take twenty, get meself and Taser here some grub, an' thank you, you're a gentleman.'

'I told you, keep it,' Adam said.

'All right, but let me give you some advice.'

'What's that?'

'When you're dealin' with the ladies, don't make no assumptions, an' don't think you understand 'em. If you're a normal, ordinary bloke, you don't – you never will, an' that's a fact. You 'ave a bust-up with a lady, you need to give her time, and she'll come round. That's all they need, a bit of time.'

'Oh,' said Adam.

Thanks for nothing, he thought bitterly as he walked off down Millbank.

It must have been an hour, two hours – he wasn't counting – since the killer punch had landed. But he still had the feeling he'd just done ten rounds with … he didn't follow boxing, but with some big geezer who had really hammered him.

He'd planned the evening with such care, right down to the last detail, starting with the play.

Maddy had wanted to see the play for ages, so she'd said, because it was significant and important. So he had got them tickets in the stalls, and booked the biodynamic fusion vegetarian restaurant for after they came out.

She'd been looking ravishing tonight, in a pale green skirt he didn't think he'd seen before, golden high-heeled sandals and a flowery top with pretty ruffles round the neck.

He could have sat and gazed at her all night. He didn't need a play.

But he'd got a play, and very tedious it had been, full of earnest stuff about the need to save the rainforests, the tigers and the pandas, and to recycle all the earth's resources.

Adam understood that this was vital in itself. But it was not exactly gripping when two actors dressed in black were standing on a stage accusing him of crimes and misdemeanours.

Or so it had seemed.

He'd never shot a tiger or moved on any pandas to make way for a factory or motorway and knew he never would. He recycled everything – he sorted paper, cardboard, bottles, plastic, cans and put them in the big green boxes in the local Tesco car park – bought most of his Christmas presents from fund-raising catalogues supporting various charities, wasn't into gadgets made in China, and his mobile phone was coming up to four years old. A mugger with any self-respect would throw it back at him.

In the interval, they'd had a drink. Then, when the bell had rung to warn the audience to go back to their seats, Maddy had walked the fingers of one hand along his arm, her perfume had caressed him and her lips had brushed his face.

'I tell you what,' she'd whispered, 'why don't we give the rest of this a miss and get a taxi back to yours? Then we can go to bed.'

'Give me a moment, sweetheart.'

He'd taken out the little purple velvet box which contained the gorgeous antique ring and put it on the table in the now-empty bar.

'Maddy,' he had said, 'my dearest, darling Maddy, will you marry me?'

'You what?' She'd stared for ten, for twenty seconds and then she'd burst out laughing. 'Oh, don't be ridiculous.'

'I'm serious, Mads!' he'd cried.

'You can't be.' She had grimaced then. 'What is this, some stupid joke?'

'No, it's absolutely not a joke! I—'

'Omigod, don't tell me! There's a single perfect rose stuffed up your trouser leg and that's why you've been fidgeting all evening? You're going to pull it out when I say yes?'

'So is it yes?' Adam was painfully aware the barman had stopped polishing a glass. In fact, it seemed the whole world held its breath.

'Of course it isn't yes,' Maddy had snapped. 'You know I'll soon be going to Uruguay.'

'But you'll be coming back.'

'No, Adam, I might not. I might find I like it there, that I can do some good and I can help with some campaigns. The indigenous people there, you know, they need support from activists in the developed world.'

She had fiddled with her empty glass. She wouldn't look at him. 'Anyway,' she'd added, 'we hardly know each other.'

'We've been going out for months! We've been on holiday together. Maddy, we've had sex—'

'Adam, this is not the Middle Ages. It's what normal people do.'

'But I thought you liked me?'

'Yes, of course I like you! I think you're very sweet and I don't deny you're great in bed. But that doesn't mean I want to marry you, do all that boring, cosy couples stuff. You'll be saying you want to look at horrid little starter homes and put down a deposit on one next.'

Then she'd picked up her bag, a woven raffia folk art

thing she'd bought for almost nothing from some poor desperate trader at a local Sunday market. 'This is getting difficult,' she'd muttered. 'I think I'd better leave.'

'No, hang on, Maddy,' he had pleaded as the barman stared. 'I shouldn't have sprung it on you. I should have— Maddy, wait!'

But she hadn't waited and, as she'd walked through the door, the barman suddenly started polishing hard and whistling something and gazing at the cherubs on the ceiling, at anything but him.

This was not surprising, Adam thought, since he'd just made the most pathetic, stupid exhibition of himself.

What should he do now?

Go home to the first floor flat above the jeweller's shop in Camden Town, the place he shared with Jules and Gwennie, who would be agog to know how things had gone tonight?

They would be dying to open the champagne. They'd already told him Maddy could move in, it would be fine, until she and Adam found a place.

After all, she practically lived there, anyway.

It seemed she didn't live there any more.

He walked all night, head down, along Whitehall, along the Strand, into the City which smelled of deals and money even in the small hours, round and round the Barbican. Then he strode down Aldersgate and, as the dawn was breaking, he finally ended up outside St Paul's.

He stared up at the round, white dome, ethereal in the early morning light. It seemed to be inviting him to make some kind of gesture, but he didn't know what.

Then, as he stood there looking at this huge extravagance of a cathedral, the wedding cake to end all wedding cakes, he made a solemn vow.

I shall never fall in love again.

Must life go on?

It had to be Tuesday morning now.

Or Cat supposed it must be Tuesday, because her diary said so, and it must be morning, although she wasn't absolutely sure. Since Jack had gone the days and nights had blurred into a never-ending twilight of misery and despair and everything was permanently grey.

But, if it was Tuesday, she ought to go to work. She had the payments on the sofa to keep up, the rent to pay, she had to eat from time to time and so she couldn't afford to lose her job.

She got up, had a shower, drank a mug of instant coffee, dressed in she-was-not-sure-what and took herself to work in Walthamstow.

Look straight ahead, she told herself as she walked along familiar streets – no glancing right or left in case the hounds of melancholy see you, get you, drag you down into the pit of hell.

Just as she had done since Jack had left.

Since Jack had said that, 'Actually, Cat'—who actually said *actually* these days? Why did Jack say *actually*? Who was he trying to sound like?—'Actually, Cat, this being engaged, this buying sofas, this looking at matching towels and tablecloths and duvets stuff, I'm not sure if we should be doing it.'

Of course it wasn't down to Cat, he'd added graciously. She had done nothing wrong. She was sweet and beautiful and lovely. But just recently he'd come to realise that he wasn't ready to get married, settle down. He needed to put things on hold a while, sort himself out.

But could they see each other in the meantime, meet up for a drink or something, could they still be friends?

She supposed he meant that when he wanted it, could he still come and get it?

No, she'd thought, he couldn't – *actually*.

But when she didn't hear from him at all, she started feeling she'd give anything, do anything, to see his face again.

'Good afternoon,' said Tess.

Cat was a couple of minutes late and Tess was already in the office at Chapman's Architectural Salvage, feet up on the desk and flicking through *heat* magazine. 'Good Easter? Get some eggs? You went to see your parents, didn't you?'

'No, I stayed in Leyton.'

'Oh, honey pie!' cried Tess. 'You were all by yourself? I thought you were going home to Sussex – isn't that what you said?'

'I thought about it, yes,' admitted Cat. 'But if I had gone home, my mother would have realised straight away that everything was wrong. I could have told her Jack was working and we were doing fine. But she's got this spooky way of knowing when I'm lying. I didn't want Mum droning on and sobbing over me and my father saying Jack was obviously a scoundrel – yes, my dad still uses words like scoundrel – and if he were twenty-five again …'

'I suppose not.' Tess put down her magazine. 'But you could have texted me, you saddo. We could have had a takeaway and watched some DVDs. Do you know your top's on inside out, or is this a hot new fashion trend of which I'm tragically unaware?'

'Did you and Bex go to that gig?' asked Cat, pulling off her top and turning it the right side out and thinking it was time she learned to dress herself again.

She wasn't six years old.

'Yes, but if you'd called me you could have come as well,' said Tess. 'Or we would have settled for a girls' night in with you. So anyway, coming out with us this evening?'

'Why, where are you going?'

'This place in Dagenham Bex's brother goes. They've got a sixties night. It's miniskirts, white lipstick, Dusty Springfield eyelashes – that means seriously gunked-up, in case you didn't know – and diamond-patterned tights.'

'Getting off with John Travoltalikes?'

'I wouldn't rule it out.'

'Sorry, I'm not interested,' said Cat.

'Oh, go on, come out with us!' begged Tess. 'You can't stay in forever and cry all by yourself. It's been God knows how long, I've lost count. He hasn't called, he hasn't e-mailed, he hasn't even texted. You have to face it some time, girl – Jack Benson was bad news.'

'Speaking of news, I have something to tell you.'

By the time Cat had finished telling Tess about the wedding competition, Tess's eyes were bigger than her face.

'You've won?' she kept repeating, obviously unable to believe what Cat had said. 'You've won this fabulous dream wedding – ceremony, reception, all the trimmings?'

'Yes, that's what the woman told me.'

'So – confetti, wedding invitations, limousines, expensive little chocolates in pretty silver boxes, magnums of champagne and Pimms and posh designer nibbles, they're all in? This company, they'll do the wedmin, organise the wedsite, advise you on the wediquette, get you and the bridesmaids to the tanning salon, pay for all the nail art? They'll commission special wedding cupcakes, sort out readings, get some swish couturier to make your wedding gown?'

'So it would seem.'

'What are you going to do, then?'

'You mean about the prize?'

'No, about the getting married, dope.'

'I'm not getting married.'

'Of course you're getting married! Look, you've got a – what's it worth? What does a wedding in a country house hotel cost nowadays? It must be twenty thousand at the very least. Or maybe even thirty. This Melbury Court Hotel, where is it?'

'Dorset,' Cat replied.

'Brilliant, you've got yourself a bridesmaid.'

'You've forgotten something.'

'Yeah, I know. You need a man. So find one.'

'Where do you suggest I start to look?'

'Oh, they're everywhere. You must have noticed them. They come in various shapes and sizes. But if I were you I'd go for tall and dark and handsome, maybe thirty, thirty-five.'

'Tess, this isn't funny—'

'They sometimes smell disgusting. You should avoid the ones who smell disgusting. Or I would, anyway. Honey, it's not going to be a problem. All he'll have to do is hire a suit and find the place and wait until the evening to get drunk.'

'Tess, stop mocking me.'

'I'm not mocking you.' Tess looked earnestly at Cat. 'You've got the wedding sorted, haven't you? So all you need to do is sort the bridegroom. You're young, you're pretty and you're solvent, so how hard will it be?'

'I'm not over Jack.'

'You ought to be,' said Tess. 'I've told you fifty, sixty, seventy times, that scumbag isn't worth your tears.'

'I wish it was that simple.' Cat looked miserably at Tess. 'I know Jack's vain and sometimes selfish. But I love him, and you can't control these things. We don't choose who we love.'

'This isn't about love,' retorted Tess.

'Oh, isn't it?'

'Of course it's not!' Tess grinned. 'This is about a sumptuous dream wedding we'll talk about for years!'

'But, Tess, I don't—'

'I tell you what,' continued Tess as she fizzed and buzzed and sparkled with extreme excitement and googled frantically. 'We'll do some wedding fairs. See what's on offer. Okay, here's a nice big wedsite, so let's have a look. Do you fancy being a demure Victorian bride? Or a saucy, sassy rock 'n' roll one? Or perhaps a mediaeval princess, Disney style?'

'None of those,' said Cat.

'What about a fifties bride in paper nylon petticoats and sticky-out full skirts and beehive hair? Or is beehive hair a sixties look? I think it might be early sixties. I'll have to ask my mother. Or my granny, she'll remember. What about burlesque? I think you'd look great in black and red and corsets and suspenders.'

'I'm not doing wedding fairs.'

'Oh, go on – why not?'

'I just don't fancy it.'

'You've only got one life, you know,' said Tess. 'So you're coming out with us this evening.'

'No I'm not.'

'You want to bet?'

'I'm not going to talk about it, right?'

'You will, you know,' said Tess. 'When you get the brochures and the DVDs and stuff, you won't be able to resist.'

'We'll see.' Cat looked up from her keyboard. 'I just heard Barry pulling up. So we'd better get on with some work.'

Thursday, 28 April

On the road to nowhere?

Adam didn't want to talk about it.

Gwennie and Jules were being so kind, so nice, so understanding – so bloody damn considerate. So fucking well annoying, tiptoeing around him, never touching, never snogging in the kitchen, never holding hands while they were watching *Notting Hill* or bloody *Brief Encounter* for the ten zillionth time.

It was like someone had died.

Somebody had, of course, and what was walking round the place these days pretending to be Adam was a zombie, just a shell. But he didn't want an autopsy. He didn't want a wake.

'Gwennie, love, I'm fine,' he said that evening, when she offered to make his supper yet again, and he said again he wasn't hungry.

But Gwennie wasn't having it. Steak and kidney pie or egg and chips, she said – he needed comfort food. She'd just been to Sainsbury's. It wouldn't take a moment. 'Adam, you need building up,' she added. 'You've always been too thin. Or maybe that's because you're half the size of Jules and maybe you're just right? But anyway, a bacon sandwich – I dare say you could fancy one of those?'

'I've eaten,' he insisted, as Gwennie crashed and clattered round the kitchen, getting out the frying pan and turning on the oven to cook healthier-option chips. 'I stopped at Burger King on the way home.'

'Yeah, I bet,' said Gwennie, eyeing him suspiciously. 'Okay, which Burger King?'

'It – it was the one in Portland Place.'

'What were you doing in Portland Place?'

'I—'

'Adam, there's no Burger King in Portland Place, and I've never known you to eat a burger, anyway.' Gwennie pursed her lips. 'Your face looks awful nowadays. You're all gaunt and hollow eyed and even Jules has noticed, so it must be bad. I'll make you eggy bread.'

'No thank you, Gwennie.'

'Make some for me?' called Jules, who was lolling on the sofa, watching television while he read the *Evening Standard*.

'You greedy pig, you've had your supper!'

'Go on, lovely woman,' wheedled Jules. 'I'll make it worth your while.'

'Yeah, right,' said Gwennie, but she laughed, then started cracking eggs into a bowl.

Why couldn't I fall in love with somebody like Gwennie? Adam thought as Gwennie shuffled round the kitchen in her Garfield slippers, opening the cupboards and getting out the plates and cutlery – with someone warm and generous, with someone nice and kind, with someone who would care for me and love me?

Oh, for God's sake, shut up, you maudlin bastard, Adam told himself.

As Gwennie made them all some eggy bread, Adam sat down at the kitchen table. He fired up his laptop and started looking through the plans and drawings for his next few projects. These included one in Aberdeenshire which he hoped would make his name and which would occupy his mind and body for months or even years, and maybe this was just as well?

If he kept busy, it might stop him going mad.

Monday, 2 May

How do you mend a broken heart?

A week after she'd disappeared into the April night, Maddy sent a text to say she would be round on Monday morning. She still had a key, so she would collect her stuff while Adam was at work.

It would be better that way.

When he'd got home that evening, it was clear that she had been and gone. She'd done a thorough job. She must have hired a lorry. Or got Daddy to come and help her out.

Maddy and her daddy, who was something big in finance – Adam had never met the guy, so didn't really know, perhaps he was a gangster or a banker or maybe he was both, there didn't seem to be a lot of difference nowadays – were very, very close.

So close, in fact, that Daddy's girl had never had to have a job. She was a free spirit and a champion of the poor and the oppressed. She was into anything and everything to do with saving Amazonian tribes, endangered Madagascan lemurs, orang-utans, white rhinoceroses, humpback whales. She went to every festival and joined in every ecological protest she could find.

Meeting her at Glastonbury last summer – Gwennie and Jules had nagged and bossed him into going to the country's longest-running, biggest music festival, saying he was getting middle-aged before his time and needed to chill out – Adam had been hypnotised by the golden vision that was Maddy.

He'd spent the weekend in a happy daze and Jules had said he was a head case. A bird was just a bird, Jules had insisted, whichever way you looked at it, and this one talked a load of pseudo-scientific, complimentary-therapeutic eco-toss.

But Adam hadn't cared. He hadn't risen or responded to his best friend's jeers and mockery because he'd known that this was what he wanted, what he had been seeking all his life.

He was in love.

Now, looking round his room, he could not see anything of Maddy's. No books, no magazines, no clothes, no shoes, no make-up. None of the clutter she usually left lying around.

She'd put her door key on the windowsill.

She definitely wasn't coming back.

He knew he should be glad, that this meant he could start again, that he could delete her from the hard drive of his mind, empty the recycle bin and tell himself she'd been an apparition, just a dream.

The disloyal thought that Maddy was indeed an eco-tosser, rather than an eco-warrior, crossed his mind again. She liked the thought of saving tribes and pandas, certainly. But could she do without her styling products, without a fix of Topshop or Miss Selfridge once or even several times a week?

He went to have a shower, and that was when he saw it, lying on the bathroom floor. A fat, pink Velcro roller, the sort she'd used to give her hair some bounce.

He stooped to pick it up.

The scent of her was subtle, but definitely there, and some strands of dark brown hair were caught on the pink web.

He'd thought he might be getting over it – that it wouldn't go on hurting, stabbing him forever, that he would be able to convince himself that Maddy was a lazy, selfish hypocrite.

But talking to himself made no damn difference.

As he held the roller, something twisted deep inside him and made him wince in pain. Something broke, and he was almost sure it was his heart.

Let me guess, your real name's Prince Charming?

'Excuse me?' said the man.

Tess had gone to source some Georgian glass, so Cat was in the office on her own, catching up on paperwork and setting up a complicated spreadsheet, when the customer came in.

While she was at work and chasing stock or updating accounts or sorting out the payroll, she found she could forget about the wedding competition. She could forget that Jack had disappeared. Or almost forget – she could blank it from her mind for half an hour or so, before the misery came flooding back.

'Excuse me,' said the man again, and she could hear he sounded well hacked off.

'Give me just one moment, please?' She keyed in three more entries, saved the data and then looked up at him. 'I'm sorry to have kept you waiting,' she continued. 'I was in the middle of doing something and I didn't want to stop.'

'So I see.' The man shook his wet hair and Cat was suddenly reminded of a collie which had been out in the rain. 'Only it says Reception on the door,' he went on crossly. 'So I assume you must be the receptionist? But if it's too much trouble to talk to a prospective customer …'

'It's no trouble,' Cat replied, in the soothing, dealing-with-a-sarcastic-bastard voice she always used for awkward visitors to the salvage yard.

It had been tipping down all day. The man was soaked – his navy coat was sodden, his jeans were splashed with dirt churned up by traffic, and his straight, dark hair stuck to his head like a bedraggled blackbird's wings. Where was the sun they had been promised? The crystal balls had clearly been malfunctioning and they'd got the forecast wrong again. But, thought Cat, why does this so-and-so feel he has the right to take his temper out on me?

'We don't have a receptionist as such,' she told him calmly. 'I meet and greet, but I do other things as well. Did we know you were coming?'

'I rang this morning at about eleven o'clock. I spoke to somebody called Tess. I made an appointment to see a Mr Chapman at four o'clock today.'

Cat glanced at the diary on her desk.

'You must be Mr Lawley, then?'

'I'm Adam Lawley, yes.'

'I'm Cat Aston, Barry Chapman's office manager.' Cat held out her hand, and Adam Lawley shook it. Somewhat reluctantly, she thought, but the shake itself was strong and firm. 'I'm sorry, Mr Lawley, but Barry isn't here. His wife is having a baby any moment, and half an hour ago he got a call—'

'I've had a wasted journey, then?'

'Let's hope not, Mr Lawley.'

'You can help me?'

'Yes, I think so,' Cat replied. Tess had left a note to say what Mr Lawley wanted – roof tiles made of genuine Cotswold stone, and nothing else would do, he wasn't interested in reproduction. 'You need some Cotswold tiles, is that right?'

Mr Lawley shrugged, but then he muttered something which Cat took for agreement.

She found a set of keys. 'Let me get a couple of umbrellas, then I'll take you out into the yard.'

Adam followed the receptionist who wasn't the receptionist into the office lobby. Now he was embarrassed. She'd been so kind and courteous, and he knew he'd been very mean himself.

These days, however, he couldn't seem to help it.

But he had to help it.

He had to sort his life out and he had to do it soon. He must stop being such a miserable sod. Otherwise, he'd soon have no friends left. Gwennie and Jules were being very patient, but he secretly suspected they were sick and tired of having someone always dripping round the place.

Dripping, right – why hadn't he driven to the salvage yard? It wasn't as if he had the time to walk. Or to catch pneumonia. He had far too much to do to take a day off work, let alone a week.

But he'd found that walking seemed to dull the pain a bit.

'You press the little button,' said the girl.

'I'm sorry?'

'This one has a spring.' She was holding out a telescopic black umbrella and looking at him as if she thought he had escaped from somewhere and was possibly quite dangerous as well. She was hanging on to the big golfing umbrella with the vicious silver spike, at any rate. 'Mr Lawley?'

'Thank you.'

Adam took the black umbrella. Then he followed the girl into the yard, wondering what rubbish she was going to try to sell him, if she knew a genuine Cotswold tile from a modern concrete fake, if she and the boss of this place were a pair of opportunist crooks or genuine themselves.

He didn't trust anybody nowadays.

I'm doing fine, thought Cat, as they went out into the rain.

I'm operating normally, not daydreaming or fretting. I'm in control again.

Adam Lawley seemed to know exactly what he wanted, which made a pleasant change, because apart from dealers most people calling at the yard were looking for something vaguely interesting to be a focal point in a back garden – a concrete cast of Paolo and Francesca, a copy of that Belgian boy or David, an oriental Buddha, a Hindu god or goddess, an Egyptian head.

Or they were doing up their dream Victorian home and wanted cast iron fireplaces, old ceramic tiles or stripped pine doors. Chapman's Architectural Salvage did its best to find them something suitable. Barry might not stock it, but he usually knew where he could source it.

Cat led Adam through the yard, past various sheds where Barry kept the valuable stuff and things which wouldn't benefit from getting soaking wet, to where the many different kinds of roof tiles were stacked on wooden pallets.

'Okay, Mr Lawley, these are what we've got,' she said, and pointed to a pallet on his left. 'All genuine Cotswold stone and there are three hundred of them here. If they're what you want, but we don't have enough of them, we can very probably find some more.'

'I'll need about five hundred, and I'll need them quickly, so could you find them soon?'

'It shouldn't be a problem,' Cat replied.

Barry had impressed on Cat and Tess that whatever the customer said he wanted, they should always tell him they could find it, because nine times out of ten they would – eventually.

'Where are you working?' Cat enquired, thinking there's no call for Cotswold stone in Walthamstow. Or anywhere in London, come to that. Barry had expected to sell these old stone roof tiles to the National Trust or to English Heritage, and that was why he'd bought them in the first place.

'At Redland Manor,' Adam said. 'It's a Grade I listed Elizabethan house in Gloucestershire.'

'What are you doing in Walthamstow?'

'I'm involved with restoration and rebuilding projects all

over the country, but I'm based in London,' Adam Lawley said, in a what-business-is-it-of-yours-then voice. He picked up one damp, lichen-crusted tile. He weighed it in his hands and then he grimaced at it critically. 'I've seen some terrible old fakes of Cotswold tiles,' he said to Cat. 'But these look like the genuine article.'

'That's because they are the genuine article,' said Cat. 'I hope you're not suggesting we would try—'

'I'm not suggesting anything,' Adam Lawley interrupted, and he fixed Cat with a don't-get-clever-with-me stare. 'But a lot of salvage merchants try to pass off modern stuff as old. They often buy up concrete roof tiles from the 1960s, paint them with a porridge of compost and sour milk so they start growing lichen, then try to fool the punters and often they succeed. Where did you get these?'

'I think they were on a dower house near Bourton-on-the-Water. I'll have to check the book and then I can tell you definitely.'

'I'll take them anyway, that's if the price is right. What do you want for them?'

'We can discuss a price. But if you need another couple of hundred, why don't you let us source them, and then we'll offer you an all-in deal? I think you'll find we're quite competitive.'

'You're authorised to do this, are you?'

'Yes, of course,' said Cat.

'Only I don't have time to mess about, and if you need to ask your boss—'

'Mr Lawley, do you want these tiles?'

'Yes, I do.'

'Very well, let's sort it out today.' Cat turned to go back through the yard. 'Come into the office, get dried off and have a coffee while I do the paperwork,' she added. 'By the way, where did you park? Barry should have told you we have some visitors' spaces round the side.'

'I didn't drive,' said Adam. 'I walked here from Camden. But I didn't realise it would be such a way.'

'My goodness, it's no wonder you're so wet.'

Adam merely shrugged, so Cat stopped trying to have a conversation. Once she'd made his coffee, she set up an account, glancing up to ask him questions, then repeating them, because he seemed more interested in staring through the window at the rain.

He looked a sight, she thought. He'd shaved with a blunt chisel, his hair looked like he'd hacked at it himself and his boots were scuffed and down at heel. His workman's donkey jacket was fraying at the cuffs and a leather patch was coming loose.

How old, she speculated – thirty, thirty-five? No grey in his black hair, no laughter lines, but maybe that was not surprising if he didn't laugh?

She wondered what he'd look like if he smiled, but somehow couldn't see it happening.

Adam did his best to drink the coffee. It was decent stuff, not instant rubbish, and it was strong and hot. But, like everything he ate and drank these days, it tasted bloody awful, and he had to force it down.

'May we have your e-mail, Mr Lawley?' asked the girl.

'My what?' asked Adam.

'Your e-mail, do you have one?' The girl – to his dismay, he had forgotten what she was called – was clearly trying to be polite and pleasant to this idiot. 'Mr Lawley?'

'It's mail@adamprojectman.com.'

'Thank you,' said the girl.

'I'm sorry to be so vacant,' Adam added, doing his best to sound as if he meant it. 'But I'm very busy at the moment. I've got a lot of work stuff on my mind.'

'You do look tired.' The girl smiled sympathetically, and

Adam saw she had a very sweet, good-natured face and gorgeous jade-green eyes. 'You probably need a good night's sleep.'

'Yes, perhaps,' said Adam, who had hardly slept at all since Maddy left and was sure he'd never have a good night's sleep again.

'We haven't done business with you in the past, so I'll need a deposit,' said the girl as she tapped on her keyboard. 'What about a hundred pounds – would that be acceptable to you?'

'Yes, that's fine.' Adam rummaged in the inside pocket of his jacket and then in all the pockets of his jeans. 'I don't seem to have my cards,' he said.

'We do take cash,' Cat told him.

'I should have just about enough.' Adam started going through his pockets once again, pulling out some tenners, fivers, half a dozen coins, more tenners and then two more fivers, until he had managed to assemble eighty-seven pounds. He put the money on Cat's desk. 'I usually carry more than this, but I—'

'Why don't you give me eighty now?' Cat wrote out a receipt. 'Then you can pay the balance on delivery. I'd better let you get off home,' she added. She handed him a couple of business cards. 'One's Barry's and one's mine,' she told him. 'Do you have a card?'

'I'm sorry?'

'Oh, it doesn't matter – just give me your mobile number. Then we'll call you when we've found your tiles. We ought to be in touch some time next week, if not before.'

'Thank you,' Adam said. He turned his collar up and then slouched off into the rain.

As Cat locked up, she thought about the man. What a miserable so-and-so! Then she thought of Jack, who was always laughing, joking, fooling round and making her laugh, too.

Who could Jack be laughing, joking, fooling round with now? She'd give almost anything to hear one of his awful jokes again.

He'd always told her she was too damn serious. She seriously needed to lighten up a bit. If she was as grumpy as the man she'd met this afternoon, perhaps it was no wonder Jack had left? Memo to myself, she thought – whatever I feel like inside, put on a happy face.

She rummaged in her bag and found her mobile.

'Hi, Tess,' she began. 'What are you doing this evening? Do you want to go and see a film? Yeah, let's make it something funny. Something that will cheer me up a bit. I've just spent the past half an hour with a guy from Doom and Gloom R Us.'

Hey, do I see sunshine?

Adam was on the roof of Redland Manor when the guy from Chapman's Architectural Salvage brought the tiles. The previous week's torrential rain had given way to beautiful spring sunshine. The builders had their shirts off and were working on their tans.

'Mr Lawley?' someone shouted up to him.

Adam looked down and saw a stocky forty-something man standing by a pickup full of tiles. If this was Barry Chapman or one of his drivers he was early. Adam was impressed because, in his long experience, suppliers were almost always late. It was encoded in their DNA.

'I'll be with you now,' he called. He made his way along the rafters, over sheets of bright blue polythene that covered half the roof, through a dormer window and back down to the ground.

'Hello, Mr Lawley, good to meet you,' said the fair-haired man, offering his hand to Adam. 'Barry Chapman, boss of Chapman's Architectural Salvage.'

'Good to meet you, too.' Adam shook Barry by the hand. 'I'm sorry I missed you at the yard last week. But your assistant seemed to know her stuff.'

'Yeah, she's good, is Cat.' Barry Chapman nodded. 'Great all-rounder – brilliant organiser, makes the office run like clockwork, takes an interest in the stock, and she's always pleasant to the customers and suppliers. She's getting to be quite a fair negotiator, too.'

'She told me you'd been called away.' Then, feeling it would be polite, he added, 'How's your wife?'

'Annie's doing great.' Barry Chapman found his mobile

phone. 'She had a sticky time of it, though – fourteen hours in labour, ended up with forceps. God, who'd be a woman? But it was all worth it. She had a seven pound girl and she's a little darling, as pretty as her mother. Here, have a dekko – ain't she the cutest thing? We're going to call her Roxie Jane.'

'You must be thrilled,' said Adam.

As he looked at Barry's child, he felt a sudden longing, and he imagined Maddy, sleepy-eyed and pregnant with the bump just visible, summer-brown and gorgeous in a white cotton dress.

She'd be sitting on a terrace somewhere warm and Mediterranean, somewhere where the air was scented with wild thyme and lemon blossom, where the nights were velvet-soft and starry, made for love, and where—

He forced himself to come back to reality.

'These roof tiles are a find,' he said, as Barry Chapman flicked through yet more pictures of his baby daughter, the image of a proud and happy father. 'I'd rung and e-mailed all around the country, trying to track some down. Your place was my last resort.'

'Whatever you need, give us a bell. If we haven't got it, we can almost always find it and give you the best price.'

'You only had three hundred in your yard,' said Adam, glancing at the lorry. 'Where did you find the rest?'

'A mate of mine in Stroud, he had a few hundred going spare. I picked 'em up as I drove over here.' Barry Chapman grinned and then he shoved his mobile back into his pocket. 'Cash is fine,' he added casually.

As Adam checked then signed the paperwork and counted out the balance of what he owed in tens and twenties, Barry looked up at the house again. 'What's the set-up here, Mr Lawley? You're the subcontractor, project manager or what?'

'I'm the project manager,' said Adam. He found a couple of his business cards and handed them to Barry.

'So you're a freelance, are you?' Barry grinned again. 'Do you do any of the actual work yourself?'

'Yes, once in a while,' Adam replied. 'My father was a builder, and when I left school I did all my City and Guilds stuff while I worked for him. When he died I worked for English Heritage and the National Trust for several years. I set up on my own last summer. I specialise in Tudor, Jacobean and Georgian restoration nowadays.'

'You go all round the country, do you?'

'Yes, I get about. I've got two projects here in Gloucestershire, another down in Cornwall, some in Middlesex and one in Dorset. I'm going to spend a week or two in Italy next month. Then I'll be off to Scotland in July.'

'What's in Scotland, then?'

'A Victorian castle needing total restoration and it'll be my biggest challenge yet. But it'll be fantastic when it's done.'

'You're obviously a very busy man.'

'When you're a freelance and you're offered any work, you always take it. Or I do, anyway. I'm gradually getting better known, so these days I don't have to bid for jobs or send in complicated estimates, which used to waste a lot of time.'

'You see your bloke, you name your price.'

'I do.'

'Yeah, so do I – and I reckon that's the only way to run a business.' Barry Chapman nodded at the builders who were working on the roof. 'Do you think your lads could lend a hand with all this stuff?'

As he helped the men unload the tiles, Adam thought about the girl from Chapman's yard, remembering how kind she'd been, how helpful, when he had been so surly.

What was her name? Barry had mentioned it only a beat

or two ago, but it had gone again. All the same, he could recall her face – sweet and heart-shaped, lightly freckled, with the most attractive jade-green eyes, all framed with dark blonde hair.

A Celtic princess, he decided.

If she had a prince, he was a very lucky man.

Thursday, 12 May

Perhaps tread carefully now?

The chirpy woman, whose name was Fanny Gregory, wanted Cat and Jack to go and meet the team from Supadoop Promotions at the Melbury Court Hotel.

The brochures, DVDs and sample menus had arrived last week. Cat and Tess and Bex spent ages sprawled on Cat's new sofa, salivating over them. They agreed it all looked wonderful, especially the food laid out on white tablecloths with silverware and crystal, beautifully photographed by glowing candlelight.

'This smoked salmon and fresh crayfish starter,' Bex suggested, as she ran a perfect scarlet nail down the list, 'followed by rack of lamb with new potatoes – wilted greens – Beaujolais and cranberry reduction – and to finish off, the triple chocolate soufflé with chocolate and almond petits fours.' Bex looked up and grinned. 'All sorted – yes?'

'No, it's damn well not,' retorted Tess. 'What about us vegetarians? If this menu's planned around you carnivores, we veggies will be given rubbish that's been in their freezer since Jesus was in Pampers. Nasty quiches full of greyish leeks, boring pasta something, glutinous risotto. You should begin with goat's cheese tartlets, Cat, and then go on to aubergine and pumpkin gratin topped with saffron custard. Or zucchini parmigiana, that looks good as well. You can keep your soufflé, Bex, but what about this loganberry panna cotta as a second choice?'

'It's my wedding,' Cat reminded them.

'Oh, you've found a bridegroom, then?' Bex twirled an ash-blonde strand around one finger and scowled down at the vegetarian options, which Cat was inclined to think looked dull. They were mostly based on cheese, and whereas cheese was fine for rats and mice—

'The bridegroom's in development,' said Tess.

'Omigod, don't tell me Jack's been sighted?'

'No,' admitted Tess. 'But there are several other options. Quite a few, in fact.'

'Online dating, eh? Desperate of Leyton seeks anything in trousers?'

'Shut up, Bex,' said Tess.

'The Royal Marines Commando Challenge, extreme sports weekends, bungee jumping off tall buildings, right? That's a sure-fire way to meet some guys, doing something really stupid, preferably wearing awful clothes and looking like a mutant from a Steven Spielberg movie. What if you break your neck?'

'Shut *up*, Bex,' said Cat.

'Mail order, that's another possibility. What about some guy from Indonesia or Sudan? Or an asylum seeker – there are lots of them about, and maybe one would marry you?'

'Bex, could you go and put the kettle on?' suggested Tess. 'Cat and I are having a serious conversation here. Cat, I think zucchini parmigiana – don't forget.'

'Rack of lamb,' called Bex, as she turned on the kitchen tap and started rattling mugs about.

After Tess and Bex had gone, Cat had Fanny on the phone again.

God, this woman works ridiculous hours, she thought, as she realised who was speaking – it was nearly midnight.

But there was no escaping Fanny now, and so Cat went for gold. She could almost hear the soundtrack from that movie *Chariots of Fire* as she lied her socks off.

Yes, she was really looking forward to meeting Fanny and the team from Supadoop Promotions at the Melbury Court

Hotel. No, getting down to Dorset wouldn't be a problem. Yes, she'd already checked up on the trains. Yes, this coming weekend would be fine.

'As it happens,' she continued glibly, 'Jack's away on business at the moment. But I'm sure you'd like to get things moving, so I'll come to Dorset by myself.'

'We were rather hoping we could meet you *and* Jack,' said Fanny Gregory briskly – or was it suspiciously? 'What's his line of business, angel?'

'He does stand-up comedy.' Then Cat crossed the fingers of one hand behind her back and crossed her eyes as well. 'He's just beginning to make his name in pubs and clubs in Manchester and Liverpool. So he couldn't miss an opportunity which came up this week.'

'Oh, I see,' said Fanny. 'What's his name again?'

'Jack Benson,' Cat replied.

'I'm googling him now.'

'He—he's not famous yet!'

'Maybe not, my darling, but Google ought to find him.'

Okay, Cat told herself, come clean. Tell Fanny Whatserface Jack's disappeared, the wedding's off, and say the runner-up can have the prize.

But then she thought – I don't want Fanny Gregory to think I'm some sad loser who invented a fiancé just so I could win a competition. When I filled in that entry form, I did it in good faith. I did have a fiancé, and the photographs I sent, they were of Jack and me.

'You'll need to know his stage name,' she told Fanny. 'He's on Twitter, Facebook, all that stuff, as Zackie Banter.'

'Zackie what?' drawled Fanny Gregory sarcastically. 'You're sure he's not a circus clown, my sweet? I'm seeing someone in those ghastly flapping shoes, a swivelling bow tie and with electrocuted hair. The sort of man who's hired for children's parties by people who live in bungalows in Essex.'

'He does stand-up comedy,' repeated Cat. 'You could try googling Zackie Banter stand-up, that should find him.'

'Oh, yes – here he is – no tweets for weeks. He should get his act together, shouldn't he, if he wants to make a good impression on the web? So tell me, darling – what's his shtick?'

'I'm sorry?'

'What is he, alternative, political?'

'Oh, I see,' said Cat. 'Alternative, Jack's definitely alternative. All his stuff is very off the wall.'

Get out now, you idiot, she thought. Stop this insanity, confess, tell Fanny Gregory you can't meet her in Dorset, tell her why.

'You say you'll be in Dorset this coming Saturday morning?' Fanny said, and Cat could hear her tapping on a keyboard, no doubt looking through her jam-packed diary and slotting people in.

'Yes, of course,' said Cat, 'that will be fine.'

Well, she told herself, there would be no harm in going to have a little look.

Friday, 13 May

Unlucky for some?

'A little look?' shrieked Bex, when she and Cat and Tess met in a coffee shop for lunch the following day.

'Yes, why not?' asked Cat.

'You've mislaid your fiancé, that's why not.' Tess peeled the crinkled paper off her double chocolate, raspberry sprinkles and marshmallow muffin. 'I think you should call the whole thing off.'

'So why did we bother to talk about those menus from the Melbury Court Hotel?' demanded Cat. 'Last month, you were telling me to find another man and go for it.'

'But you haven't found one, have you, dumbo?' Tess shot back. 'You haven't been out anywhere to look.'

'Jack might come home,' said Cat.

'I haven't noticed any flying bacon.' Bex glanced through the café's plate glass window. 'Tess, do you see anything with wings?'

'Alas, no angel pigs out there.'

'So, as Tess has pointed out, you need to call the whole thing off,' said Bex.

'Cat, it would be for the best,' soothed Tess.

'But I'll look such a fool,' objected Cat.

'You'll look a bigger fool if you arrange your wedding and you don't have a bridegroom.'

'What will you do, rope in a waiter or a cook?'

'Or will you skip the wedding and go straight to the reception?'

'That would be rather stupid, wouldn't it?'

'Stop going on at me,' said Cat. 'Or you two won't be getting invitations anyway.'

'You could always marry Tess,' smirked Bex.

'Or marry Bex,' grinned Tess.

'Yes, okay,' said Bex. 'But I want to be the one who wears the wedding gown and carries the bouquet and there's to be no tongue stuff when we kiss.'

'Otherwise, it's off,' said Tess.

'Shut up, the pair of you,' said Cat.

'Listen, honey, this is getting serious.' Bex looked hard at Cat. 'Yeah, we had a lot of fun discussing all those menus and watching all those DVDs. The catering sounds fabulous and we don't dispute the place looks gorgeous. But we're your friends, we want what's best for you and we think you should stop this madness now.'

'We do indeed,' said Tess. 'So, bearing that in mind, we're going to keep you occupied. We'll stop you mooning round the place like some pathetic adolescent who's in love with Johnny Depp.'

'We're taking you to do some heavy-duty shopping on Saturday afternoon,' continued Bex. 'We've got three tickets for an Abba tribute gig that evening.'

'So we'll have some jolly super fun,' concluded Tess.

'But Tess, I always thought you hated Abba?'

'I do,' admitted Tess. 'But I still like them ironically, especially when I'm drunk, and I intend to be extremely drunk. I'm going to work my way through twenty pints of Guinness.'

'Tess, you're very silly.'

'Yes, of course,' said Tess. 'You should be silly too, once in a while. It might help you loosen up a bit. So – who's going to be the pretty one?'

'Me,' said Bex, 'because I've got the patent leather boots and miniskirt, because I have the longest, blondest hair, and because when we go out together guys all ask if you're my ugly sisters, anyway.'

Saturday, 14 May

Will this be a disaster?

But, in spite of being offered Abba tribute gigs and heavy-duty shopping opportunities, and in spite of Tess and Bex doing their most sarcastic best to talk her out of it, on Saturday Cat caught the train to Dorset.

As she sat there in the grubby carriage with the noisy families, with the teenage lovers plugged into the same iPod, with a million old age pensioners setting off on cut-price day trips, wondering what she'd say to Fanny Gregory and her team, she looked through all the brochures yet again.

The Melbury Court Hotel itself was gorgeous. A square and solid Jacobean mansion, it was four storeys high, it had elaborate window frames which Cat decided must all be original, and it was built of mellow, blush-red brick.

Its gardens were spectacular. There was no other word. Grand herbaceous borders, shaded tree-lined walks, carved and sculpted topiary, Elizabethan love-knots, this place had the lot.

Mum would have a great time pinching cuttings and swiping various sprigs of this and that and letting seed-heads accidentally drop into her William Morris–patterned shopping bag, Cat thought ruefully.

The lawns beyond the formal grounds were dotted here and there with summer houses and little rustic temples, all festooned with honeysuckle, roses and wisteria. In summer, they would make the place a perfumed paradise.

Peacocks strutted on the lawns, ornamental chickens with feathered legs and dappled plumage fussed around looking for worms and grubs, and doves roosted in dovecotes.

As for the garden art – you never saw anything like this

in Barry Chapman's yard. Ancient, period and modern, lichened stone and gleaming steel, there was something to please everyone.

The white marble fountain in the forecourt, with its centrepiece of gods and goddesses and mermaids, with its dolphins, cherubs, nymphs and great, carved cockleshells, must have come from some Italian villa, Cat decided, and would be worth a fortune.

She wondered what it looked like when it played. Or when its jets were petrified and it was festooned with sparkling icicles, all glittering like diamonds in the January sun?

A winter wedding, she thought dreamily.

I'll have a wedding in the snow.

Does it snow in Dorset?

If it doesn't, maybe I could hire a snow machine?

I'll wear a beaded, ice-white velvet gown, a fur lined velvet cloak and silver shoes.

I'll be a real live Snow Queen with crystals in my hair.

But you're forgetting something, said the voice inside her head. You don't have anyone to marry.

I'm working on it, lied her other self.

Supadoop Promotions turned out to be a forty-something woman in a sharp black business suit, a pretty twenty-something girl, a teenage boy photographer with half a dozen cameras round his neck and an extremely elegant and beautiful black greyhound with the most amazing amber eyes.

Cat found them waiting in the station car park, standing by a lovely gleaming purple BMW, the sort of vehicle that was clearly custom-made.

'You must be Cat. I'm Fanny,' said the woman in the sharp black business suit. She had bright blue eyes that clearly didn't miss a thing, immaculately-styled auburn hair, a lovely figure

– amazing legs, thought Cat, and what fantastic boobs, I wonder if they're real or plastic – and she was wearing pretty-near-impossible-to-walk-in high-heeled purple shoes.

'This is Rosie Denham, my assistant.' Fanny waved one white, bejewelled hand at the pretty twenty-something girl. 'Rosie, this is Cat, our lucky winner and radiant bride-to-be. She's absolutely perfect, isn't she?'

'Perfect,' echoed Rosie and then she shook Cat's hand. 'It's good to meet you, Cat. We're all looking forward to having lots of fun with you today.'

Omigod, thought Cat.

'This is darling Caspar.' Fanny stroked the greyhound's lovely head. 'Say hello to Cat, my angel.'

Caspar nosed politely at Cat's hand and then looked up at Fanny as if to say Cat seemed to be all right.

Then somebody coughed.

'Oh, poor love – I was forgetting you!' As Fanny smiled at the teenage boy, Cat found she was reminded of crocodiles and antelopes on natural history programmes in which things went badly for the antelopes.

'This is Rick,' said Fanny. 'He's our photographic genius and he'll be taking lots of gorgeous pix of you today, inside, outside, looking soulful, looking happy, looking like you've never been so thrilled in all your life.'

She gave Cat's chain-store top a vicious tweak and pulled a face. 'But of course he won't be snapping you in this, my sweet.'

'Why, what's wrong with it?' asked Cat. She rather liked her pretty lemon-coloured top which was patterned with a paler primrose and had elaborate cutwork on the sleeves.

'My darling girl, what's right with it?' Fanny shook her head. 'It's badly made and finished, which is not surprising considering it was probably stitched together by some poor child slave in a benighted Third World country. The pattern's not been matched. The cut is dreadful – it rides up at the back. It's a common little garment, you look common in it, and for this promotion we need class, class, class.

'But don't worry, angel. Darling Rosie's brought along some really super outfits. We're assuming you're a perfect ten? Or that's what you put on the entry form. So if you weren't telling porky pies …'

Cat shook her head and did her best to smile. Since Jack had gone, she'd overdosed on chocolate, custard doughnuts and vanilla cheesecake at a million calories a slice.

But if Fanny Gregory was alarming, Rosie Denham didn't seem too bad. A tall, slim girl with wild, black curling hair and sprinklings of freckles just like Cat's across her pretty face, she wore black Converse trainers, Diesel jeans and a top which Cat had seen in Gap last week and almost bought herself.

She thought – if things were different, this girl could be my friend. The dog of course was lovely, and the boy photographer seemed harmless.

As for Fanny, though – as slender as a snake and darting like a stickleback in her smart business suit – looking at Fanny Gregory, Cat felt sick. She knew, without a whisper of a doubt, that people didn't mess with Fanny Gregory and live to tell their children what they'd done.

They crept into a hole and died instead.

Rosie ushered Cat towards the purple BMW, and Cat resigned herself to going to meet her doom.

They drove along a gravelled road edged with new-mown grass and smart, white palings, Fanny issuing a stream of comments and instructions, Rosie making lots of notes, Caspar sitting quietly looking dignified and gazing through the window, and Rick the boy photographer sniggering at something on his phone.

As they came round a bend they saw the house.

'There,' said Fanny, momentarily turning round to shoot a glance at Cat. 'The perfect setting for a wedding, don't you think?'

Cat stared at Melbury Court in wonder.

It was even better than she could have imagined, even more amazing than the brochures had suggested, because it had been made out of a dream.

It was all the country houses, Hollywood recreations of old England, gracious living and unending summers magically made one.

'It's beautiful,' she breathed.

'I'm so relieved you like it.' Fanny beamed. 'Well, my angels, they're expecting us, so let's get on.'

The manager met them on the gravel sweep outside the house and smiled in welcome, congratulating them on having chosen such a lovely summer day. There was valet parking, he told Fanny, so if she would let him have the keys?

But Fanny said she didn't trust some idiot Dorset flunky to park her lovely BMW, and couldn't it stay here on the gravel, sweet? It wasn't in the way.

As Fanny laid the law down to the manager, Cat glanced at the fountain in the forecourt. The image in the brochure had been doctored, Photoshopped, she realised now, because the actual fountain was in urgent need of restoration.

It wasn't gleaming white. It was a streaked and mildewed dirty yellow, and bits of it were missing. There were cracks and holes all over it. But if it were restored it could be wonderful. It could be—

'Come along, my angels, chop, chop, chop!' Fanny swept her angels into the hotel foyer, was gracious to the housekeeper and brisk with the receptionist. She told them no, there wasn't time for coffee. She had a tightish schedule and she needed to get on.

Yes, her dog was very well-behaved. Caspar's manners

were much better than most people's, darling, and he went with his mistress everywhere.

'Of course, I'll let you know when we need anything,' she added, with a charming smile.

She seemed to have permission to go anywhere she pleased, and indeed she did, with her black shadow at her heels. So Cat walked all around the house and gardens, private conference suites and public lounges, bedrooms, bars and dining rooms, like somebody half stunned.

It was all so fabulous she couldn't take it in.

Fanny bombarded her with questions. Did she like these gorgeous flower arrangements? If she did, they would do something fairly similar on her own big day. Didn't she just love this Chinese chintz here in the morning room? Or wasn't chintz her thing?

What about the Grinling Gibbons staircase, didn't she think it wonderful, my darling? It had been badly damaged in a fire back in the 1930s. But you'd never know it, would you? It had been restored by local craftsmen, and now it looked just perfect, didn't it?

'The reception, sweetheart, where do you think you'd like to have it – in the formal dining room or in the orangery?' she asked, as Cat tried to remember if she had actually seen the orangery.

'The dining room is rather special, isn't it, my angel?' she continued, as she swept into a beautiful, high-ceilinged room which was hung with studio photographs of famous actors, all done in black and white.

'Golden greats of stage and screen,' she trilled, pausing for a moment to gaze up at a very handsome man in a tuxedo. 'Ewan Fraser, darling – do excuse my blushes, but I've always had a teeny tiny crush on him.'

As Cat looked at the photographs, she recognised James Mason, Ray Milland and Errol Flynn. She'd never heard of Ewan Fraser. But she had to admit this man was pretty damn attractive.

'Of course, the red hair made him more than usually delicious,' added Fanny wistfully. 'It's so very gorgeous on a certain sort of man. So anyway, my love, the orangery or the dining room? Do you want white table linen, silver service, finger bowls? Or do you want to go for something more informal? Of course, I don't mean chicken in a basket, obviously.'

But, to Cat's relief, Fanny didn't seem to want intense, in-depth discussion. All she needed was for Cat to nod and to agree that everything was wonderful. Cat didn't have any trouble doing this because, inside and outside, the Melbury Court Hotel was rather more than wonderful.

It was divine.

The dining room was beautiful, oak-panelled with a quite amazing icing-sugar ceiling. The orangery – she remembered now – was a vaulted vision of stained and patterned glass and intricate Victorian ironwork.

'Yes, they're both fantastic,' Cat said faintly, when Fanny nagged her for a quick decision, because she'd need to tell the hotel management, my sweet, everyone was keen to get things moving right away.

'The orangery, then,' said Fanny. 'Rosie, angel, did you make a note? I think you've made a wise decision, Cat. You can get more people into the orangery. Darling, I must press you for a date.'

'I—I need a bit more time,' said Cat. 'I'll have to ask—'

'While you're considering, we'll pencil in some possibilities, and then you can decide.'

Cat decided she felt very ill.

But, as the day went on, she started to enjoy herself. Well, almost to enjoy herself. She couldn't shift the nagging, guilty feeling that was making her feel sick.

The hotel had given them a room where Rosie did her face and dressed her up in gorgeous outfits which had clearly cost a lot of money, and Rick took lots of photographs, and Fanny said they were delightful, darlings, that Cat had perfect cheekbones, and her eyes were rather nice, as well.

'Or a good colour, anyway,' she added. 'But you need to dye your eyelashes, and you should sort your eyebrows out as well. A decent pair of tweezers aren't expensive, so don't look at me like that.'

If Cat would put her hair up, not have it loose and drooping – you look like some prehistoric hippy, or Neil out of *The Young Ones* at the moment, darling girl – she would be almost pretty.

'Cat, don't be offended,' whispered Rosie, as her boss moved out of earshot to give Rick more instructions. 'Almost pretty means you're really beautiful when Fanny says it – trust me.'

'What was that, my sweet?' Fanny turned her laser beam on Rosie. 'What did you just say?'

'We're running late,' said Rosie. 'We should have left an hour ago.'

'Oh, my angel girl, why didn't you tell me?' Fanny's bright blue eyes were narrowed now and the boy photographer looked scared.

But Rosie didn't seem fazed at all, and Cat was well impressed.

They were hurrying back towards the forecourt, Rosie tapping on her keypad, Fanny firing questions, comments and instructions like an AK-47 and Cat still feeling sick, when they all collided with a man in faded jeans, a blue checked shirt and workman's heavy boots. He had been carrying an armful of rolled-up plans and drawings, and now he dropped the lot.

They stopped to help him pick them up. As Fanny and

Rosie piled the stuff into his arms, he turned to glance at Cat.

'Oh,' he said and frowned. 'It is you, isn't it – the girl from Chapman's yard? You're a long way from home.'

Cat stared for half a moment. But then she remembered. It was the surly guy who'd bought those tiles. What was his name? Lawson, Langley, Longley? No, hang on – it was Lawley – Adam Lawley.

What was he doing here? She thought he'd said the place that he was working on – where was it? She wished she could remember! She was almost sure it wasn't Dorset. He wouldn't have needed Cotswold tiles in Dorset.

Fanny was staring at the man and very obviously assessing him. 'So you two know each other?' she demanded, speculation glittering in her eyes.

'N-no, not really,' stammered Cat. 'A week or two ago, Mr Lawley bought some tiles from where I work, for a house in – Gloucestershire!'

'But now you're working here in Dorset, Mr Lawley?' Fanny asked him, smirking as her eyes peeled off his shirt.

'Yes, I'm project-managing the rebuilding and conversion of the stables,' Adam Lawley said. 'They're going to become a health club complex with treatment rooms and plunge pools, tanning salons, saunas – all that stuff. I'm not here every day. This is a flying visit to check on work in progress.'

'So you do renovation, restoration, all that kind of thing?'

'Yes, but I—'

'I knew it – serendipity!' cried Fanny. 'I've just bought this old flint barn in Surrey. It has outline planning permission for conversion to a six or seven bedroom house with triple garage. Perhaps I'll have a swimming pool, as well.'

Now she was eyeing Adam like a vixen might eye a handsome cockerel she meant to have for dinner. 'Do you project-manage things like that?'

'Sometimes,' Adam said. 'But I'm a builder, not an architect, and it sounds to me as if you need an architect right now. What I do would come afterwards, working from the plans.'

'So could you recommend an architect?' asked Fanny, baring sharp white teeth in a big smile and flicking her pink tongue across her scarlet lip-glossed lips. 'If you and an architect—'

'We'd have to talk about it.' All his plans and drawings now cradled in the crook of his left arm, Adam fished in the pocket of his shirt and found a business card. He handed it to Fanny, absentmindedly stroked Caspar on his sleek, dark head, and then he turned to Cat again. 'What brings you here, Miss Aston?'

'Oh, Cat's the lucky winner of our fabulous competition!' said Fanny Gregory brightly, handing him her own much posher, heavily embossed and gilded card. 'She and her fiancé will be having the most fantastic wedding here later on this year. Or maybe early next year – I don't think she's quite decided yet. But what she's seen today has knocked her sideways. She's totally bedazzled, aren't you, sweet?'

Cat found she couldn't manage a reply.

'Congratulations,' Adam Lawley said, and then he smiled the sort of smile that looks like it's been shrunk, it was so tight.

She met his gaze, and there she saw – what was it, curiosity? Or was it disbelief? It wasn't congratulations, anyway.

'Th-thank you, Mr Lawley.' Cat realised she was blushing furiously, and told herself to stop imagining things.

Adam hurried on towards the Georgian stables which were round the back of Melbury Court, fifty yards or so from the hotel. They'd been far enough away to have escaped the fire which had badly damaged the original Melbury House, as it had been known before it was reborn as a hotel.

After half a century of neglect the stables were in disrepair but were now being restored. Their original Grade I listed classical façade had been retained, but inside they were being converted into a luxurious health club with a Turkish theme. This had proved to be a plumbing nightmare, as it so often was with listed buildings, and he had to sort it out today.

He had to go to Gloucestershire on Monday and then come back to Dorset later that same week, because here in Dorset there was the Italian fountain, too. He was looking forward to working on the fountain, even though it promised to be a long, involved and very complicated job.

He meant to start with Venus, who was in a pitiable state, pocked and marked and riddled with what looked like bullet holes, and so cracked and fissured that she was in danger of losing fingers, toes and several petals of the roses which were woven in her hair. Some of these roses were already missing – broken off by accident or deliberately shot away?

Rain was getting in the cracks and threatening to make everything much worse. One more cold and frosty winter would be a disaster, opening these cracks up even further and causing even more bits to fall off.

What stupid, idiot vandals had used a lovely thing like that for target practice?

Drunken, bored aristocrats, perhaps?

Or ditto soldiers?

They should have been shot themselves.

As for lovely things – the girl from Chapman's yard had looked even more beautiful out in the soft spring sunshine.

Where had he put that woman's business card?

He patted all his pockets, but he couldn't find it. But it didn't matter. It wasn't as if he needed any work.

He had more than enough of it already, and she could always call him, anyway.

'What a hottie,' Fanny said, as she watched Adam Lawley stride away.

She read the details on his business card and then she slipped it into her Versace leather handbag, smirking speculatively.

'I must get my train,' said Cat, zipping up her own bag which was made of bright pink canvas and had come from Stead & Simpson.

'Of course you must, my darling.' Fanny snapped her fingers, and Rosie and the boy photographer came hurrying up at once.

They all piled into Fanny's BMW and Fanny zoomed away at Mach 1 speed, churning up the gravel and scattering the rabbits who were venturing out to take their evening promenade.

'A good day's work, my angels,' Fanny told them, as the BMW careened along the narrow country roads. 'We've lots and lots of lovely pix of gorgeous Cat, so darling Lulu's going to be delighted – don't you think so, Rosie?'

'Yes, she should be very pleased,' said Rosie, who was clearly used to being thrown around in purple BMWs and didn't seem to mind one little bit. 'Mummy said to tell you, Fanny – if you'll let her have a snap or two, she'll write a little piece for *Dorset People*. The editor's a friend, plays golf with Dad.'

'Excellent,' said Fanny, honking at some walkers who were cluttering up the road and forcing them to take evasive action in the form of falling in a ditch.

Cat didn't know what Rosie and her boss were going on about. But she found she didn't really care. By now she'd had enough of Fanny and her gang and wanted to go home.

As Fanny brought the BMW to a shuddering halt outside the station, she turned to look at Cat. 'I'm sorry we can't take you back to London,' she said crisply. 'But we have to drive to Solihull.'

'What's in Solihull?' asked Cat, relieved. She didn't fancy driving back to London with Fanny, Rosie and the boy photographer and being interrogated all the way.

'We're seeing a woman who makes sugar flowers and sugar Moses baskets, rocking horses, bootees and the like for christening and wedding cakes,' said Rosie.

'She reckons she's the queen of sugar art,' continued Fanny. 'She's won all sorts of prizes and awards, apparently. Now she wants to move upmarket, sell her stuff to WAGs and supermodels. So she needs my help.'

'She says she doesn't mind how much it costs. We think she must be loaded,' added Rosie.

'Or maybe she's delusional,' drawled Fanny.

She's not alone, thought Cat.

As soon as she got back to London, she decided, she was going to write to Fanny Gregory. She would say that everything was off, and she was sorry for all the inconvenience she had caused. She hoped the runners-up would have the wedding of a lifetime.

She got out of the BMW. 'It's been great to meet you,' she said insincerely, shaking hands all round and stroking Caspar on his velvet head and hoping the experience of spending time with Fanny would never be repeated.

'Thank you, sweetheart, likewise,' Fanny said. She arranged her face into a terrifying grin. 'I'll finalise some details and then I'll be in touch. I'll need firm confirmation very soon, most probably Monday morning.'

'But, but,' said Cat, 'I can't—'

'I'll call you, angel. So mind you keep your phone on all the time.'

Cat watched the BMW zoom away. She knew she wouldn't write that letter. She didn't have the nerve. She wondered what the hell she should do now, apart from find a lake and drown herself?

Adam and the foreman on the site sorted out the urgent plumbing problems, so on Monday morning the men could get on with the next phase of the stables project.

Then he made his way back to the car park, mentally clicking through the list of things he had to do and places where he had to go before he went to Italy.

He was looking forward to the Italian trip, because he would be seeing a guy whose father, brothers, cousins, uncles – those who didn't run restaurants and cafés and let out apartments to Lucca's summer visitors, anyway – were all involved in building work of some kind, in various restorations and conversions, and who himself was project-managing the total restoration of a sixteenth-century manor house. Or a *castello*, or *palazzo*, or whatever Italians called such things.

Sixteenth, seventeenth, eighteenth-century domestic architecture was his own special subject. The one he'd choose if he should ever go on *Mastermind*, which of course he wouldn't, because there was no way you'd ever get him sitting in that big black leather chair.

But the thought of working in the warm Italian sunshine, of project-managing restorations for the many well-heeled British who, in spite of the recession, were still buying anything from a castle to a cowshed over there – it had a most definite appeal.

He was working hard on his Italian, listening to CDs as he drove round the country, repeating words and phrases after someone very florid and excitable, someone who used far too many exclamation marks. *Andiamo! Pronto! Presto! Arrivederci! Si, Signor, Signora, Signorina!*

He got a lot of nervous looks at traffic lights and junctions as he tried to get some *brio* into what he said and as he attempted to get the accent right.

He had been in e-mail contact with Pietro since last autumn, had told him he'd be coming to Lucca in late spring or early summer, and Pietro said that would be fine – *perfetto, ideale, assoluto*.

Of course, he'd meant to go with Maddy, to combine a bit of business with a lot of pleasure. They'd drive around the Tuscan countryside and visit hilltop villages. They'd sit in shady cafés and drink cold Pinot Grigio. They'd make lazy love on linen sheets throughout the warm Italian nights.

He'd wondered if they might find something wonderful themselves, if she would fall in love with some *castello* or *casale*. If she'd turn to him and say – this is it, my darling, this is where I want to live, where we'll bring up our children.

But of course all that had been a fantasy. He wouldn't be doing any of it now, and this would be a business trip, no fun in it at all.

He thought about the girl he'd seen this afternoon, the pretty, kind and helpful girl from Barry Chapman's salvage yard, who was getting married at the Melbury Court Hotel.

She hadn't looked very happy at the prospect. In fact, she'd looked like she had lost a grand and found a penny, and he wondered why. Where was her fiancé, and why hadn't he been there today? Why did she seem so anxious and so sad?

Then he thought – what's it to do with you? Why are you so worried about a girl you're never going to see again?

He made some notes about the stuff he'd done today, he sent some e-mails and then he rang Jules.

'I'll be back in London eightish, nineish,' he began. 'Yeah, I'm fine. Gwennie's still at her sister's, is that right? She's going straight into work on Monday morning? What do you mean, I don't sound fine? I'm doing really well today.'

Who am I trying to fool, he asked himself. 'Jules, old mate,' he added, 'do you fancy getting very drunk with me tonight?'

Cat didn't usually drink spirits.

But, once she was on the train back home, she realised she needed something stronger than rubbish-from-the-trolley instant coffee.

So she bought a shot of vodka and a can of tonic, and drank it in defiance of the sixty-something couple sitting opposite who had a squirming grandchild on each lap and were glaring at her as if she were the living incarnation of the Antichrist.

What was she going to do?

Start an online manhunt, she supposed. Post Jack's picture all over the world wide web, captioned *have you seen this man* and offering a reward for information?

'Excuse me?' said the sixty-something woman.

'Yes?' said Cat.

'There is another way, you know.' The woman offered her a brightly-coloured leaflet. 'If you're troubled in your mind, that devil's brew will only make things worse. But if you let the good—'

Cat tuned out and, when the trolley next came down the aisle, she bought another shot of devil's brew. She stared out of the window. Somebody or something was messing with her mind. But it wasn't Jack. It wasn't Fanny. It wasn't Rosie, Caspar or the boy photographer.

Who was it then, she asked herself, as she drank her vodka and wondered why she felt so very strange.

This can't be right, what's going on?

'Okay, what's the problem?' Jules enquired.

'Why does there need to be a problem?' Adam shrugged. 'Why shouldn't I get drunk with an old mate?'

'Your oldest, dearest mate,' corrected Jules.

'Yes,' said Adam, nodding. 'You're absolutely right, and it's your round. I'll have a black and tan and a Macallan chaser, if it's all right with you.'

But this had been at ten o'clock, and now it was gone midnight. Adam had passed the awkward stage of being an uptight, stiff-necked Anglo-Saxon. He wanted to confide, have therapeutic, meaningful discussion, man to man. He wanted to be in a Cheyenne sweat lodge or a Californian man cave, not in a crowded London pub with an extended licence and a football-pitch-sized pull-down screen.

Jules must have felt the same.

Or, at any rate, he put his arm round Adam's shoulders and gave him a big hug. 'What's bothering you?' he asked, as he picked up his own Macallan chaser from yet another round. 'It's not that bird again?'

'It isn't Maddy, if that's who you mean.'

'You've got yourself a different bird?' Jules grinned. 'Well, nice work, my friend! What's this one like?'

'It's not a girl, exactly.' Adam was now light-headed with fatigue and fumes of single malt. 'It's more about what girls can do to you.'

'Oh.' Jules switched his grin off and put on his family doctor face. 'Some trouble in the trouser region, right?'

'No.' Adam thought about it for a moment, wondering if he should tell his friend about the girl from Chapman's yard, the one who was engaged, but who had somehow got inside his head and made herself at home there?

But in the end he found he couldn't do it. He'd sound so pathetic, such a loser, such a fool. There's this girl, she's in my mind, he'd say, and Jules would laugh and say I can't believe I'm hearing this, why isn't she in your bed?

'If it's not a bird, and if it's not trouser trouble, it can't be too bad,' said Jules. 'Mate, I said—'

'I heard you.'

'You're overworking, though – bombing up and down the motorways, Cornwall one day, Dorset, Middlesex and bloody Gloucestershire the next. You don't know if you're coming or going. You need to take time out.'

'You could be right,' admitted Adam.

'Of course I'm right,' said Jules. 'You need to chill a bit. You need to have a little holiday.' He looked down at his empty glass. 'You need to buy a round, as well.'

This is wrong, thought Cat. It's more than wrong, it's totally insane.

Since meeting Adam Lawley once again so unexpectedly, she'd thought about him all the time. On the train while coming home from Dorset, while she ate a takeaway in front of the TV, while she took a shower, then dried her hair, then went to bed – he wouldn't go away.

She spent the whole night dreaming about Jack. But Jack was somehow all mixed up with Adam. Now the dawn was breaking, all the street lights had gone out, and she was still confused.

Why should she obsess about this man? She hardly knew him, after all. She didn't fancy him. She didn't even like him.

So why did she remember he was tall, and – if he'd been her type, which of course he wasn't – reasonably good-looking, albeit in a gloomy sort of way?

What did it matter if he had broad shoulders, if his waist was neat and well-defined, if he had dark, Spanish-looking eyes with long, black lashes – lashes which were wasted on a man?

Why had she noticed that in the bright spring sunshine his poker-straight dark hair was streaked with red, as if it had been stroked by fire? What was it Fanny Gregory had said, something about red hair being delicious on the right sort of man? She could have had a point.

Adam might be solemn, but he didn't look mean or cruel or spiteful – just serious, in fact, and surely being serious was no crime? She was always being told that she was much too serious herself.

As she mixed some muesli, adding seeds and raisins and banana slices – I must eat healthily, she told herself. I can't afford to pile on pounds. I still might need to fit into a wedding gown – she was wondering if he had a girlfriend. How did solemn, serious men find girlfriends? Did they advertise on dating sites?

If they did, how did they sell themselves?

Almost every man you saw on dating sites made a point of saying he had a sense of humour. But Adam seemed to have no sense of humour. Perhaps he said as much, and added that he didn't want a sense of humour in his girlfriends either, and serious women only need apply?

Oh, shut up, you idiot, she thought.

She was broken-hearted. Surely it had to be obscene, to take an interest in another man while she was broken-hearted? She must forget him and she had to do it now. She had to concentrate on finding Jack and getting him to talk about their future as a couple – that's if they had a future.

This Adam Lawley, he was just a sudden crush, a wild infatuation. It often happened, she was sure, especially when a girl had been just been dumped. She'd read about it in a magazine, about the need within us all to fill up psychic voids.

She must talk to somebody.

Tess would fit the bill.

But Tess was worse than useless.

'Of course he isn't dead, you muppet,' she retorted, when Cat rang and got her out of bed, wondering aloud if Jack might be in serious trouble, adding what if he hadn't rung because he'd had a breakdown or a psychological collapse? If he'd been in an accident and was lying unconscious somewhere in intensive care, unclaimed, unknown, unloved, like in that storyline in *Holby City* or was it in *ER*?

Or if he might be dead?

'Well, he could be,' Cat said, stung.

'We'd have heard,' said Tess. 'It would have been the headlines on the BBC and on Sky News – unknown alternative comedian kicks the bucket. Only the good die young, in any case. So Jack the lad will live to be a hundred.'

'But listen, Tess! What if—'

'Cat, it's half past six on Sunday morning! Please can we do this some other time?'

'Sorry, I didn't realise.'

'Why don't you buy a clock?'

'I've said I'm sorry.'

'Okay, apology accepted, now I'm going back to bed.'

'Why, have you got company?'

'Yeah, I might have, Mrs Nosy Parker.'

'Who is it, someone nice?'

'I haven't quite decided yet,' said Tess. 'By the way, what happened when you went to Dorset? I assume that's where you must have gone? I tried to call you but your phone was off. So did you see the place?'

'Yes, and it was fabulous! The hotel was gorgeous. The gardens were amazing. There was this fantastic marble fountain. It needs a lot of work done on it, but it could be wonderful. Then there's going to be this awesome health club with saunas, tanning salons, plunge pools – Tess, I've got so much to tell you! I—'

'Tell me tomorrow, eh? At this very moment, I have a pot to watch, a fish to fry.'

'A pig who needs a poke?'

'Yeah,' said Tess, then giggled and hung up.

Is this getting seriously weird?

Tess was very keen to hear about the trip to Dorset, which Cat described in detail.

Well, maybe not in detail.

Okay, leaving out a lot of things, including everything to do with meeting Adam Lawley.

When Cat had finally run out of steam and Tess had had enough of wedding stuff – or temporarily, at any rate – she nodded at Cat's mobile, which was lying on her desk. 'If you're still hot and bothered about Whatsisface, why don't you try ringing him?' she asked. 'You never know your luck. He might be taking calls today.'

'What?' said Cat, who couldn't believe Tess was suggesting this, that Tess had read her mind.

'I said, why don't you phone him?'

'But I hardly know him!'

'Sorry?'

'Oh – you mean phone Jack.'

'Who else would I mean, you numpty?'

'No one else, of course. I'm sorry, I'm just tired.' Snap out of this, Cat told herself. You're going round the twist. You need some psychiatric help. 'I – um – I don't know what to say.'

'I'll call him, then.'

'You dare!'

'Okay, okay, calm down.' Tess glanced at the phone again, her fingers twitching dangerously, or so it seemed to Cat. 'Do you, by the remotest chance, happen to have a number for his mother? Or for a relation? Does he have relations?'

'He told me he was brought up in an orphanage in Surrey. He never knew his parents because he was abandoned as a baby in a carrier bag outside a hospital near Waterloo.'

'You're sure it wasn't in a handbag in the cloakroom at Victoria?'

'What?' Cat frowned at Tess. 'Oh, don't be so mean,' she snapped. 'I think it explains a lot about him – his need for unconditional affection, his need to test his friends—'

'His need to be a big fat liar, his need to be a git.'

'Jack's not a git, he's insecure.'

'You're in denial. So maybe he was left outside a hospital, and maybe it was in a grocery bag. Or maybe he's not human? Maybe he was beamed from outer space? Maybe he's an alien, and maybe he's gone home to Planet Weird? Why haven't we considered that?'

'Why don't we change the subject?'

'Yes, okay.' Tess grinned. 'We had a great time at the Abba tribute gig. You really should have come. It was a groovy scene, as I believe our mothers used to say. I met a man.'

'You always do,' said Cat. 'What's this one like?'

'Nice smile, cute arse, but brain dead. Good sex, no conversation, and I won't be seeing him again. A shame, because he's into stock car racing and I'd quite like to have a go at that. So come on, tell me more about what happened down in Dorset.'

'Like I said, the place is beautiful, the gardens are spectacular, and later on today I'm going to ring the woman at Supadoop Promotions and tell her that I won't be getting married after all.'

'You don't mean it, Cat.'

'I do.'

'You're mad,' said Tess. 'Look, I tell you what – why don't you give that tosser two or three more days? I'd put serious money on him turning up again.'

'But do I really want to marry a man who comes and goes to suit himself?'

'You want a wedding at the Melbury Court Hotel, especially if that woman's going to get you in *Hello*.'

'Tess, I wish to God you'd make your mind up! First you're telling me to find myself another man. Then you and Bex say I should call it off. But now you reckon Jack will soon turn up.'

'Okay, I'll spell it out. Bex and I are dying to be your bridesmaids. We want to be part of your luxurious dream wedding at the Melbury Court Hotel. But sadly we're not very keen on Jack.'

'So you still think I should find myself another man?'

'Yeah, that would be good. But in the meantime, maybe keep your options open and don't close any doors?'

Cat was working on a database when Tess came up and dumped the office phone down on her desk. 'It's for you,' she said.

'Oh, God,' said Cat, assuming it was Fanny – had she given Fanny the number of the office? 'Wh-who did you say—'

'I didn't, but it's a guy called Adam something, whoever he might be? He says he bought some roof tiles here a week or two ago, and you did the paperwork for him.'

'Oh,' said Cat and breathed again, relieved it wasn't Fanny, but also hoping there weren't any problems with the tiles, that they weren't made of concrete after all. She was aware that she was colouring up. 'He's—'

'He's waiting, dummy.'

So Cat picked up the phone. She knew her face was pink, that Tess would notice, and she told herself to get a grip. 'Good morning, Mr Lawley,' she began. 'What can I do for you?'

'I noticed some Elizabethan chimneys in a corner of your yard,' said Adam Lawley. He clearly didn't believe in bothering with superfluous stuff like hi-Miss-Aston-how-are-you, or what-a-strange-coincidence-meeting-you-in-Dorset. 'I don't know if they're genuine? I didn't get a proper look at them. They might be garden ornaments from Homebase or from B&Q.'

'They're genuine Tudor terracotta, Mr Lawley,' Cat replied, as she clicked through the database. 'Barry got them from a place in Lewes. They're signed with somebody's initials, it looks like ATD, and they're dated 1565. Do you want to come and see them?'

'Yes,' said Adam Lawley. 'May I come today?'

'Of course you may,' said Cat. 'The yard is open until three.'

'I'm in Gloucestershire right now and I won't be back in London until after four.'

'That's not a problem, Mr Lawley. I'm here until half five. So just ring the bell, then I can come and let you in.'

'*Ooh, Mr Lawley*,' simpered Tess, as Cat put down the phone. '*Do you want to come and see my genuine Tudor chimneys, and would you like an after-hours appointment?* What's with all the smarm and charm, then – are you trying to pull?'

'I don't know what you mean.'

'What's he like, this Adam Lawley geezer, is he fit?'

'I really couldn't tell you. I've only met him once, and that was in the pouring rain.'

'Then why've you gone all red?'

'I haven't.'

'Yes, you have – you're blushing like a poppy. Go and look in a mirror, and you'll see.'

'Tess, I'm not remotely interested in Adam Lawley. When he comes, or if he comes, why don't you take him round the yard yourself? I'll get on with this database. Barry's messed it up. He's been putting stuff in the wrong columns and it will take a while to sort it out.'

'Sorry, but tempting though you make it sound, I can't do anything with Mr Lawley.'

'Why?' demanded Cat.

'I'm going out.'

'You never said.'

'I've only just remembered.'

'Why don't you ever put things in the diary?'

'I'm a dealer, buyer and negotiator, not an office manager. I don't write in the diary, that's what you're supposed to do. I'm almost sure I told you, anyway.'

Tess stood up and shrugged into her coat. 'I'll be out all day, in fact,' she added. 'I have an appointment with a lady who's demolishing an outhouse. She wants to know how much we'll give her for a ton of blue Victorian slates. She asked if we'd consider taking them in part exchange for a new bathroom suite – like as if we're Homebase? I explained this is a salvage yard.'

'What about this afternoon?'

'I'm calling on a man in Hillingdon. He's got some genuine Arts and Crafts stained glass. Or so he says. All studio of Rennie Mackintosh, all signed and dated. I'll believe it when I see it. So you'll have to deal with Mr Lawley all by your little self.'

'I dare say I can manage.'

'You'll have to, won't you, love?' said Tess. 'Barry's gone to Chesterfield to fetch those Georgian spindles and a big Victorian cast iron fireplace I don't think he'll ever sell. It's all in the diary, if you want to have a look. He won't be back until tonight.'

'I'll lock up, don't worry.'

'I wasn't worrying, just telling you.' Tess wound her fake

Armani scarf around her neck. 'But let me give you some advice?'

'What's that?'

'They're all hunters, men. They know by instinct when a woman's wounded. They know when they'll be able to make an easy kill. So you watch yourself with Mr Adam Lawley, right?'

I'm only going to sell him chimneys, Cat thought crossly, as she heard Tess start the flatbed truck belonging to the yard and drive away. I'm not going to offer him my body.

Now you come to mention it, that might be a plan, observed a little voice inside her head. You'd like to get his shirt off, wouldn't you?

Oh, don't be ridiculous, she muttered to herself.

She went into the cloakroom and splashed lots of cold water on her face. 'I am so not interested in Mr Adam Lawley,' she told her reflection in the glass.

'Ha, we'll wait and see,' the glass replied.

Obviously, Adam had thought while he was shaving earlier that morning, it really didn't matter if he was attracted to a girl who was engaged to someone else.

She was out of reach, he told himself and his reflection. So talking to this girl would be like talking to his granny, not that Cat looked anything like his granny, and not that he was actually attracted.

Or not very seriously attracted, anyway.

After all, his heart was broken, wasn't it? So how could he feel anything at all?

He forced himself to think about the work he had in Middlesex, where he was involved in half a dozen different projects, all in various stages of completion.

The Elizabethan manor house, whose grounds had all been swallowed up by a small estate of smart new homes, and would be a conference centre soon, didn't need replacement chimney pots. But the budget would allow for it, and he had seen the very ones in Barry Chapman's salvage yard.

When Cat let him into Chapman's yard at ten past five – the traffic had been terrible, and he'd wondered more than once if she would have locked up and gone home by the time he got to Walthamstow – he saw at once that she was looking good. A little tired, perhaps, a little pale, but she'd probably had a busy day.

She'd done something different with her hair, had pinned it up with pretty golden combs, and some of it was falling down in graceful, dark blonde curls.

His fingers itched to loop them up again.

She wore a pale pink top and smart black trousers which showed off her long legs, and her arms were dusted with light golden down, and around her neck she had a pretty silver chain which looked Victorian or Edwardian perhaps?

Why was he bothering to notice?

'Mr Lawley?' Cat was looking at him curiously. 'I assume you want to see the chimneys?'

'Yes, that's right,' he said, and told himself to get a grip.

'Okay, let's go out into the yard.'

Adam took a good look at the chimneys, satisfied himself that they were genuine sixteenth-century Tudor terracotta, not from B&Q, and told her that he'd take them, if they could agree a price.

Cat was chewing at her lower lip in a way he'd noticed some girls did when they were worried, anxious, nervous or preoccupied.

But why would she be anxious?

Well, they were alone together out here in the yard.

Perhaps she felt intimidated, even scared of him?

She didn't need to be.

'Something wrong, Miss Aston?' he enquired.

'No, Mr Lawley, nothing's wrong.'

She turned to walk back to the office, so he followed, trying all the time to think of something safe to say, something to defuse the tension he was sure he couldn't have created, but which was getting tighter by the minute.

The wedding – girls loved talking about weddings and engagements, or in his experience most girls did, even though he'd got it wrong with Maddy.

Gwennie was forever going on at Jules to get engaged, leaving wedding magazines and wedding venue brochures lying round the flat. She and her girlfriends were always going off to wedding fairs, coming home with goodie bags and catalogues and samples.

Then they'd sit for hours on the sofa all soulful-eyed and wistful, talking about corsages and cupcakes and table decorations – which were better, real flowers or high-end artificial, not orange plastic roses, obviously, and had little pots of lavender been done to death?

'Did you enjoy your trip to Dorset?' he began.

'Yes, thank you, Mr Lawley,' Cat replied. 'I had a lovely time.'

'It's a very attractive place, the Melbury Court Hotel.'

'It's gorgeous,' Cat said tonelessly.

'You and you fiancé must have a lot to do, organising something like a wedding at long distance, sorting out the guest list, working out who's sitting next to who, deciding on a menu?'

'Yes, it's quite a challenge,' she agreed and went back to chewing at her lip, gnawing at it hard enough to draw a bead of blood.

'You mustn't worry,' he continued heartily. 'I'm sure everything will work out fine.'

But she didn't comment.

'There's still a lot to do at Melbury Court. The whole

project – house and grounds and outbuildings – it's one big work-in-progress. But the interior of the house itself is nearly finished, and I'm sure the health club will be up and running in good time for your big day. You might decide to have your hen night there?'

She turned and glanced at him for half a moment. Then, to his astonishment and dismay, her eyes filled up, spilled over.

'What did I say?' he asked, bewildered.

'You—you didn't say anything at all.'

'But what's the matter?'

'I'm so sorry.' Cat groped in her pocket for a tissue. She found one, wiped her eyes with it and then she blew her nose. 'It's nothing to do with you,' she added. 'It's—please, Mr Lawley, don't take any notice. Let me have a moment and I'll be all right again.'

'Perhaps I should come back some other time?'

'R-really, it's okay,' choked Cat. 'Come into the office and I'll sort out the paperwork for you.'

Although she did her best to get a grip, Cat found she couldn't stop crying. It was as if someone had turned a tap on in her head. She sat there sobbing like a child who'd had its lolly snatched or lost its comfort blanket.

As Adam Lawley waited while she sorted out his paperwork, he looked as if he wished he could be anywhere but Chapman's Architectural Salvage yard, and Cat thought – who could blame him?

When she'd named a price, he had agreed to it at once, even though on reflection it was somewhat on the high side, and he could have haggled, and he must have known it.

'What time do you finish?' he enquired, as she screwed up yet another tissue and lobbed it at the bin.

'Ten m-minutes ago,' she sobbed. Then she started shutting

down computers, pulling down the blinds, collecting mugs and taking them into the little kitchen.

'Where are all the other guys who work here?'

'B-barry and Tess have gone to see some people who have stuff we want to buy, or who want to sell their stuff to us,' she told him, knuckling her eyes. 'But we don't have any other appointments. So when I've s-sorted out your chimneys, I'll go home myself.'

She blew her nose again. 'Do you want to take the chimneys with you now?' she asked. 'If you do, I'll need to go and find some straw or bubble wrap. Damn – I've shut the payment system down. I'm sorry, I'm not thinking straight today. I don't suppose you want to pay with cash?'

'I'm about fifty short in ready cash,' admitted Adam. 'But I'm in no hurry. If you'll mark them sold, I'll come back and pay for them and take them later on this week. Miss Aston, please don't think I'm being nosy, and I know it's not my business, but why don't you—'

'Get a grip?'

'I was going to say, why don't you come and have a drink? You sound like you could do with one.'

Cat looked at him again and saw he was concerned – that although he looked so serious and had clearly never learned to smile like other people did, that his dark eyes were kind. 'Yes,' she admitted. 'Yes, perhaps I could.'

'Do you know any decent pubs round here?'

'There's a very nice one round the corner, quite s-smart for Walthamstow.'

'You think they'll let me in?' Adam glanced down at his torn and faded jeans and at his workman's boots, which were scuffed and crusted with yellow Cotswold mud.

'There's a scraper in the yard,' said Cat. 'If you get the worst off, I'll finish locking up, and we can go.'

'Okay,' said Adam and went to find the scraper.

As Cat pulled on her coat, she thought, I shouldn't be going drinking with this man. What if, as she and Adam Lawley came out of the yard, Jack himself came walking up the road?

What if he was on his way back home, to tell her he'd been stupid, and say could she forgive him, and that of course he loved his darling Cat, of course they would get married?

What if he saw her with another man – would he have a fit?

Yes, he just might.

Jack always liked a drama – a fight, a scene, a row.

But Adam Lawley had been so sweet, so kind, and she so didn't want to be alone. The company of an undemanding stranger she probably wouldn't ever meet again – she'd send Tess out to see him when he came to fetch his chimneys – was somehow very appealing. After all, he didn't know that over the past day or two he'd been filling up her psychic void.

What the hell, she thought. She grabbed her bag and shoved the office keys into her pocket.

The Red Lion was an old Victorian pub which hadn't been done up, and Cat loved it to bits. She especially loved the beautiful ceramic tiles and the well-polished wood and gleaming brass. Barry had had his eye on all the fitments for more than a decade, but the current landlord had said he'd never sell.

'What must you think of me?' said Cat, as she and Adam Lawley walked into the saloon.

'I think you need a drink,' said Adam calmly. 'I was also thinking it was time to have a pint. But I don't like going into pubs all by myself.'

'Why, do lonely ladies sidle up and bother you?'

'All the time,' said Adam. 'I have to beat them off. How are you feeling now?'

'A little better, thanks.'

'What would you like to drink?'

'A tonic water, please, with ice and lemon,' Cat replied. 'Diet if they have it, doesn't matter if they don't.'

'What about a slug of gin in it?'

'I don't like gin.'

'Or a shot of vodka?'

'Just a tonic water, honestly.' Cat thought, I'm not going down that route. I'm not going to be one of those women who weeps pure ethanol. I'm done with weeping, anyway. What happened in the yard was just a blip, a little aberration, and now I'm fine again. 'But don't forget the ice and slice.'

'Okay,' said Adam. 'You go and sit down.'

When he brought the drinks, Cat found her purse and asked how much she owed him.

'I don't remember what he charged me,' he replied.

'All right, I'll get the next ones.' She took a sip of tonic water. 'Thank you, Mr Lawley.'

'Adam.'

'Thank you, Adam.'

'You're more than welcome, Cat – if I may call you Cat?'

'Of course you may.'

'So what's the problem? Your mother giving you grief about the catering arrangements, the wording of the wedding invitations? Mutiny among the pageboys, bridesmaids disagreeing about their outfits? Or just pre-wedding nerves?'

'No pre-wedding nerves, because there isn't going to be a wedding!'

Then, in spite of making a big effort not to cry, Cat found she was sobbing all over Adam Lawley, all over again.

Adam was silent for a minute, then he said, 'Why don't you have a handkerchief? Those paper things are useless.'

He offered her a clean blue cotton one, which Cat took gratefully. She thought, so Adam Lawley has a wife who washes handkerchiefs?

It took a while, but finally she managed to stop crying. 'I haven't used a real cotton handkerchief for years,' she told him, dabbing at her eyes. Then, screwing up the scrap of sodden cotton, she stuffed it in the pocket of her coat. 'I'll get yours washed and give it back to you.'

'You keep it, I have dozens.'

'Goodness, have you?'

'I'm afraid so.' Adam shrugged. 'My mother thinks I'm still eleven years old. So, whenever I visit Mum, she makes me eat enough to feed a dozen body-builders for a week and I always leave with a clean hankie in my pocket.'

'She sounds sweet, your mum.'

'She's very sweet. But she'd like to mother me to death.' Adam drank some beer. 'I'm not trying to force you, but if you want to talk about it?'

'You'll be bored.'

'I won't.'

So Cat told Adam about Jack, about how he had gone to find himself, about the wedding competition, about how any minute Fanny Gregory would be pressing Cat for dates.

'So now,' she concluded, 'I have my wedding sorted, everything is going ahead, and Fanny's trying to get me in *Hello*. But there's no bridegroom. Go on, laugh – it's funny.'

'It's not funny.' Adam looked at Cat, his dark eyes serious and concerned. 'This man of yours, he sounds as if he's—'

'Charming, handsome, smart,' insisted Cat. 'Yes, he could be difficult at times. Artistic temperament and stuff, you know? I loved him, though, I really did. I love him still. If he walked in now, I'd be delighted. It would make my day, my year, my life.'

'Or maybe you would look at him and wonder what you ever saw in him?'

'No, that would never happen!' Cat insisted as she shook her head. 'Or – well, perhaps it might?' she added, meeting

Adam's calm but searching gaze. 'I've always known I wouldn't have had an easy life with Jack. But you see, I thought he was the one. I thought he'd be the father of my children. I've always wanted children, and I'd like to have some soon. Or before I'm past it, anyway.'

'You're nowhere near past it.'

'Do you want to bet?'

'You can't be more than thirty.'

'I'm almost thirty-two.'

'Oh, I see your point,' said Adam gravely. 'You're practically an old age pensioner. You'll qualify for free prescriptions soon, a set of NHS false teeth, elastic stockings and a hearing aid.'

'Only a couple more years to go before I get my bus pass.'

'You'll have a Senior Railcard and get your hair done cheap on Thursday mornings, like my mother and her friends.'

'Old age and decrepitude – they're looking more attractive by the minute.' Cat fished her slice of lemon from the bottom of her glass and started chewing it reflectively. 'Adam, I've been wittering on for ages. You've been listening so patiently. Why don't you tell me something about you?'

'There's nothing much to tell.'

'Go on, there must be something. I know a little bit about your work. But are you single, married? Leisure interests – origami, bridge, calligraphy, or something more exciting like arson, robbing banks?'

'I'm single.' Adam shrugged again and gazed into his almost-empty glass. 'I don't have many interests outside work, which takes me all around the country and occasionally abroad. I'll be off to Italy when I can snatch a break from Melbury Court.'

'Oh God, Melbury Court,' said Cat and winced. 'I'm going to have to talk to Fanny soon.'

But Fanny Gregory could wait, at least until tomorrow.

She turned her full attention back to Adam Lawley. 'You might be single now, but you must have had a lot of girlfriends?' she suggested, thinking, I'd put money on you not being gay.

'Yes, but they—I'm not sure how to put it.' Adam stared up at the ceiling. 'They don't tend to stick around. Girls like spending Saturday afternoons in Oxford Street or wandering round some awful, godforsaken retail park. On Sundays they like doing couples stuff, lying in bed all day and eating croissants, watching DVDs and doing – well, you know, and it's not really me.'

'So you don't do relationships? I think you're very wise.'

'You do?' Adam met her gaze, his own eyes dark, opaque but kind. 'You will get over him, you know.'

'I hope you're right.' Cat sighed. 'But I still think about him all the time, and when I wake up he isn't there, and that's when I start hurting. It feels like someone's sticking red hot needles in my heart. But I won't start going on again. You must be bored out of your mind. Why don't you tell me more about your work in Dorset?'

'You mean at Melbury Court?'

'Yes, if you like.'

'It won't upset you?'

'No, I won't be going there again.'

'I've been involved with Melbury Court for years. My father was a builder and he knew the people who bought it back in 1990. It had always been a private house and no one but the family and their invited guests had been inside for years. But the new owners were determined they would make it the best hotel in Dorset.'

'I think they did a brilliant job, don't you?'

'Yes, they did their best, but part way through the project they ran out of money and had to sell again. So now the place belongs to a consortium of businessmen. They've plans to make it earn its keep not just as a hotel. They want to rent it out for film and television stuff – for adaptations of the classics, Jane Austen and the like, for conferences, parties, weddings—'

'Yes, of course they do.'

'I'm sorry, Cat,' said Adam, reddening. 'You already know about the weddings.'

'It doesn't matter.' Cat knew she was colouring up herself because he'd said her name again and somehow this had changed things – she was not sure how or why. 'Who owned it when it was a private house?'

'A family called Denham. A hundred years ago or more, it must have looked much as it does today. But in the 1930s there was a disastrous fire. The house – it was plain Melbury House back then, not Melbury Court, that's just a modern affectation – was very badly damaged. It was left to rot until the owner's daughter, Daisy Denham, who was a well-known actress, decided to rebuild it and live in it herself.'

'She must have been quite rich?'

'Yes, she must,' said Adam. 'But she was smart and sympathetic, too. She did things properly. She got local craftsmen to make new doors and window frames. She had that amazing staircase fixed. She made sure the old and new stuff blended perfectly.' Adam turned to glance at Cat. 'She bought that marble fountain when she was on holiday in Tuscany and had it shipped to Dorset in 1956. God knows what she paid for it. She didn't keep the bill.'

'She wouldn't, would she? Who keeps bills for holiday souvenirs?'

'Well, quite,' said Adam wryly, and Cat could have sworn he almost-cracked an almost-smile. 'As far as I can tell it's never functioned as a fountain, or not here in England, anyway. So it would need new plumbing, state of the art electrics – everything. It would cost a bomb to get it working.'

'But wouldn't it be fantastic if you could?' demanded Cat. 'I'd love to see it working. It would be spectacular! Adam, I wonder why the actress didn't get it sorted when she had it sent to Melbury Court?'

'She probably forgot about it. She was in America most of the 1950s and the early 1960s, making films and doing shows on Broadway. She had several houses all over the world.'

'What was her name again?'

'Daisy Denham, perfect English blue-eyed blonde,' said Adam. 'She played ice-cold temptresses who broke her lovers' hearts, but she did lots of comedy as well. My mother says my granny was a fan.'

'I've never heard of Daisy Denham. But I'm not into vintage movies anyway.'

'My best mate's girlfriend loves them. *Rebecca*, *Casablanca*, *Vertigo* – she knows them off by heart. So I haven't dared admit to Gwennie that I'm working on Daisy Denham's house. She'd go on at me to steal a brick.'

'Yes, she probably would.' Cat found her handbag. 'Let me get you a drink?'

'It'll have to be some other time. I've got a date.'

'Oh, why didn't you say? You'll need to get back home, get showered, get changed and stuff.'

'I won't,' said Adam and Cat saw that almost-smile again. At any rate, the corners of his mouth turned up a bit and made her want to say go on, you know you can do it if you try. 'It's a date with football and a curry. There's an important match on Sky tonight, and I promised a mate I'd join him to support our team.'

'I see,' said Cat. She pushed her chair back and stood up. 'So I've made you late. I'm sorry, Adam. I shouldn't have rambled on. I know I've bored you rigid. But thank you for your sympathy.'

'You're welcome.' Adam stood up too. 'I wasn't bored.'

'I'll bet.'

'It's been good to talk. I mean it, Cat. I'll see you at the yard later this week. I'll come and get the chimneys.'

They walked along the road and parted at the bus stop.

As Cat sat on the bus, she thought, I know that name already. Denham, Daisy Denham – I'll have to ask my mother.

Or I'll google it.

But haven't I also heard the surname Denham somewhere else, and fairly recently?

She racked her brains but got no hits at all.

Jules was already in the pub, well-placed to see the screen.

Gwennie was snuggled up against him, looking happy enough to spend the evening watching football with her man.

She'd even brought her knitting. It was a mound of something pink and fluffy with vivid purple stripes. It looked like something off the Muppet show – perhaps it had escaped? If he poked it, would it bite his hand off? He was afraid it might.

'Your day been okay?' he asked, as he slumped down on Gwennie's other side.

'Yes, thank you, Adam.' Gwennie plained and purled, her plastic needles going clack-click-clack. 'We had a man come in for an appointment who hadn't seen a dentist since 1995. So it was sort of interesting working on his teeth, like doing dental archaeology. But we also saw some children who had perfect sets of twenty. Mums are much more clued up about acid, sugar, flossing nowadays ...'

As Gwennie rattled on about her job, which sounded

very tedious, dull and boring, about her boss the gorgeous Polish dentist who all the lady patients loved but who was firmly gay, about how much she'd like to train to be a music therapist because all sorts of damaged people could respond to music, but she didn't know how she was going to find the money so she could do a course, Adam drifted off into a daydream starring Cat, only coming out of it when Gwennie jabbed a needle in his side.

'How was your day, Adam– not too bad, I hope?'

'It was all right.'

'How are you getting on with that old manor house in Gloucestershire?'

'I've almost finished there.'

He didn't add, I took a weeping girl to have a drink. If he had, Gwennie would have fallen on him like a ton of paving slabs.

What's she like (she's nice, in fact she's charming), is she pretty (yes, good figure, lovely skin, green eyes and dark blonde hair), did you get her number (no, but I know where she works). So will you be seeing her again (I'd like to meet up some day, but I don't know if it would be wise), it's time you started getting over Maddy (I don't believe that's going to be possible), you can't work all the time, you know (why not, it stops me thinking and regretting and going round the bend).

He ate his curry, sort of watched the football, wound a ball or two of yarn for Gwennie – not too loose and not too tight – and thought about the girl.

There's always someone who's worse off than you.

A trouble shared, a trouble halved.

All that stuff his mother was so fond of spouting when he had a problem or she thought he had a problem and which drove him slightly mad.

Mum might have a point?

Cat was clearly suffering. She was in that terrible dark place he knew so well, the place where it was always cold and starless, the place where gloom and sorrow had their mansions, the place where evil goblins pushed sharp skewers through your tormented heart.

But it was funny – or it wasn't funny, nothing about the situation was remotely funny – talking to the girl had made him feel a little better and less miserable than he had for days.

Maybe trying to comfort someone else had done him good? Maybe he and Cat ought to be friends? Maybe he should contact her again, invite her to a film, suggest a concert?

Yes, that might be a plan.

Why had he said that stuff about not liking lazy Sundays, lying in bed and eating croissants, watching DVDs?

While he was with Maddy, those were the best times of all. When he'd been away all week and she had been in London, doing whatever she did to save the tigers, whales and pandas, it was always great to see her on a Friday evening, and—

'Your mobile's ringing, mate.' Jules snaked his arm round Gwennie and pushed Adam's shoulder. 'Mate, I said your mobile—'

'Yes, I know.'

Adam saw that Gwennie's lips had parted, heard that she was breathing slowly, deeply. She was probably hoping it was Maddy, that a reconciliation scene would soon be under way.

'Hi, Tom,' said Adam. He listened for a minute. 'Oh, I see,' he said. 'Yeah, that's a pity. But you don't need to worry. The timbers will be fine. A bit of rain won't hurt them. I'll leave here first thing tomorrow morning. I'll have to stop and sort a few things out along the way, but I should be with you about three.'

'Do you have a problem?' Gwennie asked him, clearly disappointed that it was only business.

'Yes, a sort of problem.'

'What?'

'It's nothing very serious, but it's going to mean I get behind with other things.' Adam pushed his phone back in his pocket. 'I left a local firm in charge of the re-roofing of a country house in Cornwall, but it seems they've messed it up. I'll have to drive down there tomorrow morning, sort it out. I expect I'll be away all week, and maybe next.'

'What about that place in Dorset, shouldn't you be there tomorrow?'

'Yes, so I'll call in, but I think Melbury Court will be okay. The foreman knows his stuff and all his lads respect him. They do as they're told. They can get along without me for a week or two. I'll always be in e-mail contact, anyway.'

'God, you stupid idiot, that was a bloody gift!' yelled Jules, and now he slammed his glass down on the table, splashing Stella over Gwennie's knitting. 'Mate, did you see that?'

'See what?' said Adam.

'A fucking tragedy of a pass, that's what!'

'I must have missed it, sorry.'

'Christ in a Toyota!' Jules was glaring furiously at the giant screen. 'It was a little beauty, and the halfwit let it go.'

Adam merely shrugged.

'Lawley, what's the matter with you tonight?' demanded Jules. 'This might be the most important match you'll ever see. Our team's facing relegation. They need your support. So why weren't you watching? Why were you on your mobile, nattering like some old woman? I'll be there at three o'clock, so mind you have the kettle on?'

'Calm down, Jules,' said Gwennie as she brushed the

drops of Jules's lager off her knitting. 'Please stop going on at Adam, too. When all's said and done, it's just a game.'

'It's more like a massacre tonight,' said Adam, picking up a ball of Gwennie's yarn which had fallen on the beer-soaked carpet. 'Our team's playing like a gang of grannies who've overdosed on tranquillisers.'

'Oh, belt up, the both of you. Lawley, it's your turn to get them in. Mine's a pint of Carling and a bag of cheese and onion crisps. The jumbo size, not those pathetic tiny little packs they do for girls.'

'Okay,' said Adam, getting up. 'Gwennie, are you ready for another drink?'

'Yes, I'd like a ginger ale please, Adam – some lemon, but no ice.'

As Adam went to get the drinks, he told himself that when he'd finished with the house in Cornwall he'd give Cat a call.

He'd keep it light and non-committal, just ask her if she fancied meeting up one evening for a drink and then he'd see what happened next.

He'd like to know her better, he decided, ask her what she loved and hated. What were her tastes in music – classic, indie, pop? What sort of movies did she like? Did she love to cook and was she always trying out the latest from Jamie or Nigella? Or did she live on ready meals and burgers?

He'd find out.

He'd go and get those chimneys, too.

Thursday, 2 June

How much longer is she going to keep me in suspense?

Monday, Fanny Gregory had said.

But which actual Monday had she meant?

There'd been one short voicemail message in which Fanny said she'd be in touch ASAP, and she had lots of plans for Cat and Jack, but she was busy, busy, busy with a million other projects.

The first Monday morning came and went, and then a second Monday came and went, and then a third, and now it was Thursday, and still she hadn't e-mailed, hadn't phoned.

Cat began to think she had imagined the whole thing – that she had dreamed the conversation she had had with Fanny on Easter Saturday, had been hallucinating when she'd visited the Melbury Court Hotel, had never seen that lovely fountain, had never walked in gardens which would have shamed the fields of paradise.

She supposed she ought to be relieved.

But she couldn't have imagined it, because when she did a bit of googling she found a lot of stuff.

Daisy Denham, for example – born in the East End and illegitimate when it mattered, she'd been adopted by a Dorset couple, started acting while still in her teens, gone to America in 1946, become a huge success in Hollywood and died in a motor accident with her actor husband Ewan Fraser in 1988.

She found some images of Melbury House as well. There was the fountain in the forecourt, but it wasn't playing. Maybe Adam Lawley had been right? Maybe it had never worked since it had come to England, and perhaps it never would.

But it must have worked in Italy?

Adam should be able to find out. Surely there'd be traces of old pipe work and lots of stains and markings on the marble, even if the pipes themselves were missing, even if the fountain had been broken up and then put back together again when it arrived in England?

She'd ask him when she saw him.

But she didn't see him.

Adam didn't come to get the chimneys, and eventually she decided that he must have changed his mind. She called him on his mobile and left a string of messages, asking him to let her know when he'd be coming for his stuff, but she got no replies.

This was most annoying because Barry carried on at her for marking things as sold when she hadn't taken a deposit. 'What were you thinking?' he'd demanded as he shook his head, adding that in case she hadn't noticed, he was trying to run a business here.

She was sort of disappointed Adam hadn't come, and it wasn't just because she'd lost a sale or two.

But then, as she was locking up that Thursday afternoon, long after Tess and Barry had gone home, Adam turned up in a transit van.

'Hello, Mr Lawley,' she began, as she told herself to get a grip and not to fantasise about this man, who clearly wasn't interested in her in any case. 'You've come to get your chimneys, I assume?'

She hoped she sounded both professional and courteous, as if they hadn't ever met before, or only on a business footing, anyway.

'Yes, that's right,' he said. 'I got your messages,' he added. 'Did you get my replies?'

'You rang this landline, right?'

'Yes, and it always went to voicemail.'

'We've had some problems with incoming calls and

voicemail. I should have given you our mobile numbers. But don't worry, we've still got your stuff.'

'I wasn't worried,' Adam said. But he seemed a bit on edge, distracted. Perhaps he couldn't wait to get the chimneys in his van, pay up and drive away?

Cat was on the point of saying, that drink we had together, Mr Lawley, I didn't read anything into it, you know.

'I'm sorry I didn't come to fetch them sooner,' he continued. 'I've been very busy.'

'It's no problem.'

She offered him the paperwork.

He took it without comment. He didn't even check it. She could have stuck another couple of zeros on and he would not have known.

She handed him the card machine.

'Doing anything this weekend?' he asked as he keyed in his PIN.

'No – well, nothing very exciting,' Cat replied. 'I'll probably go shopping with some mates. Then we might go to see a film. Or we'll get a takeaway and maybe rent a couple of DVDs. What about you, Adam – got something thrilling planned?'

She'd called him Adam. She'd meant to call him Mr Lawley, keep everything all businesslike, but now …

She felt her face glow red and hoped he wouldn't notice.

'I'm going to Wolverhampton,' Adam said. 'I'll be seeing a man about a house he's just inherited from his uncle.'

'What sort of house?'

'At first he thought it was Victorian. But since he's started doing it up he's realised it's much older. So he wants advice on just how far he should go back – to the Georgian cornicing, to the original Tudor beams, should he take out an old Victorian fireplace, what might he find behind it and all that sort of thing.'

'Ooh, sounds really interesting!' cried Cat.

'You think so?'

'Yes, I do! I'd love to get my hands on an old house. It would be so exciting. I'd strip off all the woodchip. Perhaps I'd find a gorgeous marble fireplace underneath a nasty modern one. I'd pull off hardboard panels and discover the original Georgian doors. I'd rip off horrid ceiling tiles—'

'You should come with me, then.'

'I'd love to, I—'

But then she stopped. She felt her face grow hot again. She didn't know why she'd said it. She hadn't meant to say it. Now he would think she was a desperate case. Or that she was flirting, vamping him, was doing a Fanny Gregory on him, playing with him for the fun of it.

Or that she was keen to get her claws into a brand new man.

'I really meant', she added, feeling stupid, 'that if you're ever doing anything similar in London, perhaps I could come round and have a look? If I would be allowed on site, of course, and if—'

'I'll pick you up about half seven on Saturday,' said Adam, who was still staring at the card machine.

'It's just a day trip?' Cat said hurriedly, aware she was still scarlet or at least a violent shade of pink.

'I'll have you back by midnight, Cinderella,' promised Adam, looking up at Cat with an unreadable expression on his face. 'What's your mobile number, Cat? Whereabouts in London do you live?'

She told him and was shocked and horrified by the amount of pleasure she had felt when Adam said her name.

'I'm busy all day Saturday. I've got some stuff to do,' she said to Bex, when Bex and Tess suggested meeting up for lunch then serial-trawling H&M and Uniqlo and maybe

L.K.Bennett – if their sale had started – on Saturday afternoon.

'What kind of stuff?' demanded Tess.

'I'm sorting out my life,' said Cat. 'You know – decluttering?'

'Do you still want that lime-green bag you got at TK Maxx?'

'I said I was decluttering, not throwing all my decent stuff away. You can have it when I'm tired of it.'

'I won't want it then.'

'Do you need any help?' asked Bex. 'I mean with this decluttering?'

'No, because you'll only try to make me give you things. You'll say they've never suited me and will look ace on you.'

'Of course she will,' said Tess. 'Why else would she offer, putty-brain? So we'll pop round about half one on Saturday. We'll have a bit of lunch at yours and then we'll hit the shops. I'm at the yard until half twelve, so get the kettle on.'

'I could come earlier,' offered Bex.

'I want to do this on my own,' insisted Cat. 'I don't need any so-called help, especially from greedy vampire scavengers like you.'

'All right, give us a call when you've decluttered,' Bex said kindly, as if she were talking to a nervous imbecile. 'We'll meet you later, have a drink. Oh, and by the way – if by any chance you should decide you've had enough of that fake Prada satchel, I'll take it off your hands.'

'If you don't want that yellow top with cutwork sleeves, I've always rather liked it, so—'

'Yes, all right,' said Cat, to shut them up.

Friday, 3 June

What's got into me?

She knew she should be sleeping.

So why was she trying on almost everything she owned, from scruffy, casual, laid-back, lazy-Saturday, to going-to-a-golf-club-dinner-with-her-parents smart?

She put her hair up, took it down. She made her face up, wiped it off. She put on big hoop earrings, put on studs. But nothing about her face, her clothes, her hair, even her flipping earrings, looked even halfway right for a day trip out with Adam Lawley.

Why am I doing this? she wondered, as she slung her clothes back in the wardrobe, on the bed or on the floor.

The girl whose face was in her mirror shrugged and said she didn't know. But hadn't she better get some rest?

So she took a long, relaxing shower. She made herself a mug of something which was meant to help you nod off straight away. She stirred in lots of honey. She put her lavender-and-hop-filled therapeutic pillow in the bed.

The dawn was breaking when at last she fell asleep.

Why does Adam Lawley have this effect on me?

She found she was ridiculously, absurdly pleased to see him.

When she saw him standing on her doorstep on the dot of half past seven that sunny Saturday morning, looking good (but not too good) in clean jeans that fitted properly (but weren't ostentatiously designer) and a pale blue shirt which showed off his broad shoulders and his narrow waist (but didn't have any special style details that would make him look like he was trying much too hard), smelling nice (but not too nice – there was a pleasant hint of soap and shaving foam about him, but he didn't reek of aftershave or men's cologne), she didn't have any trouble smiling as she said hello.

He managed one of his almost-smiles, too.

'How have you been?' he asked.

'Okay.' She shrugged apologetically. 'I'm sorry I cried all over you that time,' she added, she hoped casually, as they walked down the street.

'You mustn't worry about it.' Adam turned to glance in her direction, and there was that almost-smile again. 'It often helps to talk our problems through. I'm sorry it's so dirty.'

'What?'

'My car, it's very muddy.' Adam shrugged apologetically. 'But there wasn't time to hose it down.'

'This—this thing is yours?'

'I'm afraid so, Cat.'

It was the most enormous Volvo Cat had ever seen. It looked as if it had been made a hundred years ago. It was all huge bumpers, a bonnet like a battering ram and giant leather seats.

Its paintwork was all cracked and scuffed and bubbled, sprayed or re-sprayed an ironic green. It was an ecological disaster, a fuel-hungry behemoth of a thing.

'Goodness, what a whopper.' Cat stood back and stared at it. 'I thought my dad's was big, but yours is even bigger.'

'Girls say that all the time,' said Adam gravely, as he unlocked her door – no central locking on this great green dinosaur, she noticed. 'It's heavy on the gas, it isn't pretty, but I need it for the stuff I cart around.'

'It's big enough to live in.'

'Sometimes, Cat, I do.'

As Adam held the door open, once again she felt that warm sensation when he said her name.

Adam couldn't believe how pleased he was to be with Cat again.

Or how much pleasure he had felt when she had opened her front door, smiling and apparently delighted to see him. Of course, he had to admit this pleasure probably had a lot to do with Cat being so pretty – especially this morning, in her washed-out jeans, white sandals, short-sleeved cardigan and flowery top.

She wasn't wearing any make-up, or it didn't show, and that was fine by him. He hated painted faces, even though he knew he shouldn't, that it was a woman's right to choose.

'*What about you, Adam – got something thrilling planned?*' she'd asked him, and his name upon her lips had seemed a kind of blessing.

'You're almost smiling, Adam,' she observed as he started to untangle the old-fashioned seatbelt.

'That's because it's such a lovely day.' Then he suddenly found that he was smiling properly, that he was grinning even, for the first time in weeks, or maybe months. 'It must be the best day we've had for ages.'

'Yes, it must,' said Cat and she grinned, too. She took the buckle and, as her left hand brushed his, he felt a pleasant shock, a jolt of happy electricity.

'Okay,' she said at last. 'I'm properly strapped in. What do you have to do to get this monster moving? Where do you keep the mice and bits of string?'

Adam turned the key in the ignition and Cat felt the huge green Volvo growl into life. 'We'll stop in Warwick, shall we, have a coffee, then go on to Wolverhampton?' he suggested.

'Great,' said Cat, and smiled. She couldn't help it. She knew today was going to be a good one. 'I've never been to Warwick. But there's a castle – right?'

'A castle, lots of Tudor buildings, mediaeval churches. It's an interesting little town. Well, if you like that sort of thing?'

'I do,' she said.

She stretched her legs out, deciding you could keep a dozen chickens in the left hand foot well. She giggled at the thought of Adam driving round the country in a mobile chicken farm, never short of eggs.

'What's so funny?' he enquired.

'Oh, I was just thinking – but I'm not going to tell you. It's too stupid, and you'll think I'm mad.'

'You think my lovely vintage Volvo is a joke?'

'Well, maybe – just a bit.'

'You're a good walker, are you?'

'Sorry, Adam.' Glancing at her feet, she realised she hadn't done her toenails for a while. The polish was at least a fortnight old and it was badly chipped.

Moving up, there wasn't much improvement – in fact, it all got worse. There was a big black mark on her left knee. A button was missing from her cardigan. But –

most embarrassing of all – she'd got a long white trail of toothpaste dribble down her top. She must look a sight, she thought, as she started scrubbing at it with a tissue, failing to make much of an improvement.

This morning, she had pressed the snooze button a time or three too many. So she'd had to rush around to dress, to eat a bit of breakfast and be ready for when Adam said he'd come. She wasn't wearing any make-up, and she hadn't done anything with her hair.

She couldn't remember even brushing it.

But it didn't matter, any more than it would matter when she had a slob-around-and-pizza day with Tess. Today, she could forget about her real life in London, about Fanny Gregory, the wedding competition, bloody Jack – especially Jack.

'Who will you say I am?' she asked as they drove through the quiet weekend suburbs.

'Who do you want to be?'

'What do you mean?' She glanced at him and saw that he was staring straight ahead, his eyes fixed on the road, and there was no trace at all of any almost-smile.

'You could be my business partner, secretary, personal assistant – or my friend?'

'I suppose we're friends?' she hazarded.

'I suppose we must be,' Adam said, but kept his eyes fixed firmly on the road.

They drove a while in silence.

Then they were out of London, and Adam said that since they had a bit of time to spare they'd go cross-country for a while before they joined the motorway.

He got tired of driving up and down the motorways. He fancied dawdling along some country lanes.

So they drove through lush and pretty Buckinghamshire, which was full of winding country roads and quiet country villages arranged round village greens. There were scatterings of ancient churches, manor houses, lovely Georgian rectories and a lot of fairly hideous modern infill, too.

'I don't know this part of England,' Cat told Adam. 'Where exactly are we now?'

'Oh, here be dragons,' he replied. 'Or reptiles, anyway – like Gordon Gekko, right?'

'I'm sorry?'

'I mean as in *Wall Street*. Do you know that movie? It's one of Gwennie's favourites. She fancies Michael Douglas. Cat, we're deep in corporate-raider-land. We're passing ordinary modern houses worth a cool five million or even fifteen million. See that one just over there with polystyrene pillars?'

'Yes, I think it's horrible.'

'It would sell for six or seven million easily. But, as I'm sure you've noticed, there are really gorgeous older houses round here, too. One day, when I'm a zillionaire, I'll—'

But Cat never found out what he would do, because as they drove round a sharpish bend they almost crashed into a Jaguar E-Type which was sitting in the middle of the road.

Adam spun the wheel. The big green Volvo veered off the tarmac and ploughed into a bank.

'Jesus,' Cat said shakily as they stopped mere inches short of an enormous oak which would have concertinaed the Volvo's steel bonnet and most probably concertinaed Cat and Adam, too.

'Cat, are you okay?' demanded Adam anxiously.

'Yes, I'm fine,' she said. 'Or at any rate, I think I'm fine. But what the hell does that fool think he's doing?'

'He must be trying to replace a flat.'

Adam left the Volvo and walked towards the E-Type – a very old and rusty one which made Adam's ancient tank look like a limousine – and asked if he could help. So she got out and followed him.

'I need to get a couple of warning triangles,' said Adam.

'Yes, okay,' said Cat, who was now looking at the man and seeing he was much older than his car and that his hands were dirty, torn and bleeding. 'What happened, then?' she asked as Adam went to fetch the triangles and put them in the middle of the road to warn oncoming traffic.

'I suppose I must have driven over a sharp stone or bit of glass.' The old man shrugged apologetically. 'I tried to steer into the verge. But the old bus started making such a ghastly noise I thought she might blow up. So I must have done some other damage when I stopped. Or rather when I skidded.'

'My friend can probably sort you out,' said Cat, nodding towards Adam as he walked back to the stricken E-Type. 'If he can't – are you in the AA? The RAC?'

'I'm afraid I'm not, my dear.'

'Oh – right.' Cat looked at the man more closely, saw his green tweed jacket was worn and patched and frayed, that he wore a moth-eaten old pullover and that his grey flannel trousers looked as if they'd come from a bazaar on Noah's Ark.

'What happened to your hands?' she asked.

'I was going to try to change the wheel. But, as I got the jack out of the boot, I slipped and fell. I'm so sorry, miss. You must be thinking, daft old bugger, having an accident himself and trying to cause another one as well.'

'I'm thinking I should clean you up.' Cat smiled reassuringly and then she led the old man to the Volvo. While Adam sorted out the E-Type, she sat its owner down and found her bag.

She took out a bottle of water and a pack of tissues. She gently wiped the old man's hands and satisfied herself that these were only surface grazes. They'd soon scab over but they'd probably be sore for a few days.

Then she noticed several clean and neatly-folded cotton hankies lying on the dashboard. Adam must have seen his mother recently, she thought. So she picked up a couple, folded them in triangles then bandaged the old man's bleeding hands.

'You have a very kind and gentle touch,' the old man said. 'I don't suppose you happen to be a nurse, by any chance?'

'No, but I'm a qualified first-aider.'

'Why is that?'

'I work in an architectural salvage yard where there are lots of hazards. So one of us has to be trained to deal with minor injuries and to give first aid.'

'Do you like your job?'

'I love it,' Cat replied. 'I meet loads of interesting people. I get to learn a lot about the building trade and I see some quite amazing stuff from years ago. Tudor terracotta, Georgian wood, Victorian stained glass.'

'You might like my house, then.'

'Where's your house?'

'It's twenty or thirty miles from here, on the way to Marlowe.' The old man shook his head. 'I'm a long way from home. I don't know how I'm going to get back. I don't think I'm fit to drive. I feel a little shaky.'

'You mustn't worry. We'll work something out.'

'Adam, have you finished?' Cat enquired.

'Yes, all done.'

As he wiped his dirty, oily hands on his clean jeans, Cat gave him a handkerchief and a my-God-you-are-a-sight-now look. It made him want to laugh out loud because for just one second she looked so like his mother.

Did all mothers teach their daughters how to do that look? He supposed they must.

'I've changed your tyre,' he told the man. 'But soon you'll

need to get them all replaced. The nearside two have hardly any tread on them at all. Also, when you skidded, you bashed the exhaust. I've moved your car on to the verge, out of the way of other traffic, but it's not fit to drive.'

'I thought I must have done a bit of damage.'

'It's all fixable,' Adam assured him. 'It's a lovely car,' he added wistfully, gazing at the E-Type 'It's one of the very earliest models, is that right?'

'Yes.' The old man nodded. 'I bought her back in 1962. We've been through a lot together, Boudicca and I.'

'Adam,' Cat said quietly, 'Mr – what's your name?'

'Moreley, Daniel Moreley.'

'Mr Moreley isn't feeling well and he isn't in the AA or the RAC.'

'Then we'll get a local breakdown service to come out.' Adam found his phone. 'Let's hope we can get a signal here. Cat, perhaps you could try your phone, too?'

Adam was the first to get a signal. He did a bit of googling, made some calls and soon he had arranged for Mr Moreley and his car to be picked up and taken home.

'But what's that going to cost?' demanded Mr Moreley. 'I don't have any money on me.'

'I can pay the men,' said Adam. 'You get home, rest up.'

'How will I pay you?'

'I'll give you my card. Then, when you're feeling better, you can get in touch with me, how's that? Mr Moreley, do you think you're going to be all right? Do you have any medical conditions – your heart, that kind of thing? We could call an ambulance?'

'Really, I'll be fine. I'm just a little shaken.'

Mr Moreley sat in Adam's Volvo, dozing in the sunshine.

Adam and Cat sat on a gate and waited for the breakdown lorry.

Cat thought, he's so kind, so generous. Some people would have shouted at the man then driven on, not stopped to help.

'Adam?' she whispered.

'Yes?'

'What if Mr Moreley never pays you?'

'Cat, it doesn't matter. It won't be very much. Less than a hundred, I imagine, or probably more like fifty.'

'I'll chip in twenty-five.'

'You won't!' retorted Adam. 'I might have killed you when we left the road and almost hit that tree. You're not chipping in a single penny.'

'We'll talk about it later. Goodness, it's so quiet here, apart from all the birdsong, obviously.'

'I can hear a blackbird. Or I think it's a blackbird, and what's that making a tap-tapping noise?'

'A woodpecker?' suggested Cat.

'A buzzard, cracking rabbit bones?'

'A vulture?' Cat said, smiling at him.

'Or a golden eagle?'

'Adam, don't be silly, golden eagles live in Scotland.'

'It must be a vulture then, or perhaps an albatross?'

'You are an idiot, Adam,' giggled Cat. 'Maybe I should try to teach you not to be so funny? Maybe I should push you off this gate?'

'Go on, then. I dare you.'

'I didn't mean it,' Cat said hurriedly, now feeling flustered and embarrassed, sensing she had crossed some boundary, or tried to cross it.

Adam made no comment.

They sat a while in silence and listened to the birds.

Twenty minutes later, they heard the breakdown lorry. Mr Moreley woke and watched the men as they put Boudicca on to the truck and chained her down. Then he let the men help him into the breakdown's cab.

'Thank you, Mr – Langley?' Mr Moreley peered at Adam's card. 'I don't have my spectacles, I'm sorry.'

'It's Lawley,' Adam told him, as he paid the breakdown men from a big wad of twenties.

Cat thought, why do builders carry so much ready cash? Barry had back pockets stuffed with tenners, twenties, sometimes even fifties. She supposed that, being in the salvage business, Adam and he were always on the lookout for a deal, an opportunity, a bargain.

They were like Boy Scouts, always prepared.

She and Adam got into the Volvo, Adam reversed it off the bank and then he and Cat went on their way.

'I suppose we'd better get on the M40,' Adam said. 'I'm sorry, but we'll have to bypass Warwick. We could go some other time though, make a day of it?'

'That would be good,' said Cat. 'Let's do it soon.'

'One weekend next month, perhaps?'

'You're on.'

Cat stretched her legs out in the foot well, flexed her toes. She'd helped somebody else and it felt good. She now knew Adam Lawley just a little better and she liked what she had learned.

Adam was the sort of guy you needed in a crisis, who wouldn't let you down, who would always know what he should do, what he should say.

They had almost reached the motorway when Cat heard a familiar jingle-jangle. She rummaged in her bag.

'It's probably just Tess,' she said as she pulled out her phone and started scrolling down her texts. 'God!' she exclaimed.

'What's wrong?' asked Adam.

'It's a text from Jack.' As she spoke, the sun was suddenly

masked by banks of cloud, and then – as if on cue – a wind sprang up and raindrops pattered on the Volvo's windscreen.

'Bloody hell, he's got a nerve,' she muttered as she read Jack's text. 'He disappears for weeks on end. He doesn't call, he doesn't e-mail and his wretched phone is never on. But then, I get this text. *Miss you, babe, where are you?*'

'Do you want to stop? Give him a ring?'

Cat started chewing at her lower lip. 'Do you mind?' she asked eventually. 'Just for a couple of minutes? I won't be very long.'

'You take all the time you need.'

'But aren't we in a hurry now?'

'Five minutes will be fine.'

Adam indicated left and pulled into a side road. By now, they'd driven through the shower, so Cat got out and walked a little way along the verge, tapping on her phone.

He watched her as she talked, as she gesticulated, as she threw her head back in – annoyance? In Christ-you're-such-a-wanker irritation? In blood-and-thunder fury?

Jack was no doubt getting the third degree, decided Adam, and it served the bastard right.

He thought, when Cat comes back, and when we're on the motorway, maybe I should tell her about Maddy? I could explain what happened, and then she'll realise I understand?

Or would that be too much like comparing battle wounds? Look, mine's bleeding more than yours? I've got a lot more stitches? Mine is going to leave a bigger scar?

If he started talking about Maddy, would he ever stop?

Cat was coming back towards the car, and he saw her face was one big smile of satisfaction. She'd obviously told Jack where he got off. Attagirl, he thought – I hope you gave the bastard hell.

'You all right?' he asked her, as she got back in. 'You're feeling better now you've cleared the air?'

'Yes, much better, thank you.' Cat was positively beaming. 'Adam, could you drop me at the nearest station, please?'

'I thought we were going to Wolverhampton?'

'You're going to Wolverhampton. I'm going back to Leyton. Jack has lost his keys.'

Adam dropped Cat off in Aylesbury where he reckoned she could get the fastest train to London Marylebone. It should take about an hour, he added. She would soon be safely home again.

As she said goodbye, she smiled at him.

He did not return her smile.

But she didn't care.

As she sat on the train going back to London, she knew that she had never been so happy – so genuinely, gloriously happy. Jack still loved her, still wanted to be with her and was sorry he had ever left.

What the hell had she been doing, driving off to Wolverhampton with another man – with a man she hardly knew, who almost never smiled, who said he didn't do relationships, who could have been a serial killer, serial rapist, anything – going off to look at some old house?

Or that was what he said they would be doing.

He might have meant to cut her up and throw her bits and pieces down a well. Then she would have made the *Daily Mail*, but not in the way her parents might have hoped to see their daughter in their favourite newspaper.

But he had helped that poor old man.

Oh, for goodness sake, she told herself – serial killer, serial rapist, good Samaritan or wolf in sheep's smart casual, Adam doesn't matter, anyway.

Adam might be the sort of man who'd make a great best friend.

But she didn't need a great best friend.

She needed Jack.

Cat and Jack arranged to meet at Mo's, a coffee shop a block or two away from Cat's own flat where Jack could get a coffee while he waited.

As she came round the corner, she saw him lolling in a window seat. He had his feet up on a stool and he was reading, lost in a magazine.

She stopped to watch him, take him in. He was still astonishingly handsome. He still had that lovely, charming smile – she knew because he smiled at the waitress who refreshed his coffee.

Then, as if on cue, he turned, he looked straight through the window. As soon as he saw Cat, his eyes lit up. He was on his feet and at the door as she walked in.

Then he was holding out his arms.

She ran straight into them.

'You've come home,' she cried, and she was almost sobbing as she breathed him in, as his familiar scent assured her that he must be real – that he was in her arms, her life again.

'Yes, sweet babe, I'm home,' he said and then he stroked her hair back from her forehead, kissed her lightly on the temples.

Cat heard the waitress sigh.

He drew back then and gazed into her eyes. 'Do you have a tenner, honeybee?' he whispered softly. 'Only I've run out of cash.'

Jack was back in London where he said he meant to stay.

He'd done a bunch of gigs in clubs up north. He'd even earned some money, so he said. He didn't add how much, of course, and Cat sort of suspected he had spent it, anyway. When they stopped off at a supermarket to get in some supplies for the weekend, she'd been the one who paid.

But this didn't matter, because to her relief and great delight he was thrilled about the competition.

'So we can have champagne?' he asked, after he and Cat had got to know each other again, which of course had taken several hours, and they were lying showered and exhausted on the sofa, looking through all the brochures while they played the DVDs, and Cat explained to Jack about the Melbury Court Hotel, about meeting Fanny and the others, and about Fanny saying she would get them in *Hello*.

'We get the bridal suite, the five course wedding breakfast for what is it, fifty guests?' demanded Jack. 'This Supadoop Promotions lot, they'll pay for everything?'

'Well, not quite everything,' admitted Cat, as she snuggled up to Jack and thought, my God, he's gorgeous. I'm so lucky! 'We might have to buy a suit for you. Or maybe we could hire one?'

'I'm not getting married in somebody else's trousers,' muttered Jack. 'I won't know where they've been. Okay, what else?'

'There'll be our rings, of course, and then there will be outfits for the bridesmaids and the pageboys. That's if we have pageboys. I'm sure my cousin Alice will expect me to ask her little boy, and I think we should, because he's cute. You mustn't worry, darling. Dad will pay for all that stuff.'

'You reckon?' Jack looked doubtful. 'Your parents, honeybee – they don't exactly like me.'

'They don't exactly know you.' Cat smiled at him and kissed him on his lovely, lovely mouth, and then she ran her fingers through his hair, his heavy mass of corkscrew curls, all glossy and blue-black. 'Once they get to know you properly, they're going to love you.'

'Do they know we've had this little blip?'

'No, of course they don't.' Cat shook her head. 'I don't go running to my friends and my relations with every little thing. I know you sometimes need to take time out. But I also knew you'd soon be coming home again. You wouldn't stay away forever. We love each other, right?'

'Cat, you mentioned being in *Hello*.'

'Yes, Fanny said she hoped she would be able to get us in the weekly magazines, and I think she has contacts at *Hello*.'

'But we're not celebrities,' said Jack. 'So how can we be in *Hello*?'

'I'm only telling you what Fanny said.' Cat could not stop touching Jack, could not stop kissing him. It was as if he were a power source and she had to be plugged into it. 'My darling, it's so great to have you home!'

'When are you going to see this Fanny Gregory again?'

'We hadn't fixed a date, but I'll call her now to say you're back.'

'But it's Saturday evening, and it's late.'

'It doesn't matter.' Cat got out her phone. 'She works twenty-four hour days. She's been dying to meet you, and I know there's lots of stuff she wants to do with you.'

'But right now I have stuff to do with you.' Jack took the phone out of Cat's hand. 'She'll have to wait her turn.'

Adam drove on to Wolverhampton in a sort of daze.

It wasn't anger. It wasn't jealousy. It wasn't even boring old resentment, the unwelcome realisation Cat preferred to be with someone else, that was gnawing, chewing at him now.

What was it, then?

He didn't know.

When it began to rain again, he welcomed it and drove on through the downpour, intimidating family saloons and even forcing lorries to give way by glaring at the drivers and flashing all his lights in a just-you-try-it-sunshine way.

He arrived in Wolverhampton, found somewhere to park and went to have a bit of lunch, then wished he hadn't bothered because it felt as if he'd eaten ashes.

He met the man with the Victorian house which was much older than it looked. The house itself was fascinating. Beautiful, in fact – it was the sort of house he loved.

Originally Tudor, it had lots of Georgian additions and embellishments which had made it even more appealing, more attractive, given it more charm, more warmth, more light.

But some of these additions were overlaid with hideous Victorian improvements. Then, at some time in the 1960s, off-white polystyrene tiles had been glued to all the downstairs ceilings, no doubt covering up some lovely Georgian plasterwork. The place would certainly repay some sympathetic restoration.

But, in Adam's present frame of mind, he was almost tempted to inform the owner it was nothing special, and – since by some planning oversight the building wasn't listed – he was more than welcome to do anything he liked.

Put in double glazing made of bright white PVC, take out all the pretty Georgian panelling, replace the rotting staircase with one from B&Q? Or even level it, and build a modern house with decent insulation, central heating, solar panels, patio doors?

He didn't envy Jack, he told himself, as he tried to concentrate on Mr Rayner's interesting old house, and to tell him yes, to keep the Georgian staircase, he could easily find replacement spindles, that would be no problem, and woodworm could be treated nowadays, provided it was not too far advanced.

'But that conservatory needs to go,' he added. 'It's a great example of Victorian jerry-building on almost non-existent bad foundations. The ironwork's rusted through and, if it isn't knocked down soon, it's going to fall down by itself.'

As he made some notes and took some photographs, he thought, it's not as if I even know the guy. This Jack – he might be genuinely charming, and genuinely sorry for going off to find himself, for making Cat so sad.

But when he had seen her back in May, poor Cat had been so miserable. So wretched, so despairing. Who had any right to make somebody feel like that, especially when the somebody in question was as kind and generous as Cat? A girl who'd help a stranger whose stupidity might easily have killed them all?

'Mr Lawley?' Mr Rayner looked at him, his eyebrows raised. 'I'd like you to help me, if you would? When could you fit me in?'

'I'll probably have some time in August.' Adam scrolled through his diary, checking dates. He had that stuff in Scotland coming up. He didn't really want any more work, and this would be a devil of a job. He'd have to find some sub-contractors, and he didn't know a single one in bloody Wolverhampton.

Perhaps he should get rid of that red button on his website, inviting anyone to contact him?

But what else could he do, apart from work?

What else was there in life?

Monday, 6 June

Confused or what?

When Cat woke up on Monday morning she couldn't quite believe Jack was still there. But she could feel him warm against her back and she could hear him breathing softly. So he must be fast asleep.

She'd dreamed about him coming back so often. Now her dreams had all come true. She was so very glad he'd walked into the yard that afternoon and bought those Cotswold tiles.

He'd bought those Cotswold tiles?

What lunacy was this?

She shook herself. She was still half asleep. She was in that state of mind when dreams and thoughts and what was real and what was just imaginary got confused, mixed up.

She raised herself up on one elbow, twisting round to make quite sure that it was Jack in bed.

Of course it was, and now he stirred. He woke up, grinned and pulled her down beside him. 'You don't need to go to work just yet,' he whispered, as he ran his fingers through her hair.

'Yes I do,' she told him. 'Jack, we haven't time for this. It's already half past seven. I'm going to be late.'

'So be late,' said Jack. 'You and I, we've got a lot of catching up to do.'

'I can't afford to lose my job.'

'You can, my darling, because I'm going places, and you're coming with me.'

Adam didn't intend to go back to the yard in Walthamstow. There were fifty other places where he could have got some Georgian spindles and he didn't need them until August, anyway.

But on Monday morning he found that he was drawn to Chapman's yard. He wanted to find out how Cat was doing, if the wedding was back on, if bloody/charming/ghastly/lovely Jack had sorted out his life.

The gates were open and so he didn't need to ring the bell. He just walked straight in. He found Cat in the office. She was looking wonderful this morning, all bright and fresh and glowing – her jade-green eyes were sparkling and her skin looked like new milk.

A dark-haired girl was sitting on Cat's desk and they were leafing through a pile of bridal magazines, their glossy pages promising – insisting – romance was a reality, that there was such a thing as genuine, everlasting love.

When they noticed Adam, they both jumped guiltily.

'Omigod, we thought you were the boss,' exclaimed the dark-haired girl, who Cat now introduced as Tess.

'Barry has the vapours at the very thought of weddings because his was a nightmare,' Cat explained, but Adam noticed that she wouldn't meet his gaze and now she'd coloured up.

'The best man got arrested for possession of an unlicensed firearm,' went on Tess.

'It was just a starting pistol he had got from eBay and he'd only brought it for a laugh. But they still cuffed him, took him in and locked him in the cells.'

'The registrar was drunk.'

'So Barry hates these magazines. But now we're wondering – satin, crêpe or velvet, which would be the best?' mused Cat. 'Duchesse satin would be good because it's thick and heavy and the wedding will probably be in winter ...'

'I'd go for duchesse satin, then,' said Adam. 'So that's the bridegroom sorted. What about the bride?'

'I'm sorry, Mr Lawley.' Cat put down her magazine, looked up, but then looked past him, still wouldn't meet his eyes. 'What can we do for you today – more Cotswold tiles, more chimneys?'

'Some genuine Rennie Mackintosh stained glass?' suggested Tess. She winked at him and grinned. 'It's on special offer, because it isn't genuine at all. It was made in China. But I bought it anyway, because it's very pretty and somebody is sure to snap it up. Or we can offer you some blue Victorian slates – two hundred quid a ton?'

'I need some Georgian spindles for a staircase. Oak, if you have them. I don't want mahogany or pine.'

Adam could not get over how amazing Cat was looking. He realised how much happiness could add to anyone's attraction, how it made a person sort of shine. So he must be really hideous these days, he decided, because he was anything but happy.

'These are for the house in Wolverhampton?' Cat enquired, as she put her magazines away and then picked up a bunch of keys.

'Yes, that's right,' said Adam, who found he couldn't drag his gaze away, that he was mesmerised.

'How many do you need?'

'Twenty-five to thirty – I'm replacing the whole run.'

'Right, let's go and have a look in Barry's special shed, where he keeps the good stuff.'

As he followed Cat into the yard, Adam saw she was almost skipping. She was almost dancing, like a child at a party. She fizzed and buzzed with happy energy.

'So you and Jack are back on course again?' he asked, as Cat unlocked the door and flicked a switch to reveal a hoard of timber – spindles, panels, newel posts and banisters, pine and oak and walnut and red Victorian mahogany.

'Yes, thank you, everything's back on,' said Cat. 'Now, let me think a moment, where did Barry put those spindles? I believe they're down here on the right.'

She led him down the central aisle, towards the gloomiest corner of the shed. 'What do you think of those?' she asked, and pointed. 'Early Georgian, English oak, and I think there are twenty-eight of them. So would that be sufficient?'

'Yes,' said Adam. 'Perfect.'

But he wasn't looking at the spindles. He was looking straight at Cat. In the dusty artificial light of Barry's shed she was so lovely that it made him catch his breath. 'How much does Barry want for them?' he managed to ask at last.

'I'll have to check the book,' she said.

She looked at him and smiled.

It was the smile that did it, the small white perfect teeth, the rose pink lips, the dimple in her cheek.

He took her by the shoulders.

He pulled her close to him.

'Cat,' he whispered, willing her to kick him, punch him, slap his face, at least push him away. 'You have to stop me now.'

But she didn't do anything at all.

So he drew her closer, closer, closer.

He looked into her eyes and saw himself reflected there. He saw her pupils had grown huge, so that they looked like pools of ink in which a man could drown himself. He thought how very much he'd like to drown in Cat's green eyes.

But, before he drowned, did he dare to kiss this woman?

Did he have a choice?

When he kissed her on the lips, she didn't seem surprised – in fact, after a moment's hesitation, she began to kiss him back, flicking her tongue across his teeth and tantalising him.

Then she put her arms around his neck. He felt her long, cool fingers in his hair. He felt them stroke his face.

Then he was in the real world again. It was as if he'd woken from a restless, troubled nightmare, had realised he'd been dreaming awful dreams. But now – thank God – he was awake, and he was kissing the most beautiful, the most gorgeous girl he'd ever known.

The minutes ticked on by, and he was still kissing Cat, and she was still kissing him with ever hungrier, more urgent passion, as if she couldn't get enough of him.

Then her hands were on his waist, first outside his shirt, and then inside it, stroking his bare flesh. She ran her fingers up and down his spine. She made him shudder with desire.

Then his hands were underneath her top, and her skin was smoother than the smoothest, softest silk, and her back was curved and sinuous, like a violin.

Then his mouth was on her neck, against her beating pulse, and he could almost hear the heavy thudding of her heart. It was banging like a marching band against his chest, and then, and then, and then —

A pickup dumping twenty tons of bricks, two vehicles colliding in the street – he didn't know and didn't care, but the crash brought Adam to his senses. Opening his eyes, he stared at Cat in horror, appalled by what he'd done.

'Adam, we — we shouldn't have done that,' she stammered, as she took her arms from round his waist.

'No,' he said. 'I'm sorry.'

'I'm engaged.'

'I know.'

'I'm in love with Jack.'

'I know that, too.' Adam raked his fingers through his hair, trying in vain to smooth it flat again. He tried to tuck his shirt back in as well, but he found his fingers wouldn't do as they were told. 'You're going to marry Jack.'

'Yes, and what's more I want to marry Jack.'

'Of course you do. I don't know what came over me just now. Cat, I'm really sorry. I can't apologise enough. Let's go and sort out the payment for the spindles, then I'll leave.'

He turned and walked back down the aisle.

She followed him.

Then she was sitting at her desk again, doing her sums and working out the VAT on Adam's Georgian spindles.

'W-what are you doing now?' she asked him, as she tapped away. 'I mean, where are you working these days?'

'I have some bits and pieces to finish here in England,' he replied. 'I need to go to Melbury Court again and check up on the next phase of the stables. I ought to go to Cornwall soon, and I have to sign off a few things at Redland Manor and make sure the owner's satisfied.'

Then he wished he hadn't used that word, because now he noticed Cat's red lips were bee-stung, swollen, and her cheeks were red as roses, and her neck was red as well, and he could see the imprints of his kisses on her throat, red, red, red, red.

'But then I'm off to Italy for a week, or maybe two. Italian craftsmen are way ahead of us with conservation, especially in marble. So I'm going to pick up a few tips. Then I'll be able to advise my clients here on marble, alabaster, gilding – all that sort of thing.'

Adam knew he was gushing like a geyser.

But he couldn't seem to stop himself. He had to say something, anything. The girl who worked with Cat was staring at him curiously now, her gaze scorching his skin, and he could hear her thinking – I know what you did in Barry's shed.

'That Italian fountain at Melbury Court, for instance,' he continued desperately. 'It's in urgent need of conservation. It's been stuck outside in our cold climate for more than half a century, and it's full of cracks.'

Just like my heart, he thought.

Or should that be my head?

'The Venus in the centrepiece, that's what I'll tackle first,' he added. 'There has been a bit of restoration, but whoever did it didn't do it very well. I'll never have the cash, time or resources to make the whole thing look like new, but I want to make the Venus beautiful again.'

'I'm sure you will,' said Cat. 'I've never been to Italy,' she added, her green eyes wide as they gazed up at him. 'I've heard it's very pretty?'

'It's more than merely pretty, it's absolutely gorgeous.' Adam gazed back at Cat and wondered where they went from here.

Nowhere, idiot, he told himself.

'What were you doing in the woodshed?' Tess demanded, as Adam left the yard, as they heard his engine firing up and heard his ancient Volvo drive away, with the spindles safely in the boot.

'What do you mean?'

'You and Mr Spindle, when you came back in here you both looked furtive. Why was his shirt untucked all round the back? Why have you got red marks all down your neck?'

'Adam was reaching for the spindles and he had to stretch. So that's how his shirt became untucked.'

'Adam, is it now? What happened to Mr Lawley?'

'I meant Mr Lawley, obviously.' Cat frowned at Tess. 'Barry had put the good stuff at the back, and Adam – Mr Lawley – had to climb over a pile of other things to get at them. I had to help him, and I grazed myself on those rough bits of planking Barry's stacked against one wall.'

'I reckon Mr Spindle was climbing over stuff to get at you.'

'Well, that's because you've got a dirty mind.'

'Well, you've been doing dirty things.' Tess shook her head. 'Look at the state of you, as I expect your mum would say. Your lipstick's been licked off. Your hair's a right old mess, all tangled up and coming down. Your top looks like you've slept in it. So something rough's been grazing you all right, but I don't think it was a plank.'

'You've finished, have you?'

'No, there's plenty more. When I said you needed to find yourself a man, I didn't mean you had to get the old one back and also grab a spare.' Tess looked hard at Cat. 'You and Mr Spindle are playing dangerous games.'

'I don't know what you're going on about.' Cat realised her cotton top was rucked up at the back, so now she pulled it straight. Then she smoothed her hair back from her forehead and clipped it up again.

She glanced down at the diary.

'You have an appointment with a Mr Walton at half past ten this morning,' she told Tess. 'He called to ask if we'd like half a dozen stripped pine doors with stained glass panels, which we would, and so I think you'd better get a move on before some other dealer beats you to it.'

'You've clearly got it bad for Mr Spindle,' Tess persisted as she fiddled with some ballpoints on Cat's desk. 'What will he be after next, I wonder? It's just occurred to me that it's quite interesting how he's been to buy the sort of stuff which also sends a message, I mean subliminally.'

'Whatever do you mean?' asked Cat and snatched her ballpoints back.

'Chimneys, spindles – think about it, phallic symbols, aren't they? Mr Spindle's obviously telling you he wants—'

'Please could you go and psychoanalyse Mr Walton, Tess? If you don't leave straight away, you're going to be late, and Barry definitely wants those doors.'

Cat got through the day by doing the most tedious, boring work, by sorting out the stationery cupboard and ordering new printer cartridges, by sharpening the pencils, getting all the filing done and throwing out the useless, dried-up pens.

She walked back home determined not to think of Adam Lawley any more, to blank him from her mind.

He'd said he was about to go to Italy, and this was just as well, because she knew for certain they must never meet again.

When he had kissed her, she'd heard angels singing – in fact, whole heavenly choirs had started up. There'd been trumpets, there'd been strings and there'd been flutes and harps. The London Philharmonic Orchestra, right there in Barry's shed.

As Adam's strong, blunt-fingered hands had stroked her face and body, as he had kissed her mouth, her ears, her neck, she had felt unreal, unlike herself, as if she were a goddess and she could do anything. As his mouth was on her throat, she'd been in ecstasy. She'd never, ever felt that way before.

If she'd stayed in that shed a few more minutes, she'd have probably ripped his shirt off, and started pulling off her own clothes, too. Yes, it had been that good.

Or rather, bad.

But she wasn't engaged to Adam Lawley.

She was engaged to Jack.

She pushed her hand into the pocket of her coat, hoping there would be some change to buy a magazine. *Marie Claire* or *Cosmo* would do nicely and would keep her occupied while Jack watched sport on Sky, as he would probably do tonight.

Or maybe she'd get *Glamour*, which was always good for fashion, shoes and wish-list handbags. She wouldn't find Adam in it anyway, his dark eyes burning, stoking her own desire.

But she didn't find any change.

She found Adam's handkerchief instead.

She must wash it, she decided, post it back to him. She could easily find out where he lived. It would be on his paperwork back at the yard.

Or could she deliver it in person?

What? You should drop it in a litter bin, she told herself. Pretend you never had it in the first place!

She held it to her face a moment, breathing in his special Adam smell, a blend of soap and wood-shavings and him.

Then she imagined she was kissing him again.

'These summer colds, they're awful,' said a woman, who had stopped to cluck in sympathy. 'You want to get an Olbas oil inhaler, darling, that'll probably shift it. My Henry swears by them.'

'I don't want it shifted,' muttered Cat. She shoved the hankie back into her pocket and walked quickly home.

As she went upstairs to her familiar little flat above the fruit and vegetable shop, the most delicious smell of dinner cooking floated down. Jack was a brilliant cook – that was on the very rare occasions when he could be bothered – and this evening he was clearly pulling out a hundred different stops.

She set her face to smile mode and then she pushed her key into the lock. Come on, she told herself, you're home. Your man is cooking you a lovely dinner. You're a very lucky woman.

You've been such an idiot today. You've given in to an absurd infatuation which won't lead anywhere.

Adam doesn't do relationships.

So what if he kissed you and it felt like you'd been born again? It didn't mean a thing to him. The man who really loves you is a couple of feet away.

As she took her coat off, she could hear Jack humming to himself. He sounded very pleased with life. When she went in the kitchen, he dropped his wooden spoon into the sink along with all the other pans and plates and cutlery and dishes, and gave her a big hug.

'Good day, honeybee?' he asked, and kissed her lightly on the cheek, a lovely, friendly, glad-to-see-you kiss.

'Yes, it was fine,' she said, while making sure she kept the happy smile glued on her face. 'What have you been doing with yourself, apart from cooking something wonderful?'

'I went to see a guy who organises gigs and got myself some dates in pubs in Essex. Then I went to Billingsgate, bought seafood, and I'm making a paella.' Jack took her face between his hands. 'Poor honeybee, you're looking really tired. Barry Whatsisface works you too hard.'

'I'm okay,' said Cat. 'Do I have time to take a shower?'

'Yes, if you're quick.' Opening the fridge, Jack took out a bottle of expensive white Rioja. 'Off you go, get showered, and then we'll have a great romantic evening, just the two of us.'

'Lovely,' murmured Cat, doing her best to sound as if she meant it, but hearing she was failing miserably. She hoped Jack wouldn't notice, wouldn't ask if anything was wrong, wouldn't spot those red grazes on her neck.

Or, if he did, he'd think he'd put them there himself.

But luckily he didn't seem to notice anything.

He sauntered back into the kitchen and carried on creating his paella, crashing pots and pans around and letting things boil over on the hob.

'By the way,' he called, as she kicked off her office shoes and stuck her tired feet into her bright pink Hello Kitty slippers – a present from her mother, to whom she would always be thirteen – 'that Fanny Gregory woman called this morning, while I was still in bed.'

'Why did she ring here, when she knows I go to work?'

'She rang you on your mobile.' Jack picked up Cat's

BlackBerry and grinned. 'When you went off in such a rush this morning, you left your phone behind.'

'Oh,' said Cat, and wondered if he'd looked through all her messages and contacts – was Adam Lawley there? She thought he must be. 'What did Fanny say?'

'She's sorry that she hasn't been in touch, but she's been busy, busy, busy. We had a little chat, and she wants to see us at her office.'

'Where's her office?'

'Somewhere off Oxford Street, she said. She gave me the address. I told her fine. It's all fixed up for Saturday at three. She had a very sexy voice, did Fanny. What's she like?'

'She's terrifying,' said Cat, and then she shuddered, thinking of how close she'd come to having to top herself. 'I'd hate to get on the wrong side of Fanny.'

'Oh, she's just a woman,' Jack said airily. 'I can deal with women.'

'You couldn't deal with this one,' Cat insisted. 'She's not a woman, anyway. She's the wrath of God.'

'I'll twist your Fanny round my little finger,' promised Jack. 'Go and have your shower and make yourself all fragrant and relaxed, and then it will be time to eat.'

Tuesday, 7 June

Why did I do that stupid, stupid thing?

At eight o'clock that morning Adam drove to Gloucestershire where he signed off the work at Redland Manor.

Then he drove on to Cornwall to make sure the project he was managing there could get on without him for a week or two.

All the time he worried about Cat, about what he had done. What had he been thinking, or not thinking?

But he also thought about what she had done. She had not been faking, he was absolutely sure of that.

Those kisses had been real.

When he got back to London, he started reading Gwennie's magazines, taking them to bed with him and studying them in detail, especially the features and the problem pages, trying to work women out.

But he only managed to confuse himself some more.

Soon he was wondering if there might be something wrong with him, because he was astonished by the things these magazines insisted most men thought (but didn't say to women), most men did (when women weren't around), and most men wanted (from a woman, especially in bed).

Position of the month – he turned one illustration round and round and tried to see how it would work in practice. But it defeated him. Whoever had cooked that one up didn't know a thing about anatomy, let alone hydraulics and suspension.

Now he could understand why Jules was grumpy and moved as if he'd done himself an injury some mornings, if Gwennie had been making him try weird stuff like this.

But he did get something out of all his in-depth study.

He read an article called *sexy signals – tell him what you really mean* and he concluded if a woman pulled your shirt out of your trousers, if she kissed you like she couldn't get enough of you, she meant she really wanted to be kissed.

But, all the same, Cat was in love with Jack.

She was engaged to Jack, and she was going to marry Jack, so he must never see that girl again.

'Adam?' As he was checking out a beauty feature on waxing as opposed to sugaring – ouch, both sounded hideously painful, he was glad he was a man – Gwennie came knocking on his bedroom door. 'Adam, are you decent?'

'Yes, come in,' he called and pushed the magazine he had been studying underneath the duvet. Then he picked up a paperback about restoring and conserving marble and tried to look absorbed.

'Sorry to disturb you. I know you're getting up at six tomorrow, but I wondered if you'd got my magazine?' Gwennie frowned at him – suspiciously? 'I haven't read it yet. I know I left it on the kitchen table, but it's not there now. I can't think where it's gone, unless we put it out with the recycling by mistake.'

'I'm sorry, Gwennie.' Adam had decided he'd give Jules a break tonight. 'I don't think I've seen it.'

'I just thought I'd ask.' Gwennie shrugged inside her fluffy towelling dressing gown. 'A bloke's bloke like you – of course it's not your sort of thing.'

Saturday, 11 June

Into the dragon's den?

'What are you going to wear?' demanded Jack.

'My plain black office trousers and my purple long-sleeved top.'

'But I hate that purple top. What about your denim miniskirt and your new green vest with lace on it? The one that shows your boobs off? They're both good on you. They make you look like one hot sexy lady.'

'Fanny will hate them, trust me,' Cat replied. 'She'll tell me they look common and I look common, too.'

'You're not dressing for some bossy bitch,' retorted Jack. 'You're my girl and you should dress for me.'

'Jack, I am a modern, independent working woman and I dress to please myself.'

'You're dressing to please Fanny Whatserface, or so it seems to me. Why have you put your hair up? You know I like it loose.'

'It looks less messy up,' said Cat. 'It isn't hanging all over my face and making me look like some sort of hippy. Jack, don't start a row.'

'Go and put your denim skirt on, then.'

But Cat wore her plain black office trousers and her purple long-sleeved top. Jack sulked all the way to Fanny's office, muttering that if anybody saw them they'd think he was dating a headmistress or a psychiatrist.

Rosie met them at the door. She took them up to Fanny Gregory's huge, palatial office. This was on the second storey of a Georgian house near Marble Arch, the beating heart of London.

But up here the noise of traffic was so muted that they could all hear each other breathe.

'Hello, Cat – we meet again,' said Fanny.

She was sitting at a great big desk which had nothing on it except for a new softly-humming laptop and the latest version of a very expensive mobile phone. The beautiful black greyhound was sitting at her side, looking at the visitors with interest and possibly amusement in his amber eyes.

'Hello, Fanny,' Cat said. 'Hello, Caspar, good to see you. Fanny, this is Jack.'

'Ah, the elusive bridegroom, our paths converge at last.' Fanny sent Rosie off to make some coffee then she looked Jack up and down. 'I must let you into a little secret, Mr Benson,' she continued. She leaned across her desk to shake Jack's hand and flash a vast amount of cleavage as she gazed into his eyes. 'When you didn't come to Dorset, I began to wonder if you actually existed.'

'As you see, I do,' said Jack, flashing back the most enormous, thrilled-to-meet-you grin. 'Please call me Jack,' he added. 'I'm sorry we couldn't meet up sooner, but I've been away.'

'You do stand-up, don't you?' As Cat stood there bemused, Fanny simpered like a teenage schoolgirl meeting Justin Bieber or his just-as-gorgeous twin. 'Gosh, I can't imagine anything more frightening! It must take such nerve, such guts, such raw, determined self-belief, to get up there in front of all those people, tell them jokes and get them laughing. What a talent you must have! But I can see you also have charisma, Mr Benson – Jack – and that's what really counts. I'll bet you knock 'em dead!'

'I do my best,' said Jack, and smirked. 'But this stand-up business – it's full of hopeless hopefuls trying to make it, even though they haven't got a chance. I have to fight for every gig. I have to prove myself against a hundred wannabes—'

'All the same, you get out there and win.' Fanny laughed a merry little laugh, and twisted one stray, clearly very expensive auburn curl around an index finger topped with a sharp, red nail. 'At Supadoop Promotions, we've been thinking of branching out a little – maybe taking clients from the worlds of sport and showbiz. Do you have an agent, Jack?'

'No, I don't.' Jack leaned across the desk and stared deep into Fanny's cleavage. 'But I'd really like one, especially one as go-getting and versatile as you. I think we could—'

'Ahem,' said Cat.

'Oh, Cat, my darling – we're neglecting you!' Fanny stopped ogling Jack at once. She took a big green folder from a drawer. 'Okay, my angels, sit down and listen up. We lost a bit of time while Jack was up in Manchester, and so we're on a tightish schedule now. Rosie, at long last, my love – what have you been doing? Pour the coffee, will you, sweetheart, then you can go home. Do we have any of those vegan-friendly, bran-rich biscuits left? The ones that man from Cheshire wanted us to try to sell to Fortnum's?'

'Yes, we do,' said Rosie. 'I tried to give them to the cleaning lady, but she said she'd rather have a Jaffa Cake, or something with a bit of taste to it in any case. Caspar doesn't fancy them at all. If you don't like them either, there are Garibaldis and some chocolate wafers in the tin.'

'What do you mean, a tightish schedule?' Cat asked Fanny, feeling anxious now.

'Monday, photo opportunity at half past ten, ideally in Hyde Park,' said Fanny briskly. 'Let's hope the sun comes out. Cat, wear something filmy, floaty, flirty – floral, if you've got it, prints are very in right now. Or don't wear that horrid purple top and those ghastly polyester trousers, anyway. You'll look like a bank clerk or a funeral director, darling heart, and that won't do at all. I'll have Rosie sort out a few outfits, keep some things on standby.'

Fanny paused for breath and then she carried on again at ninety miles an hour. 'The kind of look I'm thinking now is rosy-cheeked and dewy-eyed and kissable. Perhaps with bedhead hair? Well, not too styled and formal, anyway, nothing like you've pinned it up today, it's too severe. You look like an unsuccessful Russian dominatrix, angel, or a stern librarian, not a girl in love – and this promotion's about love, romance and fun, fun, fun.

'Jack, you must be hunky, sexy, gorgeous. But don't worry, darling, you'd look gorgeous in a bin bag. We'll need to cut your hair, so don't be late. I'll have a stylist bring some clothes, just in case yours turn out not to be exactly right. But, from looking at you today, I honestly don't think there'll be a problem.

'Tuesday, we'll be having lunch with editors from women's magazines. In the afternoon, we'll kick around publicity angles, make some calls and see who'll pay for what. The wedding gown's included in the package, obviously. But I'm hoping the designer will agree to make the bridesmaids' dresses, do an all-in deal. So fingers firmly crossed.

'Wednesday morning, we'll be seeing a literary agent who's trying to get a book deal, and in the afternoon a guy from cable. He loved your pictures, darlings, and he's thinking of a series, maybe following you both around as you prepare for your big day.

'We'll maybe get a special wedding chair for you to sit in while you do your one-to-ones to camera, video-diary style. You know the sort of thing – like in *Big Brother*? Yes, of course you do. But in this case no one gets evicted, ha ha ha. The producer said—'

'This television stuff, it's definitely going to happen?' interrupted Jack.

'Yes, of course, my darling – that's the plan! So a book will make a perfect tie-in. But don't worry, Cat. We'll pay some hack to write it. I know just the one. She freelances for some extremely tedious provincial magazine. She wants to be a novelist and win the Booker Prize. But it will never happen, unless they change the rules and give the prize to someone who can get a hundred clichés on every single page. She'll be very happy to write your book for cash-in-hand and see your names on it.

'Do you like these biscuits? I think they're rather dry. They need more syrup, butter, or more something, anyway.'

'They're okay,' said Cat.

'But they're not right for Fortnum's. Selfridges might take them, or possibly John Lewis – gift department, pretty boxes, pix of dear old biddy busy cooking in some old-style kitchen? Snow-white pinny – cameo brooch – grey hair – big, beaming smile? I'll tell Rosie to get on to it. Anyway, on Thursday—'

'But I can't take all this time off work,' objected Cat.

'I beg your pardon?'

'Fanny, I have a full-time job. I have responsibilities. I can't swan off to lunches, photo opportunities and whatnot. I can't say to Barry—'

'One moment, sweetheart,' interrupted Fanny, who had suddenly gone all gimlet-eyed. 'Somewhere, Cat, I have your entry form. Yes, here it is, and I see you've signed to say you're willing to accept all Supadoop Promotion's terms and all our conditions?'

'But I didn't mean—'

'So – in the event of winning, you agreed to make yourself available for all publicity, all photo opportunities, all interviews that Supadoop Promotions might arrange?'

'Did I, Fanny?'

'Yes, my love, you did.' Fanny pushed the entry form across the desk to Cat. 'You also said that if you couldn't meet these obligations, and if any monies had been disbursed

– that means spent, my darling – by Supadoop Promotions, you would reimburse the company – and that means pay me back. You signed there, my angel, do you see, right on the dotted line.'

As Cat stared at her signature, dashed off so carelessly so many months ago, she thought she might be sick. 'How much have you spent, then?' she enquired.

'I'd have to work it out, but I'd say the high four figures easily, or maybe even five.'

'Anyway, you don't need that job,' said Jack.

'Of course I do!' cried Cat.

'You don't.' Now Jack's arms were folded and one foot was tapping crossly. 'Listen, Cat, this is an opportunity. This whole thing will generate a mass of great publicity for me – I mean, for us. I'll be on television, for fuck's sake! But all you can do is mutter about your boring job and your responsibilities. Cat, you're not the CEO of eBay. You're not running Microsoft. You work in a scrap yard, selling junk.'

'My salary pays the rent,' Cat told him sharply.

'You mean I'm some sort of parasite?' Jack was glaring daggers. Fanny Gregory looked at Cat and pursed her lip-glossed lips. 'Cat, you set this up,' said Jack. 'You entered this fantastic competition. So why are you trying to pull out?'

'I'm not trying to pull out!'

'That's how it looks to me.' Jack scowled. 'Do you want to marry me?'

'Jack, you know I do.'

'Then help me, won't you?'

'But I can't afford—'

'It's crunch time, honeybee.' Jack turned to look at Fanny. 'Give us a couple of minutes on our own? I'll talk her round.'

Fanny Gregory stood up. 'You mind you do, my darling,' she said crisply. Then she turned to Cat. 'I'll be back in five and by then, my nightingale, I'll hope to hear you sing a different song. Caspar, angel, come with me.'

They heard her clacking down the passage. It sounded like her Manolos themselves were seriously brassed off.

'What the bloody hell do you think you're doing?' Jack demanded furiously.

'I might ask you that same question!' Cat glared back at him. 'When you asked me to marry you, I assumed it was because you loved me!'

'I do love you, Cat, and well you know it!'

'So that was why you said it wasn't working? Why you disappeared into the night and didn't call and didn't text and didn't e-mail for what was it, two months? Or was it more?'

'What's that got to do with anything?'

'Did you think of me at all? Did you wonder what I might be feeling, if I might be worrying about you, if my heart was breaking, if I could sleep at night?'

'Stop dragging up the past!' cried Jack. 'Stop opening old wounds! They're history, and now we need—'

'We need to go straight home and talk this through.'

'But Fanny Gregory, Cat – she's gone to all this trouble.' Now Jack looked like a five-year-old who'd had his sherbet fountain snatched away and chucked into a bin. 'We can't just walk out of here. Surely you see that? Fanny really wants to help us. She would be so hurt—'

'Oh, for God's sake, Jack!' exploded Cat. 'She isn't doing this because she loves us and wants to make us happy! She's done a deal with the Melbury Court Hotel! She's been busy schmoozing with the women's magazines! She's sucked up to a literary agent and a cable company! This whole charade – it's about making loads of dosh for Fanny Gregory! It isn't about us!'

'Well, that's where you're wrong.'

'What do you mean?'

'This is about my life,' said Jack. 'This is about me getting my big break. If you're so selfish and short-sighted and so mean you can't see that, perhaps I shouldn't marry you after all.'

'But do you want to marry me?' Cat looked at Jack and met his eyes, the eyes she loved. Or thought she loved. 'It seems a bit extreme, to go to all the trouble of getting married if it's just to further your career. Why don't you go to bed with Fanny Gregory, instead?'

'I don't want to go to bed with Fanny! The woman is a hideous old slapper! She's a greedy bitch with plastic jugs and nasty orange hair!'

'A greedy slapper, eh? Or somebody who really wants to help us? Why don't you make your mind up? A minute or two ago, you said—'

'I know what I said!' Jack glared. 'God, I sometimes wonder what I ever saw in you, and I—'

'The feeling's mutual, Jack.' Then Cat thought – sod all this. Sod Fanny Gregory and her tightish sodding schedule, and sod Jack Benson, too. She grabbed her bag, stood up to leave.

But Jack caught her hand and then he pulled her down again. He took her by the shoulders and gently, very gently, he turned her round to face him.

As if one of his switches had been flicked, his gaze became conciliatory, kind. 'I'm sorry, honeybee,' he said. 'My darling, I love you. I want to marry you, of course I do. I want to go to bed with you – and only you.'

'Do you, Jack?'

'I do, my darling, my precious honeybee.'

Then Jack smiled the charming smile that Cat had always loved, the smile which had bewitched her from the start, from the night she'd met him in that grubby pub in Kilburn, where she and Tess had gone to meet two guys who didn't turn up.

He'd been doing a set for half a dozen bored, indifferent regulars. The sort who had their special chairs rubbed smooth by sitting on them for a hundred years, who played with the same dominoes every night.

They'd more or less ignored him.

But Cat had thought, what nerve, what courage, to get up on that stage all by yourself. I couldn't do it in a million years.

As he'd wound up his act to sparse applause, Tess had winked at Cat. 'His stuff was rubbish, but he looks quite fit,' she'd said. 'I love those corkscrew curls. They make him look like Beethoven.'

'Beethoven?' Cat had not been able to take her eyes off him. 'Do you mean the dog or the composer?'

'No, I mean the poet. So maybe I mean Byron? Did he have loads of curls? Or was it Shelley? Oh, who cares? Let's go and buy him one and cheer him up.'

'All right,' Cat had agreed.

So that was what they'd done.

The chemistry had been there from the start. Jack had gone home with Cat that very night. But this was months and months ago, and what had happened to that chemistry?

She didn't know.

'What the hell's the matter with you now?' demanded Jack.

'What do you mean?'

'You look as if you're miles away.' Jack's tone grew sharp again. 'We have to sort this out,' he snapped. 'So let's call Fanny back in here and tell her we've made up. Then we can book a date.'

Cat dragged herself back to the here-and-now. Did she really want to marry Jack? She thought she did. She was almost sure of it, in fact. But was *almost* sure enough? Well, it might have to be ...

'You'll sort the time off work?' asked Jack.

'I'll do my best.'

'What's more important, your precious job or us?'

'Of course it's us,' she told him. 'You can go and call that woman, Jack. I'd feel such an idiot, standing in the passage, shouting Fanny.'

It seemed Jack didn't want to stand there shouting Fanny either, because he went to look for her instead, leaving the door wide open.

He was away for ages.

But at last they came along the passage.

Jack was grinning like he'd won the EuroMillions Lottery. Fanny was patting at her hair and smirking enigmatically. Caspar padded silently at Fanny's six-inch heels, giving Jack some very dirty looks and baring all his sharp, white teeth.

Fanny sat down at her desk.

Caspar chose to sit by Cat and lay his fine dark head upon her lap.

But Fanny didn't seem to mind.

'All sorted out, my angels?' she enquired.

'Yes, all sorted out,' said Jack, giving her his special, big-eyed charm-the-ladies grin, the one that melted knicker elastic at five hundred yards, that made you want to take him home and mother him and do several other things most mothers never did. Or shouldn't, anyway.

'So, first of all, we have to set a date,' said Fanny, tapping on her keyboard. 'Cat, do you have anything in mind? Most days in November are available. Nobody gets married in November unless they're in a hurry. Or they're trying to do it on the cheap and they don't want anyone to come. The weather's always horrible, and guests don't want to drive for miles in rain and sleet and snow. But I see December's filling up.'

'The fifth of January?' suggested Jack.

'Let me see, my angel.' Fanny clicked and tapped. 'It's a Thursday, isn't it? Why would you get married on a Thursday?' She glanced up and smiled. 'No, don't tell me, children. Let me guess. It's the anniversary of the first time you two met?'

'I can't remember when we met. I don't do those sorts of anniversaries, anyway. I think they're a waste of time.' Jack beamed back at Fanny. 'It's my thirtieth birthday, as it happens. I'd like it to be a special one.'

'Oh, it will be, darling,' Fanny told him, and again Cat felt she wasn't there, as if she wasn't part of this at all. 'We at Supadoop Promotions, we'll make sure of that. So, the fifth of January – that date is booked, all right?'

'Excellent,' said Jack.

'You could put it in your diary, Cat,' continued Fanny. 'Then you won't forget you'll have to ask for that day off. If you tell him now, your boss should manage to work around it, do without you for a day, even though you have such an important, high-powered job.'

'I won't forget, don't worry,' muttered Cat as she stroked Caspar's head.

'Do speak up, my darling, or don't speak at all,' said Fanny. 'When you make your vows, you'll need to make them loud and clear, otherwise the mics won't pick them up.'

'The mics?' said Cat.

'We'll be recording, sweetheart. Long before the ink on your certificate is dry you'll be up on YouTube and on Facebook, to trail the next instalment of the show.

'We'll have to think about the honeymoon. It wasn't in the package when we first set this thing up. But once all the sponsors have seen your pix, my loves, I'm betting they'll be willing to push the boat right out.

'Mauritius, do you fancy? The Seychelles? Oh, everybody

goes to the Seychelles. So maybe we could send you somewhere rather more exciting, like riding with the nomads in Mongolia and staying in a special bridal yurt?'

'A bridal yurt?' repeated Cat. 'You mean a tent?'

'I mean a yurt, my angel, something made of hides of yaks and lots of gorgeous ethnic fabrics like you see in Liberty, not orange ripstop nylon. If you look at Twitter you'll see yurts are trending and nomad chic is very in right now. Or do you fancy trekking in Namibia or Nepal? Or scuba-diving off the coast of Cape Town? We'd put you in a shark cage, obviously. We wouldn't want the pair of you to come to any harm! I'm sure we'll find a travel firm prepared to cut a deal, especially if cable is involved. There'll be lots of close-ups, Cat, so don't forget to wax. But coming back to nomads – what do you think of Finland, herding reindeer? That would make great telly, wouldn't it?'

'It all sounds bloody brilliant,' said Jack, and then he started fiddling with his hair, as if he were getting ready for his close-up now.

'I'll get darling Rosie to see about some photo shoots with nomads,' Fanny told them, tapping on her keypad. 'Let's just have a little think – lots of beads and head dresses and skins and boots and folk embroidery? I'll ring one of our stylists, we'll discuss what she could do. Cat, my sweet, do you think you could be a Laplander? You have perfect Nordic colouring. Maybe we could get you into *National Geographic* or a similar British magazine?'

'I don't think so,' muttered Cat. 'I'm sure I'd have to be a real Laplander, and I come from Sussex.'

'We might have to fudge and hedge a bit,' admitted Fanny thoughtfully. 'But anyway, my lovebirds,' she continued, 'now we have to make some wedding plans. Where are all the menus? Where did Rosie put them? Do you have any preferences for times? Maybe you should aim to have the ceremony at twelve, and eat at two? Then anyone who can't afford to stay at Melbury Court can still get home again.'

'I've got the menus in my bag,' said Cat, and handed them to Fanny. 'I've brought along the other stuff, as well. I didn't know if you would want it back.'

'Thank you, darling girl. You seem to think of everything. I can see why you're so indispensable at work.' Fanny started flicking through the menus, a critical expression on her face. 'I believe we said the orangery?'

Thirty minutes later, as Cat and Jack stood on the busy pavement outside the Georgian terrace, Cat wondered if she'd dreamed the last two hours and would eventually wake up.

If not, perhaps she ought to see a psychotherapist?

She looked at Jack, the man she was supposed to love, the man she'd said she'd marry. 'I still can't believe you said that stuff about your birthday,' she began.

'What do you mean?' demanded Jack.

'I know you have issues, and that sometimes you feel the need to say outrageous things. But to say you wanted to get married on your birthday—'

'Well, I do,' said Jack. He shrugged and shook his head, as if he didn't understand what Cat was going on about. 'What's so wrong with that?'

'Jack, just think about it! A wedding is about two people, not about just one!'

'You be nice to me, I'll let you come.'

Cat shut her eyes for three full seconds.

But then she opened them, looked hard at Jack, and suddenly she found she hated him. Or didn't hate, perhaps, but didn't like.

What was this relationship about? Where were friendship, trust, respect, affection? 'God, I've been such an idiot,' she sighed. 'Jack, this wedding's off.'

'It's what?' said Jack.

'You heard me – off, off, off.'

'I don't think so, sweetheart.' Jack shook his head again. 'You heard the lady. You signed her little form. Terms and conditions – right?'

'She can't force me to marry you.'

'But she can sue you, honeybee. She can make your life a living hell. You annoy our Fanny, and you'll soon be cutting up your cards. Your credit rating will be rubbish. You'll be in debt forever.'

'You mean we'll be in debt.'

'No, Cat – I mean just you.' Jack grinned. 'You were the one who entered Fanny's precious competition, and you were the one who signed the form. This has nothing at all to do with me.'

'Fanny wouldn't sue me,' Cat said, wondering how you sued somebody, what you had to do. Get a lawyer on the case, presumably, and write a lot of threatening letters on official-looking paper, frighten your opponent half to death?

Fanny Gregory didn't need a lawyer to frighten anybody half to death.

'I'm sure she wouldn't go to all that trouble,' muttered Cat.

'Oh, I bet she would,' said Jack and smirked. 'Old Fanny looks like she'd enjoy a fight.'

'I need to think,' said Cat, and she started walking down the street. 'I want to be by myself a bit. I dare say you could find a room or sofa for the night?'

'No problem, sweetheart. I've been thinking, too. It's time I had a bit of space.' Jack tossed his raven curls. 'You know something, honeybee? You're seriously messed up.'

Adam had messed up.

He was supposed to be in Wolverhampton this weekend,

sorting out that staircase, or finding someone local who could sort it. August, he had said originally, to start on Mr Rayner's strange but interesting old house..

But then Mr Rayner phoned, cajoled and begged and pleaded, offered to pay him twice his fee, and Adam had agreed to make a start immediately.

He was supposed to be in Dorset, too. So that was where he was right now, looking at the Venus, taking photographs and notes for when he went to Italy and could ask for some advice.

He needed to be twins.

He also needed someone who could run his virtual office, who could chase the subcontractors, source the raw materials, do the books and sort his diary out and get him to the places where he was supposed to be, when he was supposed to be there, since he couldn't seem to manage do to this himself.

He'd never been much good at time and motion. He was always underestimating how much time it took to get from place to place. He forgot to factor in the hold-ups, the awful British weather, the motorway congestion, the dealers and suppliers who were late or didn't come at all.

In fact, he needed someone like Cat Aston, someone who could organise his time, his work, his life.

Perhaps he could persuade her to do some stuff for him?

Or would that not be a brilliant plan?

They wouldn't have to see each other, would they?

Or not very often, anyway?

A brilliant plan or not, now it had occurred to him it wouldn't go away.

Jack strode off up Edgware Road, his hands shoved in the pockets of his jeans, and going God knew where.

Cat turned east and started walking, thinking she had better start economising, and she'd better start to do it now.

Jack was probably right, she thought, and sighed. She must be really seriously messed up. How else could she have got involved with somebody like Jack, with somebody so absolutely and completely selfish? A man who thought of no one but himself?

Just physical attraction, she supposed. It had to be, for even when she was annoyed with him, even when he was behaving like a hundred different sorts of git, she was still drawn to him. Whenever he was near, her treacherous, stupid body wanted him.

Jack must be some sort of roving magnet and she must be a heap of iron filings, following where he led. Well, she wasn't going to be a heap of iron filings any more.

How much money did she have in various old Post Office savings books and hardly-any-bloody-interest ISAs? No more than a couple of hundred, which was nothing, and she had the payments on the sofa to keep up. Unless the shop would take it back, of course, but she didn't think this was a possibility. It was scuffed and marked in several places. So even if she cleaned it up, it wasn't in as-new condition now.

She hadn't kept the magazine. She thought she could remember reading that the prize was worth an unbelievable twenty thousand pounds. Or was it thirty thousand?

She didn't have twenty thousand pounds. She didn't know anybody who would lend her such a sum. She didn't like to think about the sheer impossibility of raising thirty thousand.

Oh, don't be ridiculous, she told herself.

Fanny Gregory couldn't have spent twenty thousand pounds already. She could not have spent a tenth of that.

Or could she?

Cat really didn't know.

But at least one thing was obvious now.

In fact, it had been obvious from the start, since Jack had

first proposed. If you could call it a proposal. No woman with any sense at all would want to marry a man who had proposed like Jack. Just what had she been thinking?

Last year, they had spent a long weekend at Cat's ancestral home, as Jack had called the fake-beamed Tudorbethan link-detached in the golf club belt of small-town Sussex.

Cat's mother had cooked a piece of beef and made a sherry trifle. Cat had warned her in advance that Jack did not like beef. He also hated puddings, and he wouldn't eat them.

At eleven o'clock on Friday evening, Cat's father put the television off and sent them both to bed. He'd looked at Jack and told him there was to be no creeping along the landing in the night.

Jack had crept – or rather stomped and crashed – along the landing, anyway.

They'd somehow got through Saturday at the golf club, where Jack had fooled around and mucked about, charmed all the ladies in the clubroom, and got right up the noses of the men.

Cat's father had been livid.

They'd left on Sunday morning, walked straight into a pub and started drinking.

Or Jack had started drinking, anyway.

Since Cat was going to drive them back to London in a pickup from the yard and didn't want to lose her licence or destroy the pickup – Barry would go mad – she stuck to lemonade.

'Hey, honeybee,' he'd said, as he'd knocked back his second pint, 'if you and I got married, I would be your old man's son-in-law. Then I'd have a claim on all his money, if he's got any money. I reckon that would really piss him off.'

Cat had been annoyed with both her parents for making things so difficult for Jack. 'It's just as well you're not the marrying kind then, isn't it?' she'd said.

'I might be!' Then Jack had pretended to be outraged. 'So I'm not good enough for you, is that it?'

'You're lovely and I love you.'

'Why don't we make it legal, then?'

'You're serious?' said Cat, astonished.

'Yes, why shouldn't I be?'

'Okay,' she had replied. She'd been both pleased and flattered to be chosen by such a handsome, sexy, charming man. 'I'll marry you. So do I get a ring?'

'Yes, when I can afford one.' Jack had shrugged and grinned. 'But you might have to wait a while.'

'That's all right, whenever.'

'But in the meantime, honeybee …'

Jack had found a piece of silver paper from a chocolate wrapper in the pocket of his jeans.

He'd made a ring and slipped it on Cat's finger.

So they were engaged.

She stumbled on down Oxford Street, hardly noticing that she was buffeted and shoved by all the people flowing past.

What had she been thinking, she asked herself again. Married life with Jack would be a nightmare. It would be the Zackie Banter Show, starring Jack and Jack alone.

She wouldn't be his partner on life's journey. She wouldn't even be his blonde and glamorous assistant in stiletto heels and fishnet tights. She would be his cleaner, sexual services provider, washerwoman, housekeeper and bank.

But, in the meantime, what was she going to do about the money? How much would it be? How much had Fanny Gregory disbursed, as she had put it? Who was going to lend her what she owed the bloody woman?

A loan shark, she supposed.

Or could she ask her father?

She shuddered at the prospect of talking to her father,

who would say he'd told her so, even though he hadn't told her anything at all, because she hadn't dared to break the news of her engagement to her parents. On reflection, this was just as well.

When she got home, she got straight on the phone to Fanny Gregory, who didn't seem surprised to hear from Cat.

'So you and Jack, you've definitely changed your minds?' she said, sounding like a high court judge about to send you down for life with no chance of parole.

'Yes, I'm sorry,' Cat replied. 'We won't be getting married after all, so now I need to know—'

'I'll call you back ASAP,' said Fanny, and hung up.

'Okay, okay,' said Cat. She pulled a face, remembering her mother's favourite saying – or one of her mother's favourite sayings, she had a lot of them: courtesy costs nothing.

While she was waiting for her nemesis to get in touch again, she fetched a block of chocolate from the fridge.

But, far from giving her a serotonin rush, the chocolate merely made her feel sick. It tasted absolutely horrible, like a lump of cocoa-flavoured soap.

She spat it in the bin.

'I've spoken to the runner-up,' said Fanny twenty minutes later, cutting in as Cat apologised again, as she tried to discover what she owed. 'She was thrilled to win the luxury weekend in Barcelona, which you will remember was our super second prize. So she was in ecstasies to know she's won the wedding, after all. What's more, my angel, unlike you and Jack, she and her fiancé are in a position to proceed.'

'Fanny, about the money,' Cat said, for she wanted – needed – to know the worst of it. 'Please can you let me know how much I owe you?'

'I don't have all the paperwork to hand.'

'Well, when you do, please could you contact me? I'll need to make arrangements.'

'Of course you will, my angel,' said Fanny Gregory crisply. 'I'll do my sums and then I'll be in touch.'

'I'm sorry, Fanny. I mean, for all the trouble I've given you, the messing you around and all that stuff.'

'Well, sweetheart, as I say, I'll be in touch.'

'I'm also sorry about Jack.'

'Yes, the lovely Jack,' drawled Fanny. 'Quite a charmer, isn't he? I can understand why you were smitten.'

'When do you think I'll hear from you again?'

'Give me a breather, darling. I need to get this new show on the road and hope it's really going to happen this time.'

Then the phone went dead.

So Cat called Tess.

'What do you mean, the wedding's off?' demanded Tess. 'I'm in serious training! I've been doing all these exercises for the upper arms so I'll look good in sleeveless. But now you're telling me that I won't be a bridesmaid after all?'

'I'm sorry, Tess.'

'I should think so, too.'

'But Tess, you never liked him. You never wanted me to marry Jack. You said he was a scumbag and he wasn't worth my tears.'

'I fancied being a bridesmaid. I've never been a bridesmaid and soon I'll be too old for it.'

'I'll make it up to you, I promise.'

'I can't see how,' sighed Tess. 'Cat, it looked so lovely, that Melbury Court Hotel – the rooms, the grounds, the fountain, especially the fountain.'

'Yes, it was fabulous.'

'There were even peacocks on the lawns.'

'I know,' said Cat regretfully.

'I'm so into peacocks.'

'Tess, I've said I'm sorry.'

'Yeah, all right,' said Tess. 'Do a bit more grovelling and serious self-abasement and I might forgive you in about a hundred years. I tell you what,' she added, 'I'll come round to yours about half seven with a couple of bottles of that nice Chilean red. Tesco's got it on at three for two.'

'Okay,' said Cat.

'We'll send out for a pizza or a curry and watch *Notting Hill* or *Pretty Woman* or *Love Actually*. Or we could watch *Gladiator* and pretend our Jackie-boy's the bloke in white who gets it in the neck from Russell Crowe. Or what about *The Terminator*, that bit where the cyborg guy gets blasted in the guts?'

'I've changed my mind,' said Cat, who by now was feeling like she had been blasted in the guts herself and was just an empty, smoking shell.

'But you like all those films!' cried Tess.

'Yes I do, and it's very kind of you to offer to keep me company. But don't come round to mine. I'm tired and I need an early night.'

Monday, 13 June

Time for something new?

'*Dio*, Signor Lawley, who taught you to speak Italian?'

Pietro Benedetto was doubled up in agony – an agony of laughing. 'Your accent, it's so terrible! It gives me so much pain!'

Your English accent's rubbish too, said Adam, but only to himself. You sound as if you should be in a sitcom.

'I'm sorry, Adam – may I call you Adam?' Pietro looked apologetic now. 'I welcome you to Lucca.'

'Thank you, Pietro,' Adam said politely, as he looked round Pietro's busy yard where all kinds of restoration work was going on. '*I'm happy to be here*,' he added in his bad Italian.

'We hope you will much enjoy your visit,' said Pietro in his sitcom English.

'Where shall I be staying?'

'You have a studio apartment above my uncle's restaurant, which is in the *anfiteatro* in the old walled town.'

'You mean the Roman amphitheatre, right?'

'Yes, and your apartment and the restaurant are both in a building set into the Roman arches. I think you'll find it comfortable there.'

'I'm sure I shall,' said Adam. 'Pietro, did you say you have a schedule for me?'

'Yes, and it's a very busy one, starting with tomorrow morning. You have many meetings and many workshops, studios and yards where you may make your visit. But you should be able to do some tourist things at the weekend.'

'I hadn't planned to do much tourist stuff.'

'You hadn't, Adam?' Pietro Benedetto looked at him.

'I hope you will excuse me if I'm speaking out of turn – is that what you say? But when we first made contact, didn't you say you had a *fidanzata*? I thought you said you meant to bring the lady on this trip?'

'Yes, but it didn't work out,' said Adam firmly, in a tone which didn't invite discussion.

How could he have told Pietro he had a fiancée? How could he have been so certain Maddy would say yes to his proposal? How could he have been so arrogant, so stupid and so blind?

'I'm sorry,' said Pietro, and he shrugged expressively. 'The ladies, Adam – they love to change their minds.'

Adam changed the subject. 'I'll need to hire a car, so can you recommend a place?'

'You could have got one at the airport,' said Pietro.

'Yes, I know,' said Adam. 'But I thought I'd like to take the train. I'd never been on an Italian train. I'll get a car tomorrow morning.'

'Get a Fiat Bravo, they're the best.'

Adam's studio *apartamento* was high in one of the *Renascimento* tenements built into the arches of the Roman amphitheatre, where flocks of city pigeons cooed and fluttered and nested on his flimsy-looking wrought-iron balcony.

Lucca was amazingly romantic. What he had seen of it so far suggested it was made for lovers, with its colonnaded villas and secluded little gardens and its cool, dark alleys opening on to mediaeval squares.

But he mustn't think about this place being romantic, he decided, as he unpacked his stuff.

What was romance to him, when he had work to do?

Thursday, 16 June

Busy, busy, busy?

Pietro had been right about the schedule. Adam spent a lot of time in workshops, studios and yards which belonged to somebody related to Pietro, or with whom Pietro and his renovation firm did business.

In all these various workshops, yards and studios, Adam watched the work in progress, learning about marble restoration, about filling cracks and pits and fissures, finding out when this was possible and when the only remedy was replacing the original stone.

He made a list of tools he'd need to buy and took lots of photographs and notes for when he got back home to England. They also let him do some work himself.

As he worked on a cherub's damaged wing, he wondered how the girl from Chapman's yard – he must forget her name, he told himself – was getting on, and if her wedding plans for Melbury Court were going ahead.

He supposed they must be – he hadn't heard they weren't. But perhaps he wouldn't, anyway? Why would she contact him?

As soon as I get home, he told himself while he was mixing paste, I'll see if I can get that Venus fixed, fill all those cracks and holes. I'll also try to get the plumbing sorted. Then the actual fountain might be working on her wedding day.

He never should have kissed her – that had been a huge mistake. She was engaged, for heaven's sake, and she would be getting married soon.

But she had kissed him back, and she had meant it – if he knew anything at all, he knew for certain she had meant it. She hadn't been intimidated, frightened or anything like that.

He also knew she could have made a scene. She could have gone to the police. She could have accused him of a sexual assault. Then he would have ended up in court. The papers would have branded him a sex fiend, he might have gone to prison, and his poor mother would have died of shame.

He worked the filler into the hairline cracks along the cherub's broken wing.

He'd thought he might be getting over Maddy, and that he might be healing. But he clearly wasn't, because kissing Cat had opened up deep cracks and fissures in his damaged heart, which no amount of filler could put right.

It was a pity he couldn't replace his heart.

At the yard in Walthamstow, Cat had started on a massive sort-out of all the files and documents which had been in the office since Barry's father set the business up in 1962.

She got the shredder going and found it very satisfying, getting rid of all the waste and rubbish. It was consolatory, in a way – and this was just as well, because her friends did no consoling. Bridge-over-troubled-water stuff was absolutely not their thing.

Tess was a good mate. She liked a laugh. She loved a party. She'd dance the night away and she was always lots of fun. But, in spite of being desperate to be somebody's bridesmaid before she got her pension, nowadays she was very brisk and practical with Cat and kept insisting that she was well rid of Jack the lad. So Cat should now get over it, move on.

'He was a waste of oxygen,' said Tess.

'When we first met him, you thought he was fit.'

'We all make mistakes,' admitted Tess. 'It's usually because we fail to understand ourselves. I read about it in this magazine. I did a test to find out if I understand myself and you should do it, too.'

'I do understand myself.'

'You only think you do,' insisted Tess. 'So take the test and then you will be sure.'

'I don't have time to take a stupid test.'

'You'll stay in psychic limbo, then.'

'Tess, don't you have any work to do, people to see, old doors and sinks to buy?'

'I'm only trying to help you get your psyche sorted out.'

'No, you're not,' retorted Cat. 'You're mocking me again. It's what you do.'

Bex was just as bad, or even worse.

What about getting Jack some concrete high-tops?

Or they could fill his pockets with lead shot and shove him in the river, couldn't they? Or take out a contract on his head? Or on some other bit of him?

She knew a man who knew a man.

She knew a lot of men.

'Oh, don't we all?' sighed Tess, and took a bite of chocolate, pecan and marshmallow muffin.

'We do, and every one of them a bastard.' Bex dipped a finger in her cappuccino and then licked off the chocolate-dusted foam. 'It must be so much easier to be gay – not that I fancy you or Cat, of course, in spite of what I said that time.'

'You mean you don't like stubble on a girl?'

'I mean you need to get your roots done and get your eyebrows threaded. Soon you're going to look like Whatsit Baggins or his wizard buddy Voldemort.'

'You mean Gandalf.'

'Do I?' Bex dabbed at some muffin crumbs and pushed them round her plate. 'Big fat shaggy eyebrows aren't a good look on a woman, anyway.' She turned to glance at Cat. 'I meant to tell you, that red lipstick doesn't suit you. It makes your face look grey. You should stick to pink.'

Cat tuned out and thought of Adam Lawley – of kind, sympathetic Adam Lawley, the man who always carried cotton handkerchiefs to offer weeping women – he wouldn't be half as mean as Bex or Tess. She would bet on it. She wondered if he fancied meeting up to have that drink she owed him? If they did meet up, she could return his handkerchief.

She'd washed it and she'd ironed it and that had been a first. She'd had to dig through many layers of stuff to find the iron, a present from her mother ten or fifteen years ago.

It had still been in its cardboard box, entombed beneath a bag of clothes and books and other bits and pieces she meant to take into a charity shop when she got round to it.

So was this ridiculous or dangerous or what?

It didn't have to be ridiculous or dangerous. They'd meet up in a public place, of course. She didn't want him thinking she was up for any hugging, kissing, any other sort of hanky-panky.

She was still a bit ashamed of grabbing him, of kissing him, of practically eating him alive in Barry's shed. But that had been a blip. She didn't want to get his shirt off, did she?

Yes, replied a voice inside her head. I'd say that's exactly what you want.

Shut up, Cat told herself.

But they had been so promising, those kisses –

Stop it, idiot, she thought. You don't want anything to do with Adam, who practically admitted to being a commitment-phobe, and who would just be trouble if you got involved with him.

So you will not meet him, understood? You will not return his handkerchief. You will delete his number from your phone.

Make me, sneered her other self.

As she was looking for a supplier's invoice later in the

day, she found Adam's business card stapled to a copy of a VAT receipt which Barry had misfiled.

She saw his e-mail address. She decided this must be a sign. So she would send a friendly little message.

Where was the harm in that?

> You know that drink I owe you? What about tomorrow, six or sevenish, if you're free?

> Sorry, I'm in Lucca – that's in Tuscany – right now. So it will have to be some other time.

> That's a shame. I fancied a Prosecco. What's the weather doing? It's raining here, of course.

> It's gorgeous – brilliant sunshine, bright blue sky.

> I'd like a bit of sunshine. It might cheer me up.

> Why, is something wrong?

> Absolutely everything is wrong.

> Jack?

> How did you guess?

> So is it on or off?

> The wedding's off. God, I don't know how I could have been so bloody stupid, so absolutely blind!

> Cat, I'm not God.

> All blokes are God, or think they're God.

> You sound as if you need a long weekend away. Why don't you come to Lucca? You could easily get a flight to Pisa after work tomorrow. I'd meet you at the airport, find you somewhere nice to stay.

> You mean it?

> Yes, I mean it. Come and have that Prosecco in the sunshine. Book your flight and text me when you know your ETA. I'll come and pick you up at Galileo Galilei.

> Why are you being so nice to me?

> You owe me a drink. So you'd better not forget your euros, because you're paying – right?

Cat thought – what the hell. I'll put it on my card.

While I still have a card.

'A long weekend?' said Barry, when she asked him.

'Saturday to Monday, yes.'

'I see,' said Barry, and he smirked suggestively.

She hadn't confessed to Barry about Jack. She didn't want his clumsy sympathy, so she'd sworn Tess to silence.

She wasn't going to tell him about Italy. She wasn't even going to tell her girlfriends she was going to Italy. They'd only say she had to bring them back a load of stuff like Fendi scarves and Gucci bags. Then they'd moan and grumble when she didn't get them cheap. They'd do better buying obvious fakes in Oxford Street.

'I don't know about a long weekend,' said Barry, who was frowning now. 'Well, not when we're so busy.'

'Oh, go on with you, it's really quiet.' Cat looked through the office window out into yard, empty but for some old guy in baggy corduroys and a cable cardigan who was probably looking for garden gnomes he could paint up. 'Barry, all the books are up to date. There are no deliveries outstanding. I didn't take any time off over Easter. So I'm due a couple of days, at least.'

'What's in the diary?'

'You're in London for the next few days. Tess has no meetings booked with anyone who'll want to sell us stuff. So she'll be at the yard.'

'Oh, all right,' said Barry and sighed a martyred sigh. 'If you twist my arm. But it's Saturday to Monday, right? No sloping in at two o'clock on Tuesday afternoon.'

'I wouldn't dare.'

'Where are you going?'

'Sussex – I want to see my parents. I haven't been to visit them for ages, and my mother's noticed I've been neglecting them.'

'So are you taking lover boy along?'

'No, he's busy,' Cat replied. 'He's got a gig in – Birmingham, and that's why I thought I'd go to see my mum and dad.'

'A likely story,' Barry said, and then he grinned again.

'What's that supposed to mean?'

'You don't usually go the colour of a London Routemaster when you talk about your mum and dad. What are you really up to, eh?'

'I told you, Barry – I'm going down to Sussex.' Cat thought it was time to change the subject. 'Anyway, how's Annie, and how's Roxie Jane?'

'They're good. I've got some pix.' Barry found his phone and started scrolling through his gallery. 'Roxie's smiling now. Or Annie says she's smiling. But I think it's wind. Okay, here's Daddy's little girl – adorable or what?'

'She's absolutely gorgeous. When's Annie coming back to work?' asked Cat, as she looked through Barry's photographs.

'Pretty soon, she reckons. She's bored out of her mind at home. She'll bring Roxie in her Moses basket and do two days a week.' Barry put his phone away. 'I know why you're asking. You and Tess, you want more weekends off.'

'The thought had never crossed my mind.'

'You've gone all red again.'

Tess didn't buy the Sussex story, either.

'You're up to something wicked,' she said, smirking when Cat mentioned she was going to see her parents.

'God, you're so suspicious. Why shouldn't I go and see my parents?'

'Parents are like Blackpool – they're all right for a day trip but not a long weekend. So is it all on with Jack again?'

'No, it's not,' said Cat.

'Okay, if you're going to Sussex, bring me back a souvenir? What about a snow globe of the Brighton Royal Pavilion? I fancy one of those.'

Friday, 17 June

At last, the prospect of some decent sunshine?

'Hi, Cat,' said Adam, who hadn't quite believed that she would come to Tuscany, and also couldn't quite believe he'd asked her in the first place.

It had been different in the days of letters, when you'd had more time to think, cross out, rip up and chuck into the bin. Nowadays, one click, one touch, one mad, impetuous impulse, they were all it took to change your life for good – or bad.

'Hi yourself,' said Cat, and smiled at him.

As usual, she looked adorable – her eyes were bright and glowing like the rarest Chinese jade, her skin was lightly tanned from walking in the summer sunshine, or what there had been of it this year, which in England wasn't very much, and there were Redouté roses blooming in her cheeks.

One stray lock of hair had fallen down and lay against her cheekbone, and he got a sense of déjà vu as it took all his willpower not to reach out to loop it up again.

But he'd decided in advance that there would be no touching and definitely no kissing. Cat was going to have a break. He meant to make her life less complicated, not foul it up some more.

He took her case and carried it through Arrivals. She was travelling very light, he thought. Where was all the stuff that women usually lugged around? The styling products, the good-hair-day equipment, the million little travel jars of gunk, the clothes for all occasions from masked balls to slobbing round on Sunday mornings, the fifteen pairs of shoes?

Since he'd sent that e-mail, he'd been thinking he had

made a terrible mistake, inviting Cat to come to Italy. But, now she was here, he found he was delighted she had come, and realised he had been inspired.

They'd do all the usual tourist stuff, he told himself. They'd see the sights of Lucca. They'd drive into the countryside, go round a few *castelli*, have lunch in family-run *trattorie*, chill out and have some fun.

It would be no big deal.

If he didn't touch this girl, if he didn't think about how lovely it had been to kiss her on her lovely mouth, and if he could forget she was a woman, it would work out fine.

'How long will you be staying?' He hoped that she would say until the Sunday afternoon, or even Monday morning.

'I'm flying back on Monday,' Cat replied. 'I hope that's going to be all right? I had to bite the boss's arm off – more or less – before he'd let me have a long weekend. You'd think I'd asked him for three months, not just three days.'

'You're indispensable, that's why.'

'Well, of course,' said Cat. 'I'm the only one who has a clue about the payroll, how to keep the diary, all that stuff. What about you, Adam, when are you going home?'

'I must be back in England on Tuesday afternoon. No, not that way, Cat,' he added, and he put his hand between her shoulder blades. Just to guide her in the right direction, obviously.

This didn't count as touching, he assured himself, even though his hand was tingling now and he felt like he had slapped his palm down on a hotplate and could almost feel the blisters rising. 'Over to the left – that's the way out.'

'Oh – *uscite* – that's exit, right?' Cat turned and shrugged apologetically. 'Sorry, you're going to think I'm very stupid. I've never been to Italy before. I don't know any Italian.'

'I know a bit,' said Adam. 'But my accent's rubbish, so Italians laugh at me and beg me to speak English. Pietro, that's the guy I came to see, says it hurts to listen to me trying to speak Italian.'

'He speaks perfect English, then?'

'It's better than my Italian, anyway.' Adam led her through the busy concourse, out into the petrol fumes and the intoxicating summer atmosphere of Tuscany. 'Pietro's a nice guy. I'm sure you'll like him. We've fixed up a good place for you to stay.'

Pietro and his uncle were sitting at a table outside the uncle's restaurant, drinking coffee in the summer twilight, and when Adam and Cat turned up they both jumped to their feet.

'Pietro, this is Cat, my friend from England,' Adam said in English, because he was reluctant to provoke another round of ridicule about his bad Italian.

Pietro shook Cat's hand and said hello, adding in perfect but accented English that he hoped she'd had a pleasant journey.

'Yes, it was fine,' said Cat. She smiled at him, then at his uncle, who was trying to tidy up his shaggy grey moustache, combing at it with his fingers, twirling up the ends.

Adam saw at once she was a hit, that these two men were smitten. So perhaps, he thought, she had this effect on every single man she met?

Maybe what he felt for Cat was friendship? Just ordinary, everyday affection, the kind he felt for Gwennie, after all?

Pietro introduced her to his uncle, who took her hand and kissed it, then turned back to Pietro to tell him in Italian that he was impressed by Signor Lawley's choice of *fidanzata*.

'Excuse us just one moment,' said Pietro.

Then he and his uncle had a shrugging and gesticulation-laden conversation in the local dialect. Adam understood the gist of it – this *bella signorina* wasn't Signor Lawley's *fidanzata*. She was Signor Lawley's friend, which was why she needed her own *apartamento*. She wouldn't wish to share.

Pietro's uncle looked again at Cat and then at Adam. He muttered something about certain people being lucky bastards, having friends like these. If he himself was ten years younger ...

Then he shuffled off into the restaurant, coming out ten minutes later with a mediaeval-looking key.

'My uncle says the *signorina* has the *apartamento* which is right above your own,' explained Pietro, as his uncle beamed and rattled on in voluble Italian and offered Cat the key, a scrolled and curlicued affair similar to the one which opened Adam's own front door.

'We hope she will be comfortable there,' Pietro added courteously. 'She'll find milk and fruit and basic groceries in the kitchenette. The bed will be made up. But if she needs anything else, or she has any questions, she only has to ask.'

'Thank you, Pietro,' Adam said, as Cat looked at the key. '*Mille grazie*, Signor Benedetto.'

'What were those two saying?' Cat enquired, as Adam led her through a vaulted archway into an oval space, which on this summer evening was still full of market stalls.

'You're a very beautiful young lady, and they hope you'll have a lovely time in Italy.'

'Yeah, I bet.' Cat's green eyes narrowed. 'Why did they take half an hour to say it?'

'Italian's quite a convoluted language. It often takes six words to say what English says in one.'

'I see,' said Cat, but she still sounded unconvinced. 'Adam, what is this amazing place?' She stared up in astonishment at the yellow stuccoed houses built into the ancient arches, towering to a height of three, four, five, six storeys high.

'The Roman amphitheatre,' he replied. 'Lucca was a Roman city, a provincial capital, and here was where the people came to get their entertainment on Saturday and Sunday afternoons.'

'Oh, like we go to the Dome or Wembley?'

'I expect so, yes.'

Opening a dark green door which looked as if it had been there since Roman times itself, Adam led Cat up a narrow flight of concrete stairs – up and up and up, past many other doors and sounds of people singing, arguing and shouting in Italian, of televisions blaring, of barking dogs and pots and pans and crockery being bashed around.

She was breathing hard, as if she couldn't manage one more step, when he stopped outside a plain black door. 'This must be it,' he said.

So Cat unlocked the door and walked into a little sitting room, with a tiny kitchenette and bathroom leading off.

'Come in,' she told him.

He went into the sitting room and opened up the heavy shutters to let in the dying light, together with the evening sounds and sights and smells of Lucca.

Cat gazed all around the room.

'But there's no bed,' she told him, frowning.

'It's probably through here.'

Opening another door he peered into the murk. Cat followed him and, as her eyes adjusted, she gasped delightedly, staring at the high, white bed which was carved with cherubs, satyrs, goddesses and fauns, at the chestnut-beamed and lime-washed ceiling, at the painted chairs and dressing table, at the patterned terracotta tiles on the floor.

'It's lovely,' she said, smiling at him. 'Where will you be, Adam?'

'In the room right under you, so no midnight dancing on the ceiling – understood?'

'I'm not going to promise, but I won't wear my tap shoes, anyway. Okay, what's the plan?'

'I don't have any work appointments until Monday morning, so if you like we'll do some tourist stuff?'

'I like,' said Cat. 'I definitely like. But now—'

'You're tired?' said Adam, as she yawned and rubbed her eyes.

'Yes, I am – a bit,' admitted Cat, and then she shrugged apologetically. 'I know I'm very boring, but would you mind if I went straight to bed?'

'I wouldn't mind at all,' he lied. 'You get a good night's sleep,' he added. 'If you want anything to eat or drink, there'll be tea and coffee and biscuits in the kitchen cupboards, peaches and bananas in the fruit bowl, and milk and bread and butter in the fridge.'

'Pietro and his uncle have thought of everything,' said Cat, impressed.

'They might have forgotten the champagne and caviar.'

'I'll let them off, but just this once – and Adam?'

'Yes?'

'Thank you for inviting me to Lucca. You can't imagine how good it feels to get away from London.'

'You're welcome,' Adam said, and then he put his hands behind his back, standing like a senior member of the British Royal Family, so he couldn't touch her, so he couldn't take her in his arms and kiss her on the mouth, the neck – or even at all.

'There should be some towels in the bathroom, and spare pillows in that chest of drawers,' he added briskly. 'So now, you get your head down. I'm going to walk you off your feet tomorrow.'

Then he went downstairs.

'Where's your pretty friend?' enquired Pietro, as Adam sat down at his usual table and began to study a menu which he knew by heart.

'She's tired,' said Adam as he looked intently at the list of *primi piatti*. 'So she's gone to bed.'

'I see,' Pietro said, and then he grinned. 'I hope she won't be lonely, Adam, up there in the roof all by herself.'

Saturday, 18 June

Why do I feel so pleased with life?

When Cat opened the shutters the next morning, the sun came streaming in like liquid gold. She heard the cries and clatter of the market which was set up in the oval of the Roman amphitheatre far below. She could smell coffee roasting and realised she was hungry.

It must be time for breakfast, she decided. What would there be for breakfast here in Lucca – fresh-baked rolls and froth-topped cappuccinos? She hoped so, anyway.

She leaned out of her window, looking at the pigeons which roosted on the ledges all around the amphitheatre, and cooed and preened and swooped on anything they thought was edible.

She wondered if the little wrought-iron balcony which led off her kitchenette was safe for anything heavier than a pigeon? Maybe not, she thought – she wouldn't risk it.

'What are we going to do today?' she asked, when Adam rang to ask if she was up.

'We'll have some breakfast in Pietro's uncle's restaurant. Then we'll go and have a look at Lucca. We'll walk all round the city walls, perhaps? We'll go inside some churches and some mansions which are open to the public. We'll go and see a garden in the sky.'

'We'll see a what?' asked Cat.

'A garden in the sky.'

'You're kidding.'

'No, I'm not.'

'Where is it, then?'

'On the Torre Guinigi, the only tower in Lucca which still has a garden on the roof. In the old days, lots of towers had gardens at the top, or so Pietro says. But this is the only one that's left.'

'Adam, I know the place you mean!' cried Cat. 'I'm looking at it now. I saw it when I opened up my shutters. A red brick tower with trees on top. I didn't think they could be real. So we could go there, could we, climb up and see the garden?'

'Yes, but you'll need comfortable shoes. A tower as high as that one's bound to have a couple of hundred steps, and there won't be a lift.'

'I've brought my oldest trainers.'

'So put them on, then come and have some breakfast.'

It took a while to do the tourist stuff in Lucca – to walk all round the ancient city walls, to visit gilded mansions in whose shuttered rooms there were whole centuries of treasures, to sit in cafés shaded by green vines or foaming white wisteria which filled the air with fragrance, to drink *caffè latte*, *cappuccino* or *espresso* and eat sweet almond pastries in a mediaeval square surrounded by *palazzi* and *chiese* which were all works of art.

'Good to go?' asked Adam, as Cat licked her fingers then drained the last of her third *caffè latte*.

'Yes,' she told him, getting up and stretching. 'Good to go. I want to see inside that big white marble church we passed when we walked round the walls.'

'The one where there's the pickled body of a local saint in a glass case?' asked Adam, looking at his guide book.

'Oh? Well, maybe not!' Cat pulled a face. 'Okay, I want to go to the cathedral, and buy something for my mother and for Tess and Bex, and then go up that tower to see the garden in the sky.'

'Sit down again and have another of those pastries if you're going to do all that,' suggested Adam.

'Must I?' Then Cat grimaced, mock-dejected, and she grinned a wicked grin. 'Oh, go on, then – if you'll have one, too.'

The churches took some time, and it was almost evening before they climbed the Torre Guinigi, arriving with a scant half an hour to spare and buying the last two tickets of the day.

'Cat, I didn't think to ask, are you okay with heights?' asked Adam, worrying slightly as they scaled the narrow wooden stairs, leaving the original wide stone staircase far below.

'I'm fine with heights, but how much further is it, do you reckon?' Cat demanded, breathing heavily.

'I think we're nearly there.'

'I hope you're right,' puffed Cat.

'Come on, old age pensioner, just a few more steps.'

Several minutes later they had clambered through a trapdoor and were standing in the garden.

'What do you think?' asked Adam.

'It's just incredible.' As Cat got her breath back, she looked around the garden, at the trees which would have shaded many generations of the Guinigi family from the blistering summer sun. She scanned the Lucca skyline, then gazed towards the snow-capped Alps which closed the far horizon. 'What an amazing view!'

She turned toward the amphitheatre next. 'Adam, there's my room up in the roof!' she cried, and beamed at him. 'I can see the window. I've left one shutter open, so I know it's mine.'

'There's mine, below it.' Adam pointed. 'What a shame they don't have gladiatorial combats any more. We could have sat and watched the entertainment from our balconies.'

'So it was a real amphitheatre, then?' said Cat. 'They did have gladiatorial whatsitsnames? They threw real Christians to real lions?'

'I don't know if they had any lions. But the Romans were a brutal bunch, and Pietro says they probably had wild beast fights with lots of blood and gore. All that *Gladiator* stuff, you know?'

'I love that film,' said Cat.

'I do, too,' said Adam. 'Great battle scenes, although some of the footage looks quite dated nowadays. The CGI guys have raised their game a bit. But it doesn't seem the kind of thing a girl would like.'

'You're suggesting I'm some sort of weirdo?' Cat grinned up at him. 'You'd be amazed what girls like, Adam Lawley – stock car racing, pints of Guinness, BMWs, great big dogs. If you had a relationship with one – with a girl, not with a great big dog, that would be very wrong – you might be surprised. Anyway, after Romans had got tired of throwing lions at Christians and having wild beast fights?'

'In the Middle Ages, people started filling in the arches, and by the fifteenth century the place looked very like it does today.' Adam glanced at the holm oaks which were growing in two clusters in the rooftop garden. 'These trees, I wonder if they know what dangerous lives they're leading up here in the sky?'

'I'm sure they do,' said Cat. 'But they're still determined to hang on. They're going to push their roots into the brickwork, come what may. They know if they should go, the tower goes too.'

'As long as it doesn't go within the next five minutes, we should be all right. Cat, I'm sure I heard them ring the bell, and we're the only people still up here. It must be time to leave.'

'Just another minute or two, okay?' Cat leaned over the

parapet. 'I feel like a princess in a fairy tale, up here in this tower. I could be Rapunzel, letting down her hair.'

'Your hair's not long enough for you to be Rapunzel.'

'Do you want to bet?' Still turned away from him, Cat pulled out the clips and shook it loose, so it fell down her back in dark blonde waves. 'There – could a prince climb up it, do you think?'

'Come back from the barrier, Cat. It doesn't look particularly solid, and it's not very high. It was probably designed so people could be chucked over the edge with minimum inconvenience to the chuckers.'

'You could have a point,' said Cat. Adam saw her shudder, but she didn't move. She went on looking at the view.

'Cat, please come away!'

'I wonder, Adam, if I were to jump, if I could fly?'

Then – as she had most probably intended, he decided later – Adam found his hand was on her arm, holding it tight.

He pulled her back from where she stood against the parapet, back towards the oak trees, and then he pulled her closer, so she couldn't escape again.

The holm oaks cast a cool green shade through which the sunlight filtered here and there, dappling Cat with green and gold and making her look like an elf, a sprite, a water nymph. She raised her face to his and smiled at him.

'You're wicked, aren't you?' Adam said. 'You enjoyed it, didn't you, scaring me?'

'I didn't mean to scare you, Adam.' Now, Cat's eyes glowed emerald in the soft rays of the sinking sun. 'I only wanted to see what you would do.'

'Come on, we're going back downstairs.'

'I know, but not just yet.' She touched his forearm with her finger tips. 'You have to kiss me first.'

'I don't think so.'

'You don't want to kiss me, Adam?'

'You know very well I do.'

'So – why don't you, then?'

'I don't think I should.'

'Why's that?'

'I asked you here to have a fun weekend and do some tourist stuff, not force myself on you.'

'You're telling me I need to use more mouthwash or chew some spearmint gum?'

'I'm telling you that I don't want to complicate your life.' Adam kissed her lightly on the mouth, making sure his own was firmly closed.

But Cat refused to let him go.

She locked her hands behind his head and kissed him back, opening her mouth, inviting him to do the same, delighted to discover he could not resist her long.

This isn't about sex, she told herself, as she tasted almonds, coffee, him. This isn't about love. This is about affection. Adam likes me. I like Adam. Why should we not kiss?

There won't be any fallout. It's not as if we're starting a relationship. Adam doesn't do relationships.

Anyway, I've had enough of being in relationships. I'm through with being in love. All love has done for me is cause me pain. But Adam makes me happy.

I think it's time for happiness.

It's time to have some fun.

The holm oaks sighed and whispered in the breeze. The evening air turned cool and velvet-soft.

'It must be getting very late,' said Cat.

'It must,' said Adam.

'We'll go and have that Prosecco, shall we?' she suggested, as she took her arms from round his neck.

'Yes, okay,' said Adam, releasing her reluctantly.

Then he stroked a lock of dark blonde hair back from her forehead, and kissed her on the temples one last time.

They walked back to the trapdoor.

It was shut.

Adam grasped the handle, pulled it, but it wouldn't move.

'I think it's locked,' he said.

'It can't be locked,' said Cat. 'They wouldn't lock us in here for the night. They don't know what damage we might do. Give it one more tug.'

So Adam yanked at it again and still it didn't move.

'What shall we do?' asked Cat.

'You know you fancied being Rapunzel? I reckon now's your chance. I'll abseil down your hair. I'll go and find the guy who has the keys, then come and let you out.'

'You know you said my hair would not be long enough for all that climbing up and down it stuff? I reckon you were right.'

'Then it will have to be Plan B. We hang over the parapet and shout.'

'What's the Italian word for help?'

'It's something like *soccorso*. Or maybe it's *aiuto*. I don't think it matters. We just have to wave our arms and yell.'

'Adam, this is so embarrassing.'

'Yes, I know,' said Adam. 'Pietro and his uncle will dine out on it for weeks.'

'It's always been on my to-do list, get locked inside a tower.'

'So you can cross it off tonight.'

'Oh, Adam – don't look so annoyed. This is all so daft, you have to laugh.'

'But we could be stuck up here for hours. You're hardly wearing anything, and I bet it's bloody cold by three or four o'clock. You can have my shirt, of course, but that won't keep you warm.'

'We'll have to make a camp fire.'

'Yes, that's a possibility,' said Adam, looking at the trees. 'At least there's lots of wood.'

'We wouldn't dare.'

'They'd execute the pair of us.'

'They'd do it in the amphitheatre, wouldn't they, with lions and tigers borrowed from some zoo?'

'I expect so,' Adam said. 'So come on, Cat – get shouting.'

As it turned out, Cat didn't do much shouting. Adam's voice was stronger, carried further, and soon a small, excited crowd had gathered on the street a hundred feet or more below. People were pointing up at them and calling out advice.

'*Someone needs to go and fetch the guy who keeps the keys,*' cried Adam, hoping that was what he'd really said – he wasn't absolutely sure.

'*All in good time, my friend,*' a teenaged boy yelled up at him.

'*I see you have some lovely company!*' called out a man. '*We wouldn't want to rush you!*'

'*You stayed up there on purpose, didn't you?*' shouted someone else, and all the others laughed.

'*We're sending for the caretaker, don't worry.*'

'*Let's hope he hasn't lost the keys!*'

'*You'll have to stop up there all night.*'

'*You'll be pretty chilly by the morning.*'

'*No, you'll have your love to keep you warm!*'

'What are they saying, Adam?' Cat demanded. 'It sounds as if they think we've been—'

'They say the guy who has the keys is on his way.'

But then he put his arm around Cat's shoulders, and all the people on the ground began to cheer and whistle.

'*Go on!*' called the teenaged boy. '*Give her one, why don't you?*'

'*Give her one from me, as well!*' shouted somebody else.

'They're saying he won't be long,' translated Adam.

'Yeah, right,' said Cat suspiciously, as more cheers and whistling floated up from far below.

The caretaker arrived at last, pushing his head up through the trapdoor and opening it wide.

'*Signor, signorina*, I'm so sorry, how can you forgive me?' he began, wringing his hands and looking as if at any minute he would start to cry.

As Cat and Adam followed him down the creaking wooden staircase, he carried on talking twenty to the dozen in Italian, repeating he was sorry, but he knew he'd rung the bell. He'd never left anyone in the tower before. He called on all the patron saints of Lucca to confirm this was the case.

'It's okay,' said Adam. 'It's no problem, doesn't matter, we're not blaming you. We're grateful you could come and let us out. I didn't notice everybody else had gone.'

'You were with a lovely girl, that's why,' the caretaker told Adam. 'This *bella signorina*, she would make any man lose track of time.'

As they left the Torre Guinigi, the people on the pavement clapped and cheered.

A few men made comments which Adam was glad Cat didn't understand, although he knew she couldn't fail to get the gist of them, especially when the comments were accompanied by explicit gestures and a lot of grinning.

As the crowd dispersed, Adam gave the caretaker some euros, thanked him once again and said goodnight.

'What shall we do next to draw attention to ourselves – fall down a well?' suggested Cat.

'Or what about free-climbing up the tower of the cathedral as an encore – that should draw a crowd?'

'Or we could be boring and go and have some supper, couldn't we?'

'Then do more tower stuff tomorrow, right?'

They walked back through the darkening streets, past restaurants and cafés full of people eating, drinking, all enjoying sitting out under the bright, white stars.

'Where would you like to eat?' asked Adam.

'What about that place with the white flowers and all the vines where we had coffee earlier today?'

'Yes, that sounds perfect,' he agreed.

So they ate their supper sitting in the perfumed twilight, beneath a heavy canopy of white wisteria blossom that filled the night with scent, where moths as big as sparrows fluttered, batting their soft wings.

'You okay?' asked Adam as the waiter brought their coffee.

'Yes, I'm fine,' said Cat. 'Why do you ask?'

'You've gone very quiet.'

'I'm very tired.' Cat yawned behind her hand. 'All that exercise I've had today – I'm not as fit as you.'

'I've worn you out.'

'I've had a lovely time,' insisted Cat.

'But you got locked inside a tower.'

'It was sort of fun.' Cat smiled at him. 'It was a big adventure, wasn't it?'

'It was a big embarrassment as well.'

'We might end up on YouTube. There were lots of people filming us on mobile phones. Let me get this,' she added, as the waiter brought the bill.

But Adam covered her hand to stop her reaching for her bag and then got out his card.

'We'd better get you home to bed,' said Adam.

He led her through the narrow winding streets, which were

full of things to look at, wonder at – fountains, churches, palaces and statues, gardens rich with perfume and cafés full of noise and merriment. It was the sort of night when anyone with any heart could very easily fall in love.

But you will not fall in love with him, Cat told herself. You will not hold his hand.

So whose hand was she holding, then?

I'm tired, she told herself, and Adam walks so fast. I need to slow him down. Otherwise I'll lose him and then I won't be able to find my way back home.

'Who's the fella with the fiddle?' she enquired, stopping to admire a fine bronze statue of an eighteenth-century musician. She realised she was a little drunk – but happy drunk, not maudlin drunk, just glad to be alive.

'Luigi Boccherini,' Adam said as he read the inscription. 'He was a composer born in Lucca in 1743, and it's not a fiddle, it's a cello.'

'Oh, I beg its pardon.' Cat looked up at Adam. 'I expect he wrote a lot of highbrow, very intellectual stuff?'

'Perhaps,' said Adam. 'I've never heard of him. I'll look him up. Cat, what sort of music do you like?'

'Lady Gaga, Amy Winehouse, Coldplay – I change my mind according to my mood. What about you, Adam?'

'I like almost everything – rock, some R & B, some jazz, some folk, some classical. I'm promiscuous, me.'

Promiscuous, thought Cat. It gets worse and worse. I'm falling for a guy who doesn't do relationships and now says he's promiscuous.

'Tell me about your family,' she said, to cool the conversation down. 'Where were you born, and were you happy when you were a child? What did your parents do before you came along?'

'I was born in Middlesex,' said Adam. 'I had a happy childhood. My father was a Russian double agent. My mother was the daughter of a Transylvanian countess and a big game hunter from Brazil.'

'So that explains the Spanish eyes.'

'I beg your pardon?'

'Oh, nothing, Adam.' Cat felt her colour rise. 'Please, take no notice. I've had too much to drink and I'm just wittering on. What about when you were growing up? Did you get in trouble with the law? Did you get expelled from half a dozen different schools?'

'No and no. I'm sorry, Cat,' said Adam. 'I don't know what to tell you that won't put you to sleep. My mother came from Stockport and I think I told you my father was a builder, that he ran his own small business, doing mostly bathrooms, kitchens, home extensions, boring stuff like that?'

'Yes, I think you mentioned it. Mr Brick the builder, Mrs Brick the builder's wife and Master Brick the builder's son,' said Cat. 'What about Miss Brick the builder's daughter?'

'I'm an only child.'

'What about your parents – do you still have the set?'

'Dad had a fatal heart attack when he was fifty-five. My mother never came to terms with it. She's never thrown out any of his stuff.'

'That's why you have so many hankies, right?'

'I've dozens of the bloody things,' said Adam ruefully. 'Do you have brothers, sisters?'

'No, I'm an only one, like you.'

'It's a big responsibility.'

'Yes,' said Cat, and sighed. 'I've always felt there was this sort of pressure. Do well at school, get married, be a doctor or a lawyer, get a mortgage, have some children, do us proud. It must be the same for you.'

But then she blushed again, embarrassed. 'God, what am I saying? I didn't mean anything, you know. I don't want you to think—'

'Cat, it's all right.' Adam gave her hand a friendly squeeze. 'I wasn't thinking anything at all.'

By the time they reached the amphitheatre, Cat was busy having a violent argument with herself.

She wanted him, she really did, and she was almost sure he felt the same. She somehow knew he wouldn't make assumptions. He wouldn't think that just because she'd kissed him she'd given him the right to take things further, do anything he liked.

Glancing at him in the scented darkness, she saw his eyes were bright. His pupils were dilated. She knew that if she offered him the slightest of encouragement—

But should she, shouldn't she?

As he unlocked the dark green door, she looked at him again. It will be okay, she told herself. Just remember that he doesn't do relationships and it will all be fine.

As they reached his landing, she touched Adam's arm and smiled at him. 'Let's go upstairs,' she whispered.

'I—maybe not,' said Adam. 'You're a lovely girl. You're beautiful, you're fun. But when I said come to Italy, all I wanted was to make you smile.'

'You did,' said Cat, and now she wound her arms around his neck. 'See how I'm smiling? Let's see you smile, too?'

'You're sure you want to do this?'

'Yes, I'm sure.' Cat looked up at him, into his eyes. 'Adam, I've just thrown myself at you. I'd appreciate it if you'd catch me?'

Adam unwound her arms from round his neck and took her hand.

He led her up the stairs.

Cat meant to take it slowly, do the sexy siren thing, to drive him wild with desire.

She meant to have him snorting like a stallion as they

reached a shuddering, mutual climax, complete with Dolby Digital of waves crashing on shores and angels singing, obviously.

But she'd overdosed on the Prosecco. So she could not stop giggling and laughing, and making him laugh, too.

As she undid a button on his shirt, she wondered why he made her feel so happy – so ridiculously, brilliantly, wonderfully happy – when she had so many worries, problems and anxieties back at home.

She'd think about it later, she decided, as he slid his hands under her top.

She had other stuff to do tonight.

She spent a lot of time exploring him. She found a mole shaped like a crescent moon on his left shoulder, gravel marks from a forgotten accident sprayed like a constellation on one forearm, a whorl of curling hair around his navel. 'I think you'll do,' she said.

'It's kind of you to say so.' Adam had also been undressing Cat, and now he peeled her knickers off so she was naked, too. 'Do you know you have the most attractive belly button in the world?'

'I didn't know women could do that,' said Adam thoughtfully, as he and Cat lay tangled up in white cotton sheets upon the carved and gilded bed.

'What do you mean?' asked Cat, her green eyes narrowing suspiciously, but looking playful, too. 'What did I do?'

'Some sort of magic.' Adam was lying on his side, gazing drowsily at Cat and playing with a strand of hair, curling it around his index finger, pulling it straight, then letting go again. 'I don't think you're real. You're a ghost, a goddess. I'll wake up in a moment and you'll vanish, like a dream.'

'I'm not a dream,' she said. 'But I am going to vanish for a moment. I need a drink of water.'

Cat swung her legs out of the bed. She pulled the sheet off too and wrapped it round her body, leaving Adam naked.

He rolled on to his stomach and smiled lazily. 'Make me some coffee, could you, goddess?'

'Yes, all right – one sugar, isn't it?'

'Make it two,' he said. 'After all that exercise I feel I need a carbohydrate hit.'

'You poor old thing,' said Cat. 'I've worn you out.'

'You have indeed,' said Adam, and he groaned theatrically. 'I'll be good for nothing for a week – or even three.'

'I hope it was worth it, then.' Glancing back at him, Cat started to giggle naughtily. 'My goodness, Mr Lawley – you've got a lovely bum!'

'Thank you very much, Miss Aston.' Adam reached languidly across the bed – and then, as quick as lightning, he yanked the sheet off Cat, who squealed in protest. 'So have you.'

Sunday, 19 June

Surely this must be a lovely dream?

They woke in the cool, grey dawn, made early morning love then dozed again.

Since all the wedding, money, Jack and Fanny Gregory stuff, Cat had been a virtual insomniac, a clock-watcher, a midnight wanderer. But today she realised she'd had a whole six hours, and she felt wonderful. She curled up next to Adam and fell into a dreamless, tranquil sleep.

They woke an hour later to a deafening cacophony of bells, crashing and reverberating round them, making the whole amphitheatre shake.

She thought – it took them several centuries, but in the end the Christians won.

'What shall we do?' she asked, or rather shouted.

'I'll take you to Fiesole.'

'Where or what is that?'

'It's a little town up in the hills.'

'It's in the what?'

'I'll tell you in a moment. Thank God for that,' he added, as the bells stopped clanging and now began to toll lugubriously. 'It's a very old Etruscan town. It's in the hills above the valley of the Arno, overlooking Florence, and it's very pretty, or so the guidebook says.'

'Do we drive there?'

'We could go by bus and train, mix with real Italian people, get a flavour of the country?' Adam glanced at Cat. 'Italian trains are really something. Lots of them are double-deckers, fast, luxurious and comfortable. But if we drive we won't be tied to timetables.'

'I don't mind,' said Cat and smiled at him. 'You make the decision.'

'Okay, we'll drive,' said Adam. 'We can have a look around and then go on to Florence, if we've time, and if you'd like to do more tourist stuff?'

'You mean there'll be more towers?'

'Oh, absolutely – lots more towers. You can't move in Tuscany for towers. We can go up the tower of the *Duomo*.'

'Ooh, me knees,' said Cat.

'I think there's a lift for old age pensioners like you.' Adam grinned. 'But you might have to prove you're over sixty before they'll let you use it.'

'Stop calling me an old age pensioner.'

'Well, you're not far off – how old did you say you were that time we had a drink in Walthamstow?'

'You watch yourself,' growled Cat.

'Or you'll do what?'

'You wait and see.'

'Yeah, right – I'm scared.'

'You ought to be.' Cat hit him with a pillow, a very heavy, hard Italian pillow, and it knocked him flat on to his back.

He grabbed her as he toppled backwards.

She collapsed on top of him, convulsed with fits of giggles.

'I'll show you,' he muttered.

'Show me what?'

They didn't get up again for half an hour or more.

Cat decided Italy was magical, that it must be enchanted.

Lucca was most certainly a city made for lovers. She knew she wouldn't, couldn't have felt the way she'd felt last night – the way she still felt now – in any other place.

She could not imagine living here and not being happy. No wonder Mrs Gallo, who was the cleaning lady at Chapman's

Architectural Salvage, always looked fed up. She'd been born in Tuscany, but now she lived in Walthamstow.

'What's next, after Italy?' she asked, as they drove out of Lucca. 'Where will you be working?'

'I'll still be in Dorset for a couple of days a week. I have some stuff to do in Cornwall, too. But then I'm going to Scotland.'

'What will you do in Scotland?'

'I'll be working on a very grand Victorian castle thirty miles from Aberdeen. Or rather it was grand a hundred years or more ago, but now it's falling down. A businessman from Surrey saw it while he was on holiday up there. Now he's decided he wants to be a laird.'

Adam glanced at Cat and made a face. 'Mr Portland and his wife are loaded. I think he made his money in casinos and now he has a chain of betting shops. They live in a modern house near Guildford which was built for them. They showed me round. They've got a billiard room, a gym, a cinema, a Hawaiian cocktail lounge, an indoor swimming pool shaped like the ace of clubs, chandeliers in almost all the rooms, gold plating everywhere.'

'Ooh, it sounds divine.'

'I know it's going to be difficult to get them to agree to sympathetic restoration of a crumbling Scottish castle. The last time I spoke to Mr Portland, he told me Mrs Portland wants a luxury Jacuzzi on the roof and she'd like a swimming pool with underwater lighting and mosaics of their children and their dogs. She's insisting all replacement window frames are made of PVC, because her brother's in the trade and he can do a special deal for them. She's ordered double glazing made to look like Tudor latticing.'

'I'm sure you'll be able to talk them out of stupid stuff like that.'

'Maybe, Cat – I hope so, anyway. But Mrs Portland's

clearly used to having her own way, and Mr Portland listens to his wife.'

'If the castle's listed, she can't have PVC. Adam, you don't sound very keen on them.'

'I'm keen to do this job.'

'Why's that?'

'It's a long term project. I'll be paid a lot of money. So, after I've finished with the Portlands and their castle, I should have the capital to rent some premises, an office, yard and stuff. I'll start employing other people and building up my business.'

'You'll be the king of project managers.'

'Yeah, that's the plan.'

'I hope it all works out, then.'

'I do, too,' said Adam. 'Cat, look over there – do you see that hilltop village, with the tower and houses clustered round it?'

'Yes,' said Cat.

'What about us stopping there for coffee?'

'Do we get to climb the tower?'

'If you like,' said Adam.

'Lovely,' Cat replied, as she told her knees to stop complaining and assured them they were up to it.

After they had climbed the tower, they found a café shaded with a trellis of white roses which dropped their scented petals on the tables, in their coffee, in their hair.

But Cat found this romantic rather than annoying, and so – apparently – did all the other tourists in the place. The café seemed to cast a spell on them.

The chinkle of the crockery, the muted buzz of genial conversation between friends and lovers, the fragrant fumes of always-excellent Italian coffee, the feeling that she didn't want for anything, that she had all she needed and would ever need – surely this was happiness distilled?

She wished she had a magic flask so she could bottle this, what was it, atmosphere? Then she would be able to sip it or inhale it whenever times got hard, and she'd be comforted.

'Stop here a moment, Cat,' said Adam, after he had paid the bill and they were walking through the narrow streets back to the Fiat which was parked outside the walls. 'Stand still – don't smile – don't giggle – try not to move at all.'

'Why?' asked Cat, intrigued.

'I want to take your photograph against that arch with sunlight filtering down on you, with petals of white roses in your hair.'

'God, I must look a right old mess,' said Cat, and now she ran her fingers through her tangled curls, trying to dislodge the petals, shaking half a dozen of them free.

'Stop,' said Adam, catching at her wrist. 'You look like an angel, like a spirit, with those petals in your hair.' Then he took his photograph and slipped his camera back into his pocket.

'Let me see?' demanded Cat.

'No,' said Adam firmly. 'If I let you see it you'll say you look a mess and you'll delete it, and I want to keep it.'

Fiesole was magical and lovely, as beautiful as Lucca, but a very different place.

Lucca was an ancient Roman city with mediaeval walls, built on a plain. Bicycles went hurtling along the narrow streets, and the smaller Fiats could squeeze along its slightly broader thoroughfares, but a BMW would have almost no chance. Lucca was enclosed and secret, hiding many things.

Fiesole had wider streets and open spaces but was even older, built by the Etruscans in the hills. So many of its houses clung precipitously to slopes, and from its high vantage points there were quite amazing views of the valley and the River Arno far below.

'How are your knees?' asked Adam as they walked along a switchback road, doing a circumnavigation of the town.

'They're fine,' said Cat and told them to shut up, promising them she'd join a gym when she got back to London. 'Adam, this is wonderful! We can see for miles and miles and miles!'

'Do you want to see a theatre built into a hillside?'

'Yes,' said Cat. 'Well, provided you'll agree to do a song and dance routine and I can take a photograph of you looking ridiculous as well.'

'It's a deal,' said Adam as he took her hand.

As they sat in a restaurant in Fiesole's town square, eating perfect pasta and drinking Pinot Grigio – Cat was drinking most of it, she realised, for Adam had drunk one glass of wine and then he'd stuck to water – Cat realised she was happy still.

Yes, Italy itself was quite amazing.

But as for feeling happy – she knew that this was mostly down to Adam.

He was the sort of man who could make any woman happy.

Some men could put up shelves. Others knew how to fix a dripping tap or build a garden wall. Adam could no doubt do all that, she thought, but his special superpower was making women happy.

So maybe it was right, and maybe it was only fair, that he didn't tie himself to any single woman, but spread himself around? When they had a drink that time, didn't he say he'd had a lot of girlfriends?

Yes, she thought he did.

She couldn't believe how wrong she'd been about him the first time they had met. She'd thought he was a grumpy, surly bastard who had never learned to smile. She reflected now that if she had been soaking wet herself – and tired and overworked – she probably wouldn't have been a little ray of sunshine, either.

She couldn't help comparing him with Jack.

Whenever she had been in bed with Jack, he'd always needed pleasing and he'd always had demands.

After these demands had all been met, he'd fall asleep, while she'd lie in the darkness feeling thwarted, cheated, more alone than if she had been by herself.

She'd always thought she was to blame, had told herself she shouldn't have so many unrealistic expectations – that she was very lucky to be with a man who looked like Jack.

But maybe Jack was lucky to have been with Cat?

Why hadn't she ever thought of that before?

Adam didn't have demands. Adam didn't need pleasing. Adam liked to please, to make a woman feel that she was special, that she was beautiful, that she was the only woman in the world for him.

Ladies first – his mother must have drummed it into him while he was still a toddler, she decided, as she drank more wine, for which she knew she wouldn't have to pay.

Jack was always scrounging fivers, tenners, borrowing and never paying back. But Adam wouldn't let her put her hand into her pocket for anything at all.

He doesn't do relationships – she kept repeating it. She kept insisting to herself that this was it, that this was all she would be getting, just one lovely, beautiful weekend.

All he had wanted was to make her smile. He'd told her so himself, and now he'd done it – God in heaven, how brilliantly he'd done it, he'd won Olympic gold – he would be moving on.

'You're very thoughtful, Cat,' he said, forking up the last of his tomato pappardelle.

'On the contrary, my mind's a blank.' Cat knew she was

blushing like a poppy and hoped he wouldn't notice. 'I'm just sitting here and chilling out.'

'You're all right, though?'

'Yes, I'm fine,' she said, and smiled at him. 'I'm full of perfect pasta. I'm sitting in a lovely restaurant with a lovely man.' Oh God, she thought, a lovely man, that's the Pinot Grigio talking now. I mustn't rabbit on like this – he'll think I'm such a fool. 'The sun is shining, so I'm warm and comfortable and happy.'

'Good,' said Adam. 'Go on being happy while you can, because it never lasts.'

She realised she was being warned.

So she was surprised when later, after they had spent a lovely afternoon in Florence, after they'd had dinner in Lucca, after they'd made love – she couldn't bring herself to say had sex, she would never demean what they'd just done by saying they'd had sex – instead of rolling over on his side and going straight to sleep, as Jack would certainly have done, Adam sat up and said they had to talk.

'What about?' asked Cat.

'You and me, of course,' said Adam.

'What is there to say?'

'Oh, for God's sake, Cat!' Adam's dark eyes narrowed as he frowned. He gave Cat a gentle but insistent little shake. 'What are we going to do?'

'You mean tomorrow?'

'Of course I mean tomorrow, and the next day, and—'

'Do we have to talk about it now?' Cat was feeling all blissed out and drowsy. What she really wanted was to curl up next to Adam for their last night together and then to fall asleep.

'You probably won't believe this,' she continued, smothering a yawn, 'but I'm not a clinger. I'm not a needy person. So you mustn't worry I'm expecting this weekend to be the start of something. I remember what you said.'

'What did I say?'

'How you don't like doing couples stuff, how you hate going shopping, how your relationships with girls don't last.'

'But I didn't mean—'

'Adam, it's okay, it's not a problem.' Cat closed her eyes and snuggled down beneath the fat, white duvet. 'It's late and we're both tired. Let's get some sleep.'

'Cat, wake up!' Adam shook her harder. 'You misunderstood me. If you go shopping on a Saturday afternoon, I'll come along. I'll even push and shove my way down bloody Oxford Street. I'll do couples stuff on Sunday mornings.'

'You don't have to, Adam,' Cat assured him, hardly taking in what he was saying, anyway. 'I don't go shopping on Saturdays myself. Or not in Oxford Street, at any rate. Some Saturdays I'm at the salvage yard, flogging old Victorian skirting boards or stripped pine doors to DIY fanatics, or helping people find a garden ornament that isn't made of concrete.' She yawned in earnest then. 'Some Sunday mornings, I go to see my parents. But if we're going to stay in touch when we get back to England, I'd really like to learn about your work.'

'I'll learn you,' promised Adam. 'Cat, I'll—'

'—teach me, even?'

'Learn you, teach you, anything!'

'Good,' said Cat. 'So now we've got that sorted, we're going to sleep, all right?'

Monday, 20 June

How did this weekend go by so fast?

The morning light came slanting through the dark green painted shutters. Adam had been awake all night, watching Cat as she lay sleeping peacefully and wondering what to say, how much to say, and when to say it.

He got up, pulled his jeans on and went to make some coffee.

He wasn't very good at making coffee. It always seemed to come out far too weak or far too strong. Today it looked like treacle and there were some gritty speckles floating on the surface.

But it would have to do. As he stirred in milk for Cat and sugar for himself, he decided he would take it slowly. He'd get to know this girl and not go rushing into things. He wouldn't make the mistakes he'd made with Maddy. He wouldn't make assumptions, and he wouldn't frighten Cat away.

After all, there wasn't any hurry.

He carried the laden tray into the bedroom and put it on the nightstand. Then he stroked Cat's hair back from her forehead until her green eyes opened and she smiled at him.

'*Buon giorno, caro mio,*' she began. She giggled as her hair tickled her face. '*Come sta?*' she added doubtfully.

'Good morning, Cat,' said Adam. 'It should be *come stai*, I think. But I don't do Italian this early in the day.'

'You don't do Italian any time, according to Italians. Or that was what you told me, anyhow. Do I smell coffee, Adam?'

'Yes, I made some – milk, no sugar, right?'

'I think I'll drink it later.'

'Oh, why's that?'

'I want something else right now.'

Cat's smile became seductive and, as she walked her fingers down his chest and reached the whorl of hair around his navel, he began to shiver with desire. 'Adam, come to bed?'

Afterwards, he told her – this was the real thing.

'You know what I'm saying, don't you?' he continued, as he tilted up her chin and as he made her look into his eyes. 'I'm in love with you.'

'I don't think I believe you.'

'Why?'

'You told me, didn't you? You said you don't—'

'Cat, I've met a lot of girls, but never one as gorgeous, as desirable, as smart, as sweet as you. Every single moment I've spent with you has been a perfect pleasure, an absolute delight.'

'Stop it, Adam, I can't deal with this.' Cat looked away. 'You're only trying to make me say I love you.'

'I don't need to try. You're the sort of person who can't hide what you feel. Cat Aston, you're in love with me.'

'You sound very confident, but how can you be sure?'

'I'm only *almost* sure – so tell me so yourself?'

'I'm in love with you.' Cat looked at him and sighed. She knew there wasn't any point in arguing with Adam or in trying to deceive him. He was an enchanter who could see into your heart. 'I think I fell in love with you when you were so kind to that old man. You changed his tyre. You called the breakdown lorry. You even paid the men to take him home.'

'Anybody would have done it.'

'No they wouldn't, Adam. When did you decide you might like me?'

179

'The evening you were crying in the pub.' Adam looped Cat's hair out of her eyes. 'I wanted more than anything to see you smile again.'

'You got what you wanted, then.'

'I did.'

'What are we going to do about it?' Cat asked doubtfully. 'I mean about this being in love?'

'We'll have to decide where we should live.'

'We're moving in together, are we?'

'Yes, I think so,' he replied.

'Where do you live now?'

'When I'm in London, I share a flat in Camden with Jules Devine and Gwennie Smith. They're two of my best friends.' Adam smiled reassuringly at Cat. 'You'll love them, they'll love you. I know they will.'

'What are they like?'

'They're fun, they're generous and they're kind. They buy coffees, cakes and sandwiches for street musicians, homeless people and *Big Issue* sellers. They stick fivers in collecting tins.'

'What do they do – for work, I mean?'

'Gwennie is a dental nurse and Jules is a rep for Bayer, Pfizer, Glaxo – one of those. He's always changing jobs, so I lose track. The flat's awash with pencils, ballpoints, notebooks, post-its, key-rings – all the promotions stuff he gives away to doctors. Cat, what are your favourite things? What's your favourite food, your favourite colour, favourite scent?'

'Pasta, purple, you,' said Cat. She shook her head at him. 'So you do have relationships with girls?'

'I never said I didn't.'

'You implied it.'

'You jumped to conclusions.'

'Did I, Adam?'

'Or you deliberately misunderstood me.'

'I don't think so,' Cat insisted.

'What's so funny?' he demanded as she grinned at him.

'I believe we're having our first row.'

'No we're not because I don't do rows.'

'What do you do?'

'I do proposals.'

Adam had decided he would take it very slowly, but now he couldn't seem to stop the words from tumbling out.

'Cat Aston,' he said softly as he gazed into her beautiful green eyes. 'Cat, will you marry me?'

'I—Adam, are you serious?'

'I've never been more serious in my life.'

'We hardly know each other.'

'We know all the important stuff.'

'We do?'

'Of course we do.' Adam kissed her on the forehead then drew back to look at Cat again, to drink in her beauty, stamp her image on his heart. 'I love you, Cat, and so what else is there to know?'

'Well, nothing, I suppose.' Cat gazed back at him. 'Adam, are you really asking me to marry you?'

'I'm asking you to marry me, to be my wife and have our children.'

'Then – yes, I will.'

'You're sure?'

'I'm sure.' Cat smiled at him. 'You took me by surprise, that's all. But you've also made me very happy.'

'Good,' said Adam. 'You've made me happy, too.'

'What time's your flight?' asked Adam, as they ate their breakfast in Pietro's uncle's restaurant.

'Ten past eight this evening,' Cat replied.

'Mine's not until tomorrow, but I'll change it.'

'There's no need,' said Cat. 'I'm going to Heathrow, not Kazakhstan. I can get back to Leyton by myself.'

'But I don't want to be away from you.'

Adam leaned towards her, then he kissed her, and she smelled the wonderful, just-shaved-and-showered scent of him.

I've never been so happy in my life, she thought, as she tasted coffee, honey, buttered croissants, him, and decided this would always be the taste of happiness.

Then, glancing up, she saw Pietro's uncle smirk. It was as if he said, I told you so.

'What will you be doing this morning?' she enquired.

'I have two appointments then I've finished.'

'Who are you going to meet?'

'The manager of a quarry at eleven – I need to make some contacts here in Italy, you see, and get stuff shipped direct, rather than buy what I need from a supplier in London at an enormous mark-up. Then I'm calling on a master stonemason who has a yard a few miles out of Lucca. Pietro says he's got some tools I'll need and he'll be happy to sell to me. I'll be away for two, three hours, no more. I won't be apart from you a minute longer than I have to be.' Adam stirred his coffee. 'You could look round the shops again, perhaps? Buy some of that glass you thought your mum and dad might like?'

'Or I could come with you to the quarry?'

'You'd probably be bored.'

'I wouldn't, Adam,' Cat replied. 'I work in an architectural salvage yard, remember? I often see Italian marble in an awful state, green and cracked and crumbling, ingrained with soot and dirt.'

'Yes, I suppose you must.'

'So, while I'm in Italy, I'd really like to see where marble

182

comes from, find out how it's quarried, how it's carved, how Italian craftsmen repair it and restore it.' Cat met Adam's gaze. 'I'm interested in what you do. I told you so last night.'

'Okay, you come along,' said Adam, nodding. 'Then, after we've seen Ricardo Angeli and Giancarlo Russo, we'll drive on to Pisa and have a look around.'

'Maybe I'll get to see a few more towers, then?'

'I wouldn't be surprised. We can't leave Pisa, can we, without going to see the leaning tower and taking a photograph of you holding it up?'

'Of course we can't,' said Cat, as she poured out more coffee. 'Adam, do you know what stops the tower from falling down?'

'It goes round in a circle, so it's always moving. If it wasn't moving, it would fall.'

'I don't believe you.'

'It's the truth.' Adam took another croissant, buttered it and loaded it with honey. 'It's a very interesting theory, anyway.'

'Go on – explain?'

'When the sun heats up the marble on the south side of the tower, it expands and makes the tower lean even more.'

'So why —'

'But when it gets dark, the marble shrinks, and the whole building changes its position, completing a small circle. It's to do with equilibrium – disturbing and restoring it.'

'Adam, you're amazing, you know everything,' said Cat. 'If I ever get to be on *Millionaire*, you'll definitely be my phone-a-friend.'

I'll never fall myself, she thought, as long as I have you.

Tuesday, 21 June

Back to reality?

The plane was late, and it was well past midnight before they left the burger-scented chaos of Heathrow.

'We'll get a cab,' said Adam.

'It will be expensive.' Cat was rummaging in her bag and thinking, do I dare to use a cash machine, or will it spit my card back in my face? 'Taxi drivers always stick it on for airport rides. They all think we're stupid foreigners who can't get the hang of British money. Why don't we get the bus?'

'Cat, it doesn't matter about money,' Adam said. 'So please put your purse away, or somebody will snatch it.'

'You can't pay for everything,' she said. 'I owe you for my room, my meals, and how much did it cost to go up all those towers and into all those palaces and galleries and things?'

'We'll talk about it later. Now, we're going to find a cab.'

'Okay.' Cat was very tired, and she could see that Adam was determined, so she stopped arguing.

Adam couldn't wait to get back home to Camden Town.

He hoped Jules and Gwennie would be up. The chances were they would be. They sometimes lounged around and watched old movies starring Bette Davis or Clark Gable until well past two or three o'clock.

Gwennie was addicted, and Jules was always happy to stay up with Gwennie, provided there were also bacon sandwiches, a big bag of Doritos, a tub of Ben and Jerry's Fossil Fuel and a pack of Heineken to ward off night starvation.

We'll get another sofa, he decided, a big, fat squashy one

with lots of cushions. Then all four of us can loll around, eat bacon sandwiches and watch Gwennie's movies half the night.

Cat and Gwennie – they would get on fine, he knew they would. They'd like each other straight away. As for Jules – he'd take the piss a bit. He always did when Adam got involved with anybody new. But that was Jules for you, a wanker with a heart of gold.

So maybe getting a new place for just the two of them was not the way to do it, after all? Maybe Cat could move into the flat in Camden Town, where there was loads of room? Then they could save for a deposit on a house?

'God, I'm so sleepy,' murmured Cat as she climbed into the taxi cab. 'It was all that exercise. I'm so not used to it.'

'I'll get you fit, you'll see.' Adam kissed her forehead. 'But I've already told you, I'm not God.'

'You're so not funny, Adam.' Cat could not stop yawning. It was as if she'd caught a yawning bug. 'I need to go to bed.'

'But in the meantime have a little doze.' Adam put his arm around her shoulders so she could rest her head against his chest. He stroked her hair until she fell asleep. He stared out of the window at the bright lights of Heathrow, and realised he had never felt so blessed.

More prosaically – he hoped he hadn't left his bedroom looking like a rubbish dump. But he was almost certain it was more or less respectable, that there would be no pizza boxes, Stella cans or rotting Chinese takeaways composting on the floor.

He might not be taking Cat back to a scented bower of summer roses, but hopefully there wouldn't be a tangled mess of jeans and socks to kick through before they went to bed.

He'd changed the sheets before he'd gone to Italy. He definitely remembered doing that. He was almost sure he'd stuffed his washing in the basket which his mother bought for him last Christmas, probably more in hope than expectation – thank you, Mum.

Stop worrying, he told himself, everything is going to be all right. After all, there's nothing to go wrong. We understand each other perfectly, and we're in love.

He closed his eyes and slept.

'Hey, mate, is this the place?' the cabbie asked him, startling him awake.

He looked out of the window, and saw to his surprise that he was suddenly home again. He shoved a bunch of tenners at the driver and helped a sleepy Cat out of the cab.

'The view's not quite as special as the one we had in Lucca,' he told Cat as he took out his keys.

'It doesn't matter, Adam,' she assured him. 'Anyway, I can always look at you.'

'I need a shave.'

'But I always think the Desperate Dan look's very sexy, especially on a man.'

'I need a shower, as well.'

'Okay, shall I come back some other time?'

'You're not going anywhere tonight.'

They made their stumbling way upstairs, a laughing, hugging, whispering, kissing huddle of coats and carrier bags and other luggage.

Cat was already pulling grips and clips out of her hair – the gorgeous hair that curled in sinuous ringlets, wound itself around his fingers, just as Cat had wound her lovely self around his heart.

The heart he'd thought was broken and would never mend. But it obviously had, for these days it was singing.

The flat was dark and silent.

Jules's and Gwennie's bedroom door was open. So they

must be out, he thought, and they might stay out all night if they'd gone somewhere miles away from home. They'd probably stay over with relatives or friends.

But perhaps that would be for the best, and maybe introductions could wait until the morning, anyway?

Or the following evening, if they went straight into work?

'Do you want anything to eat?' he asked, as he began to turn on lights – and turn some off again, because the kitchen was a tip. There were empty packets, cartons, bottles everywhere, and it looked like nobody had washed up for a week.

'I'm not hungry,' Cat replied, and smiled a feline smile. 'Well, not for food, in any case.' She slid her arms around his waist. 'I'm shattered, though, aren't you? Adam, I've been thinking – it would be so lovely to be under a duvet, curled up with someone nice.'

'I was sort of thinking that, as well.'

'We'd better go to bed, then, hadn't we?'

Adam's bedroom door was firmly closed. As he opened it, he realised there was something wrong.

The curtains were pulled tight – he'd left them open.

There was a burger box, some sandwich wrappers and a Coke can on his desk – he hated burgers and could not remember the last time he had bought a can of Coke.

There were piles of books and magazines and clothing scattered, jumbled, heaped up on the floor – he'd put almost everything away.

As his eyes adjusted, as light from the landing spilled in a white arc into his room, he saw there was someone in his bed.

Bloody Jules, he thought, he might have asked, he might have texted, before he let his bloody mate crash here.

Or maybe it was one of Gwennie's friends? Or Gwennie's

sister Lauren, come to the big city for a week to do some serious shopping? There were lots of carrier bags from Topshop and Miss Selfridge littering the floor.

'Excuse me,' he said loudly, as he turned on the light.

Then he thought, why am I saying excuse me? It's my bedroom and I need this bed. So whoever's in it can doss down in the sitting room tonight.

As he was about to speak again – to tell this interloper to get up, get out, and sound as if he meant it – the body in his bed began to move.

It raised its head and stared at him, shielding its eyes against the light.

'Adam?' it said sleepily. 'What a nice surprise! I wasn't expecting you until tomorrow at the earliest. But don't just stand there, darling – come to bed?'

Then he was falling down a lift shaft, down and down into a pit of snakes. He tasted dread and panic like hot metal on his tongue, and smelled a sweet, familiar female scent.

He told himself he must be seeing, must be hearing things. But as he stood there staring at the person in the bed, he knew this was no vision from a nightmare.

'Adam?'

As he tried to grope his way out of a fog of horror, he became aware that Cat was speaking, that her hand was on his arm.

'Adam,' she repeated, 'who's this woman?'

'I'm his girlfriend,' Maddy said. She yawned and stretched seductively. 'I'm his fiancée, actually.'

'You can't be!' Cat stared, shocked and horrified.

'Oh, but I can,' said Maddy. She smirked complacently. 'Adam, darling, could you tell this person we're engaged?'

'We're not engaged!' cried Adam.

He turned to Cat and took her by the shoulders. 'Cat, let me explain,' he said. 'Long before I met you, I asked Mads to marry me, but she turned me down. She went away, she left the country, she told me she was going—'

'I'd better leave,' said Cat, pulling away from him.

'I'm coming, too,' said Adam. 'Mads, when I get back, I want you to have gone. By the way, who let you in?'

'The fat girl who's shacked up with Whatsisface.'

'Where is Gwennie now?'

'They've gone to see some friends. I didn't catch their names. So anyway, I got myself some supper, had a shower, and then I came to bed.'

Maddy lay back against the heap of pillows, grinning like a vixen who had slaughtered a whole coop of chickens and meant to eat the lot.

'Dear old Gwennie,' she continued, looking at her nails, which Adam saw were long and painted red. 'She was so pleased to see me. She gave me a big hug. She told me you've been absolutely miserable while I've been away.'

'Maddy, that's enough!' snapped Adam.

'Moping around the place, she said you've been, not eating properly and getting thinner every day. Jules has been quite worried. He thought you ought to go and see a doctor and get some medication, although of course he didn't like to say. He knew you'd bite his head off.'

'Mads, get up, get dressed and leave,' said Adam. 'Cat, could I come back to yours tonight?'

'No, Adam, you could not.' Cat's expression was unreadable. 'I think you should stay here, don't you, and sort things out with Maddy?'

'I can explain,' cried Adam, as Cat turned on her heel and then went clattering down the stairs. 'It's not what it looks like!'

'Yeah, yeah,' muttered Cat. 'It's what you bastards always say. *It's not what it looks like.* Or, *I can explain.* I can't believe I almost fell for you.'

'Cat, please listen!' As she reached the hallway, Adam grabbed her arm and spun her round to face him. 'I didn't know Mads was coming home. I didn't know she'd want to see me. I—'

'So you do know her, then? She's not a nutter who's been turfed out of some bin? She's not in the care of the community?'

'No, she's not a nutter.'

'She said she's your fiancée.'

'I did ask her to marry me. But, as I explained, she turned me down.'

'So you're on the rebound and I'm a consolation prize – is that it?'

'No!' cried Adam, as he raked his fingers through his hair and tried to think, as he tried to put his words together so they'd make some sort of sense. 'I don't know what she's doing here in London. She told me she was going to Uruguay.'

'Why would she go to Uruguay? It looks to me as if she went to Topshop.' As Cat glared at him, he could see her eyes were sparkling bright. If they had been a pair of lasers they'd have burned a hole in him. 'You—you lied to me.'

'I didn't lie to you!'

'Then you forgot to mention certain things, like you were still in a relationship, like you were living with a woman.'

'Cat, it's not like that – Mads and I split up before you and I met, I swear to God.'

'Let's leave God out of this, we don't want him involved.' Cat's eyes grew hard as chips of Dartmoor granite. 'Adam, in my admittedly non-professional opinion, you do need medication. You also need some psychiatric help.'

'What's that supposed to mean?'

'You proposed to Maddy. You proposed to me. You've probably proposed to half a dozen other women, too. You said yourself you do proposals, plural. So you're a serial proposer and you should see a shrink.'

'I don't need a bloody shrink!' cried Adam desperately. 'We can sort this whole thing out between us. It will take five minutes. If you'll just hang on a moment, I'll get Mads to tell you it's all over between her and me.'

'Get off me,' Cat said coldly, trying to squirm out of Adam's grasp. 'Stop shouting, too. You're going to wake your neighbours.'

'Damn the neighbours! Maddy?' shouted Adam. 'Get down here this minute and help me to explain!'

'I can't, my love, I'm naked.' Maddy's voice came floating down the stairs like a carillon of silver bells. 'Adam, are you coming up to bed?'

'Cat, don't leave!' cried Adam desperately.

'Oh, go and stuff yourself,' snapped Cat. 'Or go and stuff that woman in your bed. She's obviously gagging for it.'

'Cat, my darling, wait!'

'Adam, don't you *Cat, my darling* me!' She slapped his hand away and, as he stood there helpless, willing her to believe him, she jerked the front door open.

She ran off up the road.

She hopped on to a bus which had appeared as if by magic and then she disappeared into the night.

Adam went back upstairs and glared at Maddy.

She was walking round his bedroom naked, grinning like a gargoyle and kicking clothes aside like someone paddling in a stream. 'You took your time,' she said. 'Who was that common-looking trollop? Where did you pick her up?'

'When did you get back from Uruguay?'

'I didn't go to Uruguay,' said Maddy. 'I flew to Mexico, and it was horrid. There were flies and dirt and filth and

191

squalor everywhere. I went to work on an organic farm run by a couple from Seattle. It was full of beads-and-bangles hippies and soya-drinking vegans who were all backpacking around the world for free, or almost free.'

'I'd have thought they would be like your friends in the UK?'

'They were nothing like my friends!' Maddy looked disgusted. 'They were the most tedious, boring people I have ever met. All so grim and serious and earnest, and you should have seen their clothes. Charity cast-offs, stuff they'd found in skips – not an ounce of fashion sense between the lot of them.'

'What about the local people, then? The ones you said needed the help of the developed world?'

'I didn't have much to do with them,' said Maddy, wrinkling her nose and shuddering. 'They live in the most awful places, Adam. Shanty towns and huts made out of rubbish, mosquitoes everywhere, no running water, or only in the gutters, anyway.'

She started stroking Adam's arm. 'So anyway, my darling, are you tired? You look exhausted. Gwennie said you'd gone to Italy. But she didn't know you took some slapper who must have worn you out.'

'Get dressed, Maddy,' Adam said, 'then leave.'

'Oh, Adam, don't be angry,' wheedled Maddy. 'I know I went away – I had to find myself, you see – but I thought about you all the time. I'm still in love with you.'

'I don't believe you. I don't think you were ever in love with me.'

'Of course I was, my darling. I might not have said the actual words. But surely lovers know these things?'

'I want you to leave.'

'But I don't have anywhere to go,' said Maddy, sticking out her lower lip and making Bambi eyes. 'Where's your sense of chivalry? Do you really mean to throw me out into the cold, dark night?'

'It isn't cold, it's June,' said Adam, as he found his phone. 'Mads, you have five minutes. Get your clothes on, pack your stuff. I'll call a cab for you.'

Cat wouldn't answer calls or texts.

She wouldn't answer e-mails.

When Adam called at Chapman's yard first thing on Tuesday morning, delivering her luggage which she'd left behind in Camden Town, he found his way was barred by Tess, who told him Cat was out.

Did he have any business at the yard, she added, was there anything he wanted, tiles, spindles, chimneys?

'No, thank you,' he replied.

'Then you mustn't let me hold you up.' She looked at him as if he were a slug she'd just discovered in a lettuce. 'You can't go through the office,' she continued. 'Go back through the yard, if you don't mind. The gate is on your right.'

'I need to have a word with Cat.'

'She doesn't want to see you.'

'She's here, then?'

'She might be.'

'I thought you told me she was out?'

'She's out to you,' said Tess. 'I think you ought to go away,' she added. 'There are laws, you know.'

'What do you mean by that?'

'This may come as a surprise to you, but stalking girls, harassing girls, molesting girls – they can have you for it. Lock you up and throw away the key.'

Adam realised he would have to wait.

Let Cat calm down, he told himself. Then try again next week – if he could hang on that long. If, in the meantime, he could stop himself from going mad.

He thought about the night on the Embankment, when he'd met that homeless man. What had he said?

'You 'ave a bust-up with a lady, you need to give her time, and she'll come round. That's all they need, my son – a bit of time.'

He hoped the homeless man was right.

'You're not going to tell me any good stuff about what you did in Italy, then?' demanded Tess as she sauntered back into the office. 'Cat, are you still here?'

'Yes, but keep your voice down,' muttered Cat.

'It's all right, he's gone.'

'I wouldn't put it past him to come back.'

Cat was hiding in the shrubbery, behind a huge asparagus fern which grew in an enormous Chinese pot.

Barry's granny had donated it to Barry's business. She said it gave the place a touch of class. Cat and Tess both hated it because they knew they would be carrion if they failed to keep the thing alive.

'You should discuss what happened with a sympathetic listener, and I'm offering,' said Tess. She flicked a rubber band across the room. 'It's the first rule of therapy, you know. I read about it in a magazine. When you talk, you purge yourself of all your bad emotions.'

'Or give your mates a laugh at your expense.'

'You vocalise your inner conflict,' Tess said solemnly. 'You cleanse your soul and find your way to peace. Anyway – this WAG, she said that doing it in hourly sessions with her therapist was the most amazing, brilliant thing.'

'What happened, then?'

'It sorted out her head – like, totally.'

'I don't think it's going to be that easy,' muttered Cat.

'Why, what did you do? What did he do?'

'I'm not entirely sure.' Cat looked at Tess and sighed. 'I

sometimes wonder if I might have dreamed it, or some of it, at least.'

'If you think you dreamed it, you could go and see this guy in Catford who's a tantric disentangler.'

'Who's a what?'

'He sorts the real stuff from the dreams.'

'How does he do that?'

'I think it's something to do with smoke and chanting. He charges fifty quid plus VAT. So he's not expensive, and for another tenner he'll sort your chakras, too. Or you could see this shaman guy in Neasden who'll analyse your aura, then get you to inhale all sorts of vapours to detoxify your mind. Or—'

'What have you and Bex been up to while I've been away?'

'We're talking about you and Mr Spindle, Cat. What did you two do in Tuscany?'

'We walked around. We drove around. We went to villas, palaces and beautiful old churches. We ate in lovely restaurants.'

'Come on, Cat – I want more than the tweet.'

'We climbed up half a dozen towers.'

'Ah, towers – they're significant,' said Tess. 'They're like spindles, chimneys. Towers symbolise all sorts of stuff. If Mr Spindle took you up a lot of towers, it must mean he—'

'Tess, I have a pile of work to do. Barry's accountant's coming round next week. Barry doesn't have a clue about Excel, and so I'm going to have—'

'I'm only guessing here, of course, but I'm assuming you had lots of sex?'

'I don't wish to discuss it.'

'Cat, what did that scumbag do to you?'

'Tess—'

'You can tell me, honey,' wheedled Tess, who had stopped flicking rubber bands. 'This Adam bastard didn't hurt you, did he? If he did, then Bex and I will sort him out. We'll go and cut his bits off. Or we'll get our brothers on the case. All you have to do is say the word.'

'Adam didn't hurt me,' Cat insisted.

'You're sure?' demanded Tess.

'I'm sure,' said Cat. 'I had a lovely time.'

'So why won't you see him?'

'I can't tell you yet.'

'Okay, tell me tomorrow.'

'Yeah, I might.' Cat tried again to change the subject. 'How was your weekend?'

'Well, we met these Scottish guys. They'd come down for a match or something and they were both seriously loaded, wallets full of Scottish funny money and they spent like there was no tomorrow.'

'So you all had a fantastic time?'

'Yeah, too right we did! Anyway, these guys were brothers. Or did they say cousins? They both had bright red hair, in any case. I've never really gone for redheads, but these blokes were seriously hot.

'They said they would be going to Las Vegas in July. I'd love to go to Vegas. Lots of millionaires hang out in Vegas, so maybe I could even find myself a millionaire. Most Americans love British girls. They like our accents. I read about it in a magazine. They think we're well cute—'

As Tess rattled on and on, Cat began to wish she had said nothing about Adam and going to Italy.

Tess came from a family of tough market traders who lived in Bethnal Green. One older brother had done time for grievous bodily harm, a younger one had just come out of prison, and Tess herself had qualifications in some martial art.

Bex was just as forceful, five-feet-two of Rottweiler belligerence and sassy disrespect. She treated men and dating like fussy children treated tubes of Smarties, picking out and gobbling up the orange ones and leaving all the purples, pinks and reds.

Cat thought it would be just as well if Adam didn't show his face in Chapman's yard again.

Maybe she should warn him?

But why she should be bothered about lying, cheating Adam Lawley's safety, she really didn't know.

She shook her head and sighed. What she did know was the thought of him, the touch of him, the lovely memories of how he'd made her feel in Italy were going to be difficult to shift.

Maddy had been difficult to shift.

Adam had called a cab, but Maddy had refused to take it, sitting on the stairs surrounded by her Topshop carriers and other bags and baggage and sobbing that she didn't know what had happened to her sweet and lovely Adam. He used to be so good, so kind, so generous, and now he was so horrid, cruel and mean.

She'd been so distressed that in the end he had relented. 'Mads, go back to bed,' he'd said at last. 'We'll talk about it in the morning.'

'You promise, Adam?'

'Maddy, go to bed!' He'd fixed himself a bowl of cereal, grabbed some cushions and a blanket and he'd spent the night – or what remained of it – sleepless on the sofa in the living room.

'We've both moved on,' he said to Maddy as they ate breakfast in the kitchen and listened to the Tuesday morning news.

'One of us might have done,' she wept. 'Adam, I admit I got it wrong. When you asked me to marry you, I panicked. I said some awful things. But can't we be friends?'

'Maddy, it's all over.'

'Did you take that girl to Italy?'

'I don't wish to discuss it.'

'What's her name? I didn't catch it.'

'You don't need to know.'

'She looked surprised to find me in your bed. You didn't tell her you'd asked me to marry you?'

'It didn't seem important.'

'Do you mean I'm not important?'

'As I told you, it's all over.'

'You're the most important person in my life!'

'You'll find someone else to jerk around.' Adam got up and put his breakfast dishes in the sink. 'I have to go to work,' he said. 'You'll need to find a place to stay.'

But when he got home again that evening, Maddy was still there. Jules had gone to Liverpool on business, but Gwennie was at home and looked at him uncomfortably, as if she were saying, is this okay?

He glanced down at his phone and saw that it was almost midnight.

'You can stay tonight,' he said to Maddy. 'But first thing tomorrow morning I shall call another cab.'

Maddy looked at him and shrugged.

The following morning she collected up her stuff and left before he was awake, before the day was light.

Thursday, 23 June

How long will it take?

It was like a tooth that needed filling.

If she didn't poke at it or bite down really hard on it, it didn't hurt too much. While she was busy doing boring stuff like spreadsheets or the payroll it didn't hurt at all. When something jogged her memory, of course, or when she was trying to get to sleep, it hurt like hell.

But she was dealing with it. She was trying to stay angry rather than be sad, and she was sure that being angry helped.

Adam Lawley, he'd been just a blip, she told herself, a mad infatuation. You can deal with mad infatuations, she insisted. You don't need to see him. You don't need to think about him. He's psychotic, anyway. He should be locked up.

As for the other scumbag – while she was in Italy, Jack had been round to the flat. He'd taken all his stuff. He'd also taken half a dozen tenners she'd left behind the radio in the kitchen.

But she didn't care. She didn't begrudge him sixty quid. She was just glad he'd gone away. She would have paid him twice as much to go away. She was so over him she could not believe how much she'd loved him.

She must have been bewitched.

She'd woken late on Tuesday, and again on Wednesday, but she got up early Thursday morning.

She had a shower and washed her hair and drank a mug of caffeine-free tisane and ate a bowl of whole-grain, fair-trade muesli. She wasn't eating junk food any more, she had decided, as she'd washed her hair with additive-and-chloride-free shampoo. It was clearly scrambling her brain.

So there'd be no more chocolate, pecan and marshmallow

muffins. She would detoxify her body, mind and soul. She would do it by herself. She wasn't going to pay some guy in Neasden, anyway.

She put her breakfast dishes in the sink and then she had a chuck-out. After all, she thought – I might as well detoxify my living space.

Jack had taken all his clothes and all his shoes and half Cat's DVDs. But he had left a lot of rubbish. Magazines with pouting models on their covers, cardboard sandwich boxes, all those bits of packaging from shirts, plastic bags and empty water bottles, lager cans and cigarette ends, pizza boxes and half-eaten pies.

As she was collecting up this litter, the postman rang the bell.

There was a squashy parcel from her mother which felt like something useful – a cute-puppy-motif shower cap or a kitten-patterned washbag, maybe – and a letter addressed to Jack at Cat's, the first she'd ever known him to receive.

Adam picked up the last of Maddy's non-recyclable rubbish – ice-cream tubs and yogurt pots and a broken pottery pig he'd cut his foot on when he'd trodden on the blasted thing – tied the plastic sack and put it out for dustbin day.

Gwennie met him coming up the stairs, carrying the morning post – junk mail, bills and flyers mostly. But there were a couple of cheques for him, together with a thick, cream envelope embossed with a heraldic crest.

It was probably some daft promotion, he decided. Or a scam to say he'd won a million quid, and if he'd send a cheque for twenty and an envelope addressed to him to this post office box in Birmingham, the lovely people at the other end would send the cash.

'Adam, about the other day,' said Gwennie.

'Don't you have to go and catch your bus?' Gwennie had

put her serious-talking face on, but he didn't want to be interrogated now. 'If you miss the 8.15 you'll probably be late for work.'

'I'm not due in until half nine today. Marek's got a meeting.' Gwennie looked at Adam with big, mournful eyes. 'I thought you'd be so pleased to have her home again. You were both so very much in love and you were so miserable when she went away.'

'We all move on,' said Adam. 'Gwennie, you watch too many vintage movies. Real life's not like in those films, you know.'

'Yes, Adam, I do know,' said Gwennie sadly. 'But that doesn't stop me wishing real life wasn't about going to the pub, and doing Jules's washing because the lazy bastard can't or won't, and working in a job that bores me rigid, sorting people's manky teeth and telling them to brush and floss more thoroughly in future, when I know damn well they bloody won't.'

'Why don't you investigate that music therapy course?' suggested Adam. 'Do you play an instrument yourself?'

'Yes, the piano and the classical guitar.'

'You never said!'

'I haven't played since I left school. I'm very out of practice.'

'You could soon polish up your skills. Listen, Gwennie, if you want to do it, go for it.'

'I can't afford to go for it,' said Gwennie, pulling on her jacket and picking up her handbag. 'I have rent to pay.'

'I could help you with the rent.' Adam looked earnestly at Gwennie, touched her lightly on the shoulder, made her meet his gaze. 'Jules would help as well, if you told him it was what you'd really like to do. But we both know he's a village idiot when it comes to intuition. So you'd have to tell him, spell it out.'

'But he'd only mock and sneer,' said Gwennie. 'You know how he feels about alternative and complimentary therapies. Anything that isn't science-based, anything that doesn't feature downing lots of drugs made in some sterile factory – it's all a load of rubbish according to the Gospel of Saint Jules.'

'He wouldn't mock and sneer,' insisted Adam. 'He's not into candles and rebirthing, but I'm sure he must have heard of music therapy. We'll talk about it later, shall we?'

'Do you mean it, about helping me?'

'Yes, of course I do.'

You know you're not supposed to read another person's letters, diaries, e-mails, texts, Cat told herself. It's worse than stealing stuff from charity shops.

But in the end she couldn't resist temptation. So she peeled open the self-seal envelope and then took out the single sheet inside. She saw it was a woman's handwriting. Some girl he had been seeing while he was supposed to be with Cat, she thought, and sighed.

She didn't want to read it, but of course she did.

She had the biggest shock.

It wasn't from some girl, or even boy. It was from his mother, and she lived in Manchester – she'd written her address out carefully, in capitals. She'd underlined the postcode, like somebody who wasn't very used to writing letters, and who was remembering what she'd been taught at school.

She'd written to tell him that she'd tried to get him on his mobile. But it was never on, so she was hoping he was still at this address?

She thought he ought to know his sister was at last engaged to Steve MacShane. Nana said it was about time, too. Harry was getting on for six, was growing up and asking awkward questions every day. He got on really well with Steve, who wanted to adopt him, and who behaved like he was Harry's father, anyway.

They were hoping Jack could soon come up for a weekend. Then they could have a party. Jack was more than welcome to bring along that lady friend he'd mentioned once or twice. Cat was it, or maybe it was Bunny?

There was a photograph, as well. It was of a twenty-something woman who looked just like Jack – high cheekbones, big grey eyes, black corkscrew curls and everything – a thirty-something fair-haired man, and a good-looking, dark-haired little boy. She turned the picture over, saw somebody had written on the back – *Harry, Steve and Crystal in Majorca.*

So, thought Cat, Jack hadn't been a foundling. He had not been left inside a bag at Waterloo, or brought up in an orphanage. He had a mum, a sister, a nana and a nephew, and they lived in Manchester.

What a lying, posturing, self-dramatising git.

She glared up at the ceiling.

She realised she was not upset, or bothered, or especially surprised. She wasn't going to have a nervous breakdown, cry, ring counselling help-lines or do anything else which was a waste of precious energy and more precious time.

Jack and Adam Lawley – what a pair of devious, lying bastards. One who fantasised about himself, and one who got his kicks from asking girls to marry him.

Why had he come after Cat?

She decided Tess must have been right, that Adam was attracted to the fact that Cat was wounded. A tiger following a deer which was already crippled, he was a lazy predator, and she'd been easy prey.

Well, she wasn't wounded any more. But it was a shame he was a head case, for sex with Adam had been wonderful.

Adam could have given Casanova basic lessons in making girls feel special, cherished, loved.

Cat could not believe she'd cried for Jack. She wasn't going to cry for Adam. God in heaven, she'd been such a fool, the sort of woman she despised. The sort who let men walk all over her and then looked sad and martyred.

How could any man respect a woman who behaved like that?

Jack and Adam – sewer rats, the pair of them, and that was dissing rats.

She chucked the stuff to be recycled in the colour-coded plastic boxes in the kitchen. She sealed Jack's letter up again, wrote *not known at this address* and put it in her bag to post it on her way to work.

She stuffed the rest of his old rubbish in a big black sack, shoved it in the wheelie bin then went to catch the bus.

'Men,' she growled, when Tess was up to speed again and knew all about Cat's long and interesting weekend in Italy. 'But I've made my mind up, and from now on I'll be like you and Bex. I'll pick them up and use them, chew them up and spit them out.'

'Attagirl,' said Tess. 'Ooh, new ring tone, eh?' she added, as Cat's phone began to jingle-jangle.

'Yeah,' said Cat, but she let the Valkyries ride on and continued scrolling through the e-mails on her desktop. 'I thought it was time for something different, something with a bit of zip and zing to it, you know?'

'So answer it?'

'I know who it will be.'

'Yes, he's quite persistent, isn't he, your Adam? Whatever else is wrong with him, you have to give him that.'

But when Cat glanced at her phone she saw it wasn't Adam.

It was Fanny Gregory.

'Omigod, that's all I need,' she said.

She thought she might be sick. She had been so preoccupied with not being preoccupied with Adam that she had forgotten about the other little problem in her life.

Fanny Gregory wouldn't have forgotten. Fanny would be calling to talk about the money which Cat didn't have.

But then she squared her shoulders, and she thought what are you – a strong, independent, modern woman or a little mouse? The new, kick-ass Cat – surely she could deal with Fanny Gregory, and there would be no messing?

So she snatched up the phone.

'Yes?' she snapped. 'What is it?'

'Good morning, angel,' said Fanny genially. 'We get to talk at last. Where have you been?'

'Italy,' said Cat, but then she cursed herself. She didn't want to tell this awful woman anything, least of all about her personal and private life. Memo to myself, thought Cat – when I talk to Fanny, I must be on my guard.

'Ah – *bella Italia*, how delightful,' burbled Fanny. 'So tell me, where exactly did you go?'

'Lucca, it's a town in Tuscany.'

'Yes, I know, my sweet. I did geography at school, and it's common knowledge among intelligent, cosmopolitan people, anyway. I'm so in love with Tuscany, aren't you? The men are all adorable and the food's divine. Did you go with someone nice, my angel?'

'I went on my own.'

'Oh yes, my love, of course you must have done. What a wicked waste, though, going jetting off to Italy alone. You always need to take a gorgeous man to Italy.'

'Fan, I'm very busy—'

'Darling girl, don't be so curt with me. Manner maketh man, you know – and maketh woman, too. But we'll let it pass. I need to let you know I've met with your fiancé. Or rather, ex-fiancé, isn't he? Jack and I have sorted something out, and we're both very happy with what we have arranged. So that leaves you. My princess, could you come into the office?'

'I don't want to see him.'

'You won't have to see him, sweetheart,' Fanny said, and her voice became all soft and cooing, like a dove. 'Jack is very busy, as it happens.'

'Busy?' echoed Cat. 'Why, what's he doing now?'

'He has auditions everywhere, my sweet. I'm finding people just can't get enough of lovely Jack. They're beating down my door, to coin a very clichéd phrase. But that's enough of him. I was also ringing about you.'

'You want to talk about the money?'

'Yes, the money. We must have a little chat.' Cat heard Fanny tapping keys. 'So let's have a look. When I am free?'

'Fanny, I do work!'

'I know you work, my darling, you keep reminding me. You're running eBay. Or is it Microsoft? But I need to see you. Of course, you're miles from Oxford Street, the tube's so slow, the buses are a joke, and I know you can't afford a cab. But you do have lunch hours? So why not take a couple the same day? Ah now, here's a window – next Wednesday, one o'clock.'

'Yes, all right, I'll try.'

'You will do rather more than try, my angel,' Fanny Gregory said silkily. 'You will be here at one o'clock on Wednesday and you will be punctual – or else.'

'Fanny, like I said—'

But Fanny had already disconnected.

'She wants to see me,' Cat told Tess. 'I expect she'll have the bailiffs there and she'll make me sign my life away.'

'Oh, don't be so daft,' said Tess. 'Listen, you've got Jack and Adam sorted, haven't you? So don't let this woman do you down. If you make it clear that you won't stand for any messing, you'll be fine.'

'It won't be so easy. She's a witch. She casts spells on people, makes them do all sorts of things they didn't mean to do, and say things they didn't mean to say. You think you and Bex are hard, but compared with Fanny you're as soft as candyfloss.'

'She can't be as hard as Bex,' scoffed Tess. 'What does she look like anyway, you've never said – is she huge and does she frighten you, is she some enormous tattooed jelly-belly, is she like a weightlifter in drag? Do you think she'll sit on you and squash you if you don't do as you're told?'

'Fanny's really tiny. She's nowhere near as tall as you and me, even in her six-inch-heel stilettos. But that doesn't mean she can't—'

'What's her hair like?'

'Moussed and styled until it begs for mercy and obviously dyed.'

'What colour is it?'

'Orange.'

'Does she have crimson lipstick, scarlet nails?'

'Yes, she does.'

'Eyelashes like a spider's legs?'

'You've got it.'

'God, she sounds revolting. However does she manage to run her own promotions company? Doesn't she scare everyone away?'

'No, I told you, Tess – she casts a magic spell on them and makes them do her bidding.'

'Rubbish,' snorted Tess derisively. 'Okay, here's the plan – when you go to see Godzilla's granny, why don't I come with you?'

'There would be no point, and anyway we're getting some deliveries on Wednesday. Barry's off to see a man in Chester who's demolishing a bakery, and he thinks there'll be a lot of pickings, pots and pans and stuff, and maybe ovens, too. So you'll be needed here.'

'We can change delivery dates,' said Tess. 'So tell me if you change your mind.'

'I will, and thank you, anyway.'

As a matter of fact, decided Cat, as she got started on some work, I wouldn't have minded some support.

But she didn't think it would be wise to let Tess loose on somebody like Fanny Gregory. She'd end up being billed for twice as much if Tess told Fanny where she could get off.

'She told me she and Jack have sorted something out, or come to an arrangement, and I don't quite like the sound of that,' she added as she keyed in figures.

'They're ganging up against you, do you mean?'

'I wouldn't put it past them.'

'Omigod,' said Tess. 'So do you think she's – do you think he's – are they?'

'Yes, I think they might be.'

'But she's old enough to be his mother, isn't she?'

'She'd have had to have had him very young. But yes, it's very likely.' Cat reached for a Kleenex. 'Oh, this is awful, Tess!'

'Come on, Cat, you're over him, you said so.'

'Yes, I'm over him, of course I am. But it doesn't stop me thinking about when we were together first of all and everything was lovely.'

'But it was a mirage, wasn't it? He's a git and she's a bitch.' Tess looked hard at Cat. 'So if they want to shag each other senseless, let them both get on with it. Good riddance to bad rubbish, that's what I say. If you have any sense, you'll say it, too.'

'You're right, of course,' said Cat.

'I'm always right,' said Tess. 'Oh, and by the way – Barry said to tell you the Anderson account needs sorting out. He says he entered something on a spreadsheet while you were away, and he thinks he might have put some figures where they didn't ought to go.'

'God, I wish he'd leave the books alone.' Cat sighed and tapped some keys and made a mental note to change the password for the customer accounts so Barry couldn't get at them and foul them up again. 'I wish he'd stick to buying paving slabs and garden ornaments, and let me do the job I'm hired to do.'

'Well, of course that's men for you,' said Tess. She shrugged her shoulders. 'Go blundering in there like a blind assassin, foul it up, then leave the mess for some poor woman to sort out.'

Adam kept on calling, texting, e-mailing.

Cat kept on ignoring him.

But she knew she was weakening.

As she was scrolling through the fourteenth, fifteenth text that day, she thought, I don't know what to do.

He wasn't whingeing, moaning, carping, grumbling. He didn't make excuses. Or justify himself. Or suggest that it was all her fault for reacting to the sight of Maddy like a jealous cow. Or tell her she should get a grip.

'Please could we meet up and talk?' he texted.

'Cat, I'd love to see you when you have a spare half hour,' he e-mailed.

'May I buy you lunch some time?' This was on a voicemail, and when she heard him speaking her thumb was on the icon straight away, ready to press call.

The latest text said he was out of London for the next few days. But he'd be in the bar of the Red Lion in Wayland

Road next Wednesday lunchtime and he'd hope to see her there.

She couldn't meet him then.

She had a date with Fanny Gregory in her office.

She couldn't quite decide in which place she most didn't want to be.

Let's get it over, shall we?

The meeting came too soon.

'Hello Fanny, hello Caspar,' Cat began as she breezed into Fanny's den. Or as she tried to breeze, but sadly failed.

'Sit down, Cat,' said Fanny, sounding like Judi Dench as M in the more recent James Bond movies, with her eyes still fixed upon her screen.

'I'm sorry about all this.' Cat tried again. 'I know I've messed things up for you. But I—'

'Spare me the sob stuff, sweetheart.' Fanny glanced up now, and the expression on her face was one of deep displeasure. 'Cat, my angel, if you think that doing the big-eyed, Puss in Boots routine is going to get you off the hook, you'd better think again.'

'Fanny, listen!' Cat retorted, stung. 'I want to sort this out! I want to make it up to you! I want to know about the money!'

'Do you have any money, darling?'

'No,' admitted Cat.

'Then we'll have to think of something else.' Fanny smiled her vixen's smile and stroked her greyhound's head reflectively. 'You do remember I have this barn in Surrey?'

'Do I, Fanny?'

'Yes, my sweet, you do.' Fanny gave one laptop key a sharp, staccato tap. 'I mentioned it when we met up in Dorset.'

'Yes, of course you did,' said Cat, thinking that perhaps she would be wise to be a bit co-operative now.

'As you know, my angel, I don't mess about. That man we met when we were all at Melbury Court in May – Adam something, wasn't it? He said I should get an architect. I don't have time for architects. I always know exactly what I want and how to get it. So I – do stop smirking, Cat. It really doesn't suit you, makes your mouth look like a meerkat's.'

'I'm sorry, Fanny,' Cat said meekly. But she hadn't been smirking. She'd been wincing. The unexpected sound of Adam's name had pushed a red hot skewer straight into her heart and had made her realise she was so not over him.

She wished there were injections you could have, to stop you catching love. One shot, she thought, that would be all it took, and you'd be immunised for life, like you were immunised for German measles when you were fourteen. 'You were saying?'

'So,' continued Fanny, 'I got a local master builder in. We did the plans ourselves. His cronies on the council took the sweeteners, and they passed our drawings straight away. An extraordinary evening session, I believe they called it, hardly anyone turned up. Or they weren't invited, possibly.'

'You're saying you and your builder fiddled it?'

'I'm saying I don't believe in wasting time.' Fanny tapped three keys in quick succession, clack, click, clack. 'I must admit his boys have earned their bonuses, and more. They've cracked on with the work at record speed. The rooms downstairs are ready to be decorated now.' Fanny did a good impression of a judge about to send a criminal down for life. 'Cat, my love, my princess – that's going to be your job.'

'What do you mean?'

'I mean that on bank holidays and at weekends, my angel, you'll be at my barn. As the plasterers, electricians, plumbers and the other men move out, you will move in. You'll be glossing woodwork, emulsioning my walls and painting ceilings, and maybe even choosing colours, too.'

Fanny paused to look Cat up and down, like a farmer sizing up some livestock and trying to decide if it was fit for breeding or should be sent for slaughter straight away.

'I've noticed that you have an eye for colour,' she continued. 'You look particularly nice today, in that pale pink and darker pink and green, and that yellow top you wore in Dorset really flattered you.

'Your clothes are rubbish, obviously. They're cheap and mass-produced in Third World countries or bought from market stalls. You ought to buy a classic piece or two, my love, at least once in a while. It's often quite amazing what's going in the sales. But you always look well put together, even dressed in tat. I'll tell darling Rosie to send you a few shade cards and some charts.'

'What if I'm no good at glossing?'

'If you're not already, you will be very soon, my sweetie pie.' Fanny took out a file and tapped it with one long, red nail. 'You signed the entry form, remember? In the event of any monies being disbursed by Supadoop Promotions?'

'Yes, all right,' said Cat and sighed, accepting she was beaten. Or that she'd got off lightly? She wasn't really sure. 'When shall I start?'

'As soon as possible, my love,' said Fanny, and her mouth curved in her trademark vixen's smile again. 'What do you have planned for this weekend?'

'Well – nothing, I suppose,' admitted Cat.

'Excellent,' said Fanny as she tapped more keys. 'So now it's set in stone. Caspar, angel, it's a lovely day. So you shall go out and have a little fun with Rosie. You can both go running in the park.'

As Cat left Fanny's office she met Rosie coming in, carrying a dozen bags from very expensive stores.

'Hello, Cat,' said Rosie. 'I'm sorry I wasn't here to let you in, but I've been collecting samples for her ladyship. How are things with you?'

'Oh, you know – pretty bad.' Cat shook her head. 'I wish I'd never heard of Fanny Gregory!' she cried. 'I wish I'd never entered her bloody competition!'

'Why, what did she say to you today?'

'I can't pay back the money she spent on me that day at Melbury Court and so I have to go and paint her barn. She's going to let me choose some colour schemes. You're going to send me shade cards.'

'I'm going to send you what?'

'Some charts, some shade cards, so she said.'

'Oh, I see.' Rosie dropped her bags on to the pavement and then gave Cat a sympathetic hug. 'You mustn't let her bully you,' she said. 'Fan's all mouth and bluster, and that's why she's so good at what she does. She can talk anybody into doing anything. But with Fan you have to stand your ground, otherwise she walks all over you. Come and have a coffee?'

'What about that woman, isn't she expecting you? She was saying something about you and Caspar going to the park.'

'Oh yes, I'm in training for a fun run. It's for charity and Fanny's doing the promotion. They can wait ten minutes.' Rosie kicked the bags into the hallway. 'There's a Starbucks down the road. Come on, I'll treat you to a chocolate muffin and a cappuccino.'

'I'd better not,' said Cat. 'I must go back to work. I'm late already and I can't afford to get the sack.'

'I tell you what, I'll call you,' Rosie said.

'Okay,' said Cat and forced a smile.

'You mustn't worry, it's going to be all right.'

A few weekends in Surrey, Cat thought grimly, as she made her way into the dirty, crowded, nasty-smelling Underground.

They might be exactly what I need.

Some country air and exercise, they'll probably do me good.

It's not as if I have much choice.

'The blackmailing old witch,' cried Tess.

Cat was back at Chapman's yard, explaining what had happened and what Fanny Gregory had said she had to do. 'You should go and see a lawyer, mate. Get a solicitor on the case to send her a stiff letter – that's my advice to you.'

'I can't afford to pass the time of day with a solicitor,' said Cat. 'Let alone employ one.'

'I could ask my brother's bloke? He told Nick some useful stuff when he was up for burglary one time.' Tess looked sympathetically at Cat. 'I'll ring Mr Gibson for you, shall I?'

'No,' said Cat. 'I can't afford to pay solicitors. I'd rather sort it this way, anyhow. These days, unless I'm at the yard, I never do much at weekends.'

'But you could, you know. You and me and Bex, we could go clubbing, drinking, meeting guys. Like we used to do, remember, in the olden days, before you met that bastard Jack?'

'I don't want anything more to do with guys. I'm going to become a nun. I've been on to a website and downloaded the forms.'

'Why won't you speak to Adam?'

'You know why.'

'But maybe he was telling you the truth? Listen, I've been thinking—'

'Blimey, that'll be a first.'

'Shut up, Cat,' said Tess. 'Maybe he and Whatserface, perhaps they really had split up? Perhaps he really loves you?'

'Perhaps there's life on Mars.'

'Why don't you call him, anyway?'

'I don't know,' admitted Cat, and sighed. 'Okay, he's nice. I know he's nice, and part of me is almost sure he wasn't lying when he said he and the Maddy woman had broken up before we even met. I believe he was as shocked as I was when he found her in his bed. But I can't take the risk.'

'You can't take the risk of what?'

'Of being hurt a second time. My heart can't take the strain. What if it's all on again between him and the Maddy woman? What if they're tucked up in bed this minute?'

'At four o'clock on Wednesday afternoon?' Tess grinned sarcastically. 'I'd say it was unlikely. Our Adam's probably on a building site in darkest Cornwall. Or he'll be in Dorset or some other part of cross-eyed-peasant-country, sticking some old house or ancient monument together with spit and Araldite.'

Or could he still be waiting in the bar of the Red Lion, thought Cat, and was he still hoping she would come?

Suddenly she wanted more than anything to see him.

But she forced the longing down.

'What do you suggest?' she asked.

'You could meet him, couldn't you, and keep it light and friendly? What about a movie and a pizza, Adam, my old mate? Let's have some good, clean fun?'

'I'm not really in the mood for fun,' said Cat, wondering why merely hearing Adam's name still had the occult power to twist a dagger in her heart? 'Maybe slapping litres of magnolia or something on Fanny's sodding walls will be good therapy for me, and Surrey's probably very nice in summer.'

'Cat, if you think slapping paint on walls is therapy, you really need to buy a better class of magazine – one that isn't full of stuff about my-husband-is-a-paedophile-who's-working-for-a-children's-charity, or

216

my-council-house-is-full-of-ghosts-and-the-bishop-came-to-exorcise-them-but-it-didn't-work-and-there's-still-a-lot-of-ectoplasm-which-won't-respond-to-bleach.'

'So you'd do what?'

'Oh, I dunno,' said Tess. 'I think this Fanny Gregory woman sounds like a gold-medal-winning bitch. But I'm not doing anything this weekend. Barry's at the yard and Annie's in the office. She's bringing Roxie in her Moses basket, so she said, and they won't need me. If you want a bit of company as you do your slapping, I'll come and help you out.'

'You mean it?'

'Yes, of course I mean it. I'm your mate.'

'Do you think Bex would tag along, and then the three of us could slap together?'

'No, Bexy-girl's got other plans.'

'Oh?' said Cat.

'Yes indeed,' said Tess, and then she grinned. 'She's been giving herself the works this week – nails and hair and facial peel and spray tan. She's been Body Shopped to death, all for some new guy she met in Tesco.'

'Where are they going, on a mini-break to Paris?'

'No, just tenpin bowling.'

'Las Vegas?'

'Cricklewood.'

'You're kidding, right?'

'No, that's what she said, or maybe it was Harlesden?'

'God,' said Cat and shook her head. 'If that's the best this guy can offer, she'd be better off with the emulsion and with us.'

Saturday, 2 July

What could be nicer than a weekend in the country?

As Cat and Tess drew up in Tess's ancient Peugeot – Cat's even older Honda Civic was out of circulation at the moment – they saw at once that Fanny's barn was gorgeous.

It was built of local flint and weathered, blush-red brick. Its narrow, arching windows sparkled in the summer sunshine, and its pantiled roof was mossed and lichened to perfection. The original doors had been removed, and now one side was glass.

It was huge, as well. She wondered how much life she'd spend emulsioning and glossing this gigantic place as she repaid her debt to Fanny Gregory and Supadoop Promotions. Maybe she should go to a solicitor, after all? But what would a solicitor cost? She didn't have any money to waste on going to see solicitors.

Maybe getting some experience of DIY would stand her in good stead? She was ashamed to realise that apart from toe and fingernails she'd never painted anything in her life.

'Good morning, ladies!' As Cat stood there wondering, debating with herself, Fanny came striding from the barn with Caspar at her heels, and Cat saw she looked different today.

She wasn't in her usual business suit. She was wearing smart designer jeans and an expensive Chloe shirt that Cat had seen in *Vogue* and coveted. She wasn't wearing any obvious make-up. She looked casual, happy and relaxed, and ten years younger, too.

'Cat of course I know,' she said, 'but you are?'

'Tess,' said Cat. 'She works with me, and she's come to help me with the painting. I hope that's all right?'

'The more the merrier, that's what I always say,' chirped Fanny brightly. 'Well, I sometimes say it. Politicians, civil servants, tax inspectors, social workers, union representatives – the fewer of people like them we have, the better, obviously. Well, girls, don't just stand there, come inside – I'll show you round.'

Cat and Tess exchanged a shrug, a raising of the eyebrows and a widening of the eyes, then did as they were told. They followed Fanny and Caspar down a hallway into an enormous atrium, full of sunlight pouring in like honey through the arching windows, and they gasped.

'Fanny, this is wonderful,' breathed Cat.

'Yeah, it's amazing,' Tess said softly, like somebody afraid to break a spell.

'Do you think so, darlings?' Fanny grinned. 'I'm so glad you like it. I must admit I had some tiny doubts about the atrium. But now it's nearly finished I'm quite pleased with it myself.'

She laid her small white hand on her black greyhound's sleek dark head. 'Caspar loves it, don't you, angel?'

Caspar looked at Fanny with adoration in his lovely eyes, as usual rapt by every single word his mistress spoke.

'Cool dog,' said Tess.

Cat hadn't expected Fanny to be there.

She'd supposed she and Tess would be alone, that there'd be instructions somewhere, maybe saying the keys were with a neighbour, that the paint and stuff was in the garage, and to get on with it.

On the way they'd stopped off at a supermarket, where they'd bought some food they could eat cold – little pots of salad, pasta, yogurts, cakes and cookies (Tess had insisted on the cakes and cookies) and a big box of organic muesli (Cat had insisted on the muesli and forbidden Tess to buy a box of sugar-coated, additive-rich rubbish). They'd also bought some fruit, some smoothies and, in case there happened to be a kettle, some teabags and a couple of pints of milk.

They had been expecting to sleep on bare stone floors – they'd brought their sleeping bags – and the best they'd hoped for in the way of luxury was water, electricity and a roof over their heads.

The kitchen had been finished, Fanny told them, and so had all the bathrooms. But there was still an awful lot to do – all the painting, naturally, and the carpeting, and buying lots of lovely china, pictures, rugs and furniture. She'd have to ask a stylist, see what he could suggest. She knew most of the influential ones. She would go to Liberty because they had the most amazing things.

'I've coffee on the hob,' she added, as she led them into the most luxurious, biggest kitchen Cat had ever seen. 'Yes, my darling girls – as of today I have a functioning stove at last! Oh, the bliss, the bliss!'

'Where do you want me to start working?' Cat asked Fanny, as she poured them coffee from a very expensive-looking pot.

'Oh, sweetheart, don't you worry about work! Or not right now, at any rate.' Fanny twinkled merrily at Tess. 'This girl, you know, she's quite obsessed with work! Fanny, she says, I have to go to work. Fanny, I have a job. Fanny, I can't take time off. So conscientious – I hope her boss appreciates it. Do you work together, did you say?'

Tess was saying nothing. She was gazing round in awe like someone in an abbey or cathedral, taking in the huge American appliances, the polished granite surfaces, the gleaming chromium fittings and the snow-white porcelain sinks.

'Sit down, darlings,' Fanny told them, sitting down herself at an enormous kitchen table. Cat guessed it must have come from France, from some old farmhouse in the Lot or the Dordogne.

Or maybe it had come from China? You could get some brilliant stuff from China nowadays, and not even Barry could always tell the genuine from the fake or reproduction.

Last week, he'd almost bought some chairs which he had been convinced were genuine Victorian balloon backs. But when he had upended them to check, he'd found them stamped with Chinese characters.

'The milk is in the frother, and there are some biscuits in that yellow box,' continued Fanny. 'I had them from a client yesterday, so they should be all right. They won't be going soft yet, anyway.'

She took a couple of sips of coffee, dunked a biscuit, took a bite. 'Why do you look so jittery, my angels?' she enquired. 'Cat, my sweet, stop staring at the ceiling. There are no hidden cameras there, you know.' She twinkled merrily again. 'Do you think, my love, with your suspicious mind, you ought to work for MI5?'

'I'm sorry, Fanny.' Cat had just been wondering how long it would take to paint the bloody ceiling, not looking for cameras or bugs. 'This is delicious coffee, by the way.'

'Thank you, Cat. It comes from Italy. You were probably drinking something similar yourself a week or two ago. That's if you went to any decent restaurants, of course.' Fanny sighed. 'I don't know what's going on in Italy nowadays – I really don't. Italians have the best cuisine in Europe, but there are American fast food outlets everywhere. When I was last in Rome, there was one right opposite the Pantheon – talk about putting diamond buttons on a pair of ghastly chain store jeans. I was so relieved when someone told me it's not there any more.'

'What's the Pantheon?' Tess asked Fanny, making Fanny sigh again and roll her big blue eyes.

'Google it, my angel,' she told Tess.

Cat was hoping coffee would help her to relax a bit before she started painting. But before she and Tess had finished drinking, Fanny was on her feet again.

'My darlings, we must dash,' she said. 'We need go to Marks and Spencer straight away.'

'Do they sell paint?' asked Cat.

'I don't think so, sweetie pie.' Fanny frowned and looked at Cat in puzzlement. 'Why do you ask?'

'I thought – why are we going, then?'

'I need to buy some food,' said Fanny, in the tone of voice some people used when talking to the stupid, very young or elderly bewildered. 'Luckily for us, the biggest M and S in Europe's down the road in Camberley. You girls can come and help me. You can push the trolleys, angels – that's if you don't mind?'

She stroked her dog's dark head then took his face between her hands and gazed into his amber eyes. 'Caspar, darling heart,' she whispered, 'they won't let you into Marks and Spencer. So you'll have to stay and guard this place for us. We won't be very long.'

'We'll bring you back a treat, mate,' promised Tess.

'You said she was a cow,' said Tess, as they got out of Fanny's gorgeous purple BMW and headed for the trolley park.

'I never, ever told you that,' hissed Cat. 'So keep your voice down, can't you?'

'But you made me think she was a bitch.' Tess released a mega-giant-size trolley and pulled one out for Cat. 'I was expecting some horrible old vampire, with yellow teeth and hair like frizzy orange candyfloss and liver-spotted hands like rotting claws. But she's really pretty and she's very nice as well.'

'I dare say even Stalin had his less psychotic days.'

'She calls us angels, too.'

'She calls everybody angel, darling, sweetheart, love, even when she's tearing out their throats, my loves, and barbecuing their livers on her flash new high-speed grill, my angels, sweethearts, darling girls.'

'I say Fanny Gregory's all right. I like her dog, as well.'

'We're not in dispute about her dog.'

'I think you're over-sensitive,' said Tess. 'You should be less defensive and less prone to take offence. You should have done that psychic test and analysed your personality. If you could only understand yourself, you would be less likely to have such extreme reactions to everyone you meet.'

'Okay, have it your way,' muttered Cat. 'Come on, she wants to get her shopping.'

So Tess and Cat pushed trolleys round the store, and Fanny filled them up with food and wine and bunches of delicious-smelling white and pink and cream and purple flowers.

'This is the sort of stuff you buy for parties,' whispered Tess as Fanny stuck more bottles in her trolley – half a dozen magnums of respectable old brandy, four dozen bottles of pink champagne – then scurried off towards the dips and salsas.

'Or for wakes,' said Cat.

She glanced down at the contents of her trolley, seeing all the bottles of expensive blood-red wine and plastic packs of blood-red strawberries, pots of clotted cream and boxes of exquisite cakes – the bite-sized sort you ate in just one mouthful – tiny scones already filled with cream and blood-red jam, puddings slashed with blood-red raspberry coulis.

She realised she felt sick.

'Anything we can find for you?' asked Tess, as Fanny dropped a giant box of savoury crackers in her giant trolley.

'No thank you, darling,' said Fanny with a twinkle. 'All you have to do is follow me.' Then she was off again.

'I know she's up to something,' Cat told Tess. 'She's got

that manic look, the one she had at Melbury Court when she was bossing me about that day.'

'Or she's stocking up her great big freezer?' Tess picked up a box of little cakes. 'You can freeze these babies. It says so on the pack.'

'They can't be for the freezer, or she'd have bought the ready-frozen versions, wouldn't she?' Cat looked worriedly at Tess. 'What's with all the lilies? They're the sort you get at funerals.'

'Or at Satanic rituals,' Tess suggested ghoulishly.

'God,' said Cat and shuddered.

'So maybe you were right,' said Tess. She glanced across the store at Fanny who was out of earshot, busy hoovering up some trays of sushi and bresaola. 'Maybe Fanny Gregory is a witch, and tonight she's having a black mass. You're going to be a human sacrifice. You'll be lying naked on a bed of pure white lilies, bound and gagged. I saw this film a year or two ago. It was on Channel 4. I think it was Romanian or Hungarian, or Eastern European, anyway. When they lit these big black candles, they—'

'Tess, don't even joke about it, right?'

'I'm not joking, mate.' Tess grinned at Cat. 'Your number's up, your die is cast, your hour is come. I reckon this will teach you to enter competitions to win luxury dream weddings.'

'Shut up, you fool, she's coming back.'

Twenty minutes later they were at the checkout, with Cat and Tess unloading and repacking, and Fanny paying with her Amex Gold.

'Five hundred quid, and that's on food alone, not counting all the flowers and wine,' said Tess, as they loaded everything into the BMW. 'Who's going to eat it all?'

'God only knows,' said Cat.

When they arrived back at the barn, Caspar welcomed them delightedly. Fanny put Cat in charge of flower arranging. 'I want big, bold statements,' she began, pushing a huge bunch of blowsy peonies at Cat. 'Over-indulgence, overflowing gorgeousness, extreme extravagance – you understand?'

'You're the boss,' said Cat, who was now wondering if this was yet another stupid dream, if this was the year of crazy dreams, if in fact she'd ever been awake, if she'd have to go to see that tantric disentangler guy in Catford after all.

Maybe she'd been in an accident and she was in a coma and none of this was happening? If so, maybe she could write a book about it when at last she did come round? She could get it syndicated in the Sunday papers, couldn't she? She'd heard they paid a lot of money for that sort of thing.

As well as all the gorgeous flowers, Fanny had bought a dozen plain glass vases. Cat began to fill them, trying to arrange the flowers as Fanny wanted them, white lilies and pink peonies in heavenly-scented masses, spikes of mauve delphiniums with foaming greenery.

Where was Rosie, wondered Cat, as she stripped off big green leaves and snipped at ends of stems with a pair of flower arranger's scissors which had been thrust into her hand. She was Fanny Gregory's assistant, after all. So surely it was Rosie's job to go to Marks and Spencer, buy food for Fanny's freezer, do Fanny's flower arrangements, things like that?

'Come along, my angels, I'll show you to your room,' said Fanny, when the flowers had been arranged, the food all put away in two enormous silver fridges and the big American freezer, and the wines been left to breathe or chill.

They climbed the spiral staircase which rose up from hallway and ended in a gallery which was full of natural light. 'It's this one on the left,' said Fanny proudly, opening a huge oak door and leading them inside.

'Do you like the bed?' she asked, as Cat and Tess stared open-mouthed at the enormous double, an elaborate French affair complete with ivory inlay, marquetry and half a dozen gilded nymphs. It was easily big enough for both of them, but still—

'It's beautiful,' said Cat.

'Yeah, gorgeous,' Tess said faintly. 'But—'

'Tess, don't look so horrified,' said Fanny, opening a door to show them into a much smaller room which held a single bed made of plain pine, a single wardrobe and a Lloyd Loom chair. 'I was just expecting Cat, you see. But you're both very welcome.'

'You can have the big bed,' Cat said graciously.

'No, you have it.' Tess glanced at the little room. 'I'll be fine in there.'

'Sort it out between yourselves, my angels.' Fanny turned to leave. 'The en-suite bathroom's just through there,' she added. 'The power shower works. Or it had better work, considering what I paid for it. I haven't tried it yet. So come along then, girls. We need to get our skates on. There's a lot to do before tonight.'

'What do you reckon now?' asked Tess, as Fanny clattered down the spiral staircase.

'I don't know what I reckon.' Cat shook her head and sighed. 'Something's going on. But we won't be doing any painting. I'll bet my boots on that.'

'You mean your L.K.Bennett black with gold-tone hardware boots?'

'Yes, if I must.'

As Cat and Tess went back downstairs, a van drew up.

Two men got out and carried several trestle tables through the hallway into the huge atrium, then drove away again.

'Along the wall, my angels,' Fanny said, and then she disappeared in the direction of the kitchen, tapping on her phone.

'It looks like it's a party,' Tess observed, as she and Cat set trestle tables all along one wall and hoped it was the right one.

'Yeah,' said Cat. 'Godammit.'

'What's the matter now?'

'I've just pinched my finger in a hinge.'

'It doesn't matter about your sodding finger, Moaning Min. Listen, I don't have anything to wear. My hair's a mess. I need my roots done. I didn't bring any make-up. My nails are a disaster. I haven't shaved my legs.'

'What makes you think that we're invited?'

'Why else would we be here?'

'Come on,' said Cat, 'engage your brain.'

Opening a cardboard box the men had left, a box which held white linen tablecloths, she took a couple out. 'She's probably going to make us wait on everybody – pour their drinks and take round trays of canapés and stuff. I heard her muttering on the phone a minute or two ago, and I'll bet you anything she was hiring uniforms for us. Black skirts, white blouses, frilly little aprons—'

'Well, she can stick her uniforms,' said Tess. 'I tell you what, mate – when we're done in here, we'll bugger off. We'll find a pub. Or we'll go back to London. Look out, here she comes.'

'All finished, girls?' chirped Fanny as she bustled in, Caspar at her heels and her mobile in her hand.

'Almost,' Cat replied.

'Excellent,' said Fanny. 'Now, what are you two going to wear tonight? We'll need to find you both a couple of nice – oh, hang on a moment, there's someone at the door.'

'Come on, mate,' said Jules. 'Stop behaving like you won the lottery and someone pinched your ticket. I'll tell you something, Adam – Maddy was bad news, and you're well rid.'

'It isn't Maddy,' Adam told him, wishing Jules would go away, go out, drop dead, do anything provided he'd stop hanging round the place like last night's curry, looking like a bloodhound with a migraine.

He was missing Gwennie, who had gone to see her parents in the sticks, and probably wishing he had tagged along, even if Gwennie's mother had decided he was better than her doctor – more sympathetic, knowledgeable and more up to date – when it came to discussing medication for her problems down below. 'I'm over Maddy,' he insisted. 'She and I are finished.'

'I'm sorry Gwennie let her in that time,' continued Jules, who wasn't listening, who blundered on regardless as he dished out good advice like some agony aunt on crack cocaine. 'I told her, send a text – tell him she's turned up again, she's camping in his room. But Gwennie, she said no, it would be better, it would be more romantic, if you got a big surprise.'

'It was a surprise all right,' said Adam, angling his laptop so Jules wouldn't see his screen saver.

This was the photograph of Cat with petals of white roses in her hair. He didn't want any comments from his friend, not even complimentary ones, and certainly no questions like – who's that fit bird then, mate?

Then he e-mailed last minute instructions for the foreman he had left in charge at Melbury Court and touched base with all his other clients before it was time to throw some stuff into a case and go to catch the train to Aberdeen.

On Sunday morning, he'd be met by Mr Portland's driver and taken to the castle on which he would be working off and on for six months, eight months, perhaps a year or more.

This was if he could keep his sanity, and he'd realised this was going to be his biggest challenge. Mr and Mrs Portland were becoming more demanding and ridiculous all the time.

It was clearly going to be a nightmare heading Mrs Portland off and trying to convince her that a Texan ranch-style kitchen would look out of place in a Victorian Gothic castle.

The last time they had spoken, she'd asked him if he could create a cocktail lounge of the sort more suited to a beach house in Bermuda than a castle in a wooded glen near Aberdeen.

But he was still determined to do this job in Scotland. He was confident – or fairly confident, at any rate – that Mrs Portland would eventually be persuaded Scottish Baronial Gothic was a better look for Aberdeenshire than Bermudan Toddy Shack.

This was his big opportunity, his chance to prove he was a brilliant and inventive project manager, up there with the best. If he couldn't get it right with women, he was going to get it right with work. If he couldn't have a wife and family, he was going to have a great career.

As for work – he knew that he was working much too hard. But working hard was helping him to take his mind off Cat. Well, just a bit. Well, not at all, if he was honest, he still thought about her almost every minute of every day.

He'd called, he'd texted and he'd e-mailed. He'd made a thorough nuisance of himself. Soon, she'd set the police on him, complain she had a stalker. Then he would be arrested and he didn't want that. So maybe it was just as well he'd soon be off the scene?

Jules was still hovering, still looking like a collie which had had its feelings hurt but had decided it wouldn't bear a grudge or do its business on the rug.

'Listen, Jules,' said Adam in quiet exasperation, 'I'm honestly not hankering after Maddy. So please can you accept it and stop going on about it, right?'

'What's the matter, then?' Jules turned off the television, plonked himself down next to Adam, sighed like someone's mother when you'd left the front door open, letting robbers, opportunist one-off murderers and career serial killers walk straight in and get your blood all over the new suite.

'I don't know what you mean,' said Adam, making sure he kept his eyes fixed on his laptop screen.

'Something's wrong, I know it.' Jules clapped his hand on Adam's shoulder in a caring, sharing, male-bonding sort of way. 'You're my best mate,' he said. 'You always have been, always will be. It chews me up to see you looking so hacked off, so bloody miserable. Why don't you go to Aberdeen tomorrow? Come and get drunk with me and Gaz tonight? Mate, it's time you met another woman.'

'Jules, please shut up. I need to finish something here and then I have to go and get my train.'

'Only Gwennie wondered if you ought to go and see a doctor, if you need some medication? You know all those magazines she reads? They're full of stuff about relationships and what to do when one goes belly-up. Yeah, it's a load of boring girly nonsense, most of it. But about the medication – she could have a point.'

'Jules, you're in the industry. Why don't you go and get your case of samples? We could have a little private party – pick and mix.'

'Now you're being stupid, mate.'

'I thought you were going to the pub?'

'I'm not going to be a maid tonight,' Tess muttered crossly as Fanny Gregory went to get the door.

Cat couldn't think of anything to say. It looked as if a couple of maids were just what she and Tess were going to be.

'I'm not handing round champagne to Fanny's hideous mates,' continued Tess. 'I'm not going to have my bum pinched by their foul old husbands. So if Fanny Annie thinks—'

'Please, Tess, do this for me?' Cat looked beseechingly at Tess. 'I'll make it up to you, I swear to God. You can have my Jasper Conran boots, my Warehouse skirt, my Birkin bag—'

'Your Birkin bag's a fake.'

'My new Oasis top, those Office shoes you said you loved – you can have anything you like. You know she's got a hold on me. You know I signed her bloody form. I wish I'd never seen that competition. I wish I'd never entered it. But I—'

'Here we are then, girls.' Fanny swept into the atrium, followed by a tall and glamorous woman who looked like Meryl Streep. They both carried great armfuls of clothes in plastic covers, and Fanny introduced the newcomer as Lulu Minto, darlings.

'The famous Lulu Minto?' whispered Tess. 'The Lulu Minto who dresses the celebrities and royals?'

'The very same,' said Fanny, whose hearing was as sharp as any lynx which had had its ears syringed that very afternoon. 'I told darling Lulu there'd be only one of you. But luckily you're similar sizes, so you should find something here to fit.'

She glanced at Tess and then she smiled her vixen's smile. 'Tess, my flower, why do you look so horrified – again?'

'I'm not horrified,' said Tess. 'I mean, I don't—I don't know what I mean.'

'Fanny, are these for us?' asked Cat, who could see a mass of glitter, glimmer, shimmer, sparkle on expensive fabrics. She could make out beading, lace and ribbons. She realised that whatever was inside these plastic covers could not be waitress uniforms.

As Tess and Cat stood silent while Lulu took the covers off and laid a row of perfect dresses on the trestle tables, they heard someone walking down the hallway.

'Rosie with the glasses, and about time too,' said Fanny.

'I was beginning to think I'd have to go down to the village shop and buy a box of straws. Darlings, do excuse me just one moment.'

When Fanny came back in again with Rosie, followed by Rick the boy photographer with all his cameras round his neck – Cat wondered if he ever took them off – every cocktail dress had been revealed in all its gorgeous glory and Tess and Cat were drooling.

'Lovely, aren't they?' Fanny smiled at Lulu. 'But don't get too attached to them, my angels. You'll have to give them back tomorrow morning, obviously. Darling Lulu, did you bring some shoes? I was only guessing about sizes, but I'd say four or five. Rosie, darling heart, my indispensable assistant, you pick something, too.'

'The pink one,' Rosie said immediately, homing in on draped and beaded salmon-coloured satin which Cat could see was perfect for her dark, dramatic colouring.

'Cat?' said Fanny. 'Come along, my angel, do speak up.'

But Cat was so overcome with lust she couldn't speak. She merely pointed to a vision with a green and gold and beaded bodice and a tiered pale green chiffon skirt.

'Tess?' continued Fanny.

'You mean I can choose anything?' said Tess, who still looked poleaxed by all the gorgeousity on display.

'Yes, of course,' said Fanny genially. 'You choose away, my angel – ask, and it shall be given.'

She turned to smile at Lulu, then at the girls again. 'You haven't lived, you know, until you've worn a Lulu Minto dress. The cut, the quality, the finish—'

'The blue one, then,' said Tess, then added, 'please'.

Fanny sent the three of them upstairs to use her huge, luxurious bathroom, said to take whatever they could find and make themselves look beautiful, while she and darling Lulu had a catch-up and a drink.

'This is getting seriously weird,' said Tess, as she opened cabinets and cupboards, ferreting and searching frantically. 'God, where does this woman keep her razors?' But it didn't look like Fanny Gregory used anything as common as a razor. 'I mean, what is she playing at? Why all this stupid cloak and dagger stuff? Why didn't she just invite you to her party, tell you to bring a mate?'

'God only knows,' said Cat.

'I've got a lady's razor,' Rosie told them, opening her own enormous washbag and tipping several dozen samples out on Fanny's bed. 'I've also brought shampoo and mousse, the ordinary stuff that Fanny never thinks to buy, because she never does her hair herself.'

'You're a heroine,' said Tess. She grinned at Rosie. 'Do you think we could have a little rummage?'

'Of course – just help yourselves.'

'How long have you been Fanny's indispensable assistant?' Tess asked Rosie as she studied her reflection in the glass. She was clearly pleased with what she saw, decided Cat.

'About two years,' said Rosie as she hooked and eyed herself into her lovely frock.

'God, you must have nerves of steel,' said Cat.

'Oh, Fanny doesn't give me any grief.'

'But, even so—'

'She's just a softie, really.' Rosie slipped on matching satin shoes. 'You only have to look at Fan with Caspar to realise she's got a heart of gold – not that it would be difficult to love a dog like Caspar, I admit, because his temperament's the best.'

'Caspar's lovely,' Cat agreed. 'But it's not as if he's some pathetic little mongrel she found wandering the streets. Fanny wouldn't have a dog like that. Caspar's an aristodog and I'll bet he has a pedigree that's even more impressive than the Queen's.'

'Well, you would lose your bet,' said Rosie. 'Fanny was about to let herself into her flat one evening when she heard this whimpering and crying. She found him and his brothers and his sisters in a plastic bag. They'd been dumped in a skip. The others were all dead and Caspar was a sickly little scrap of skin and bone.'

'Omigod, that's horrible!' gasped Cat.

'What happened next?' asked Tess.

'Fanny took him up to her apartment then she called a vet. Over the next six months she nursed him, fed him, trained him, loved him, and of course she loves him still. Anyone who's mean to Fanny usually gets bitten where it hurts. But anyone who's mean to Caspar's dead.'

Then, as if on cue, Caspar put his elegant long nose round Fanny's bedroom door to check out what was happening in the inner sanctum.

'Come in, Caspar, sweetheart,' Rosie said.

So Caspar jogged into the room on springs, or so it seemed to Cat. He jumped on Fanny's bed, arranging his long legs into a graceful arabesque.

'It's fascinating, watching Fanny zooming round and bossing everyone about and making everyone do what she wants, especially if they don't want to do it,' added Rosie. 'I'm taking lots of notes.'

She brushed her hair back and clipped it with some pretty jewelled slides. 'One day, I'll have my own promotions business,' she continued. 'My sister will be starting her final year at Oxford in October, and when she's finished there she's going to come and work with me. She's the creative one and I'm the go-getter. She's the intrepid traveller and I'm the stay-at-home. So she can open offices for us all over the world, and between us we'll do very well. We'll be even richer and even more successful than Fanny is herself. You wait and see.'

'But won't Fanny mind you starting up your own promotions company?' asked Cat. 'You'll be competition, after all.'

'On the contrary, she's been most supportive and encouraging,' said Rosie. 'Anyway, there's loads of work for both of us, and I won't be chasing any of her high-end clients. I'll be starting small.'

'But you'll go on to bigger things?'

'I expect we will.' Rosie smiled enigmatically. 'That's certainly the plan.'

'How did you two meet?' asked Tess.

'Mummy and Fan are friends,' Rosie replied. 'They went to the same school. But Mummy was a prefect when Fanny was a frightened little first year, far away from home and missing teddy. Mummy helped her settle in, and I think Fan was grateful. They've always kept in touch.'

'I can't imagine Fanny being scared of anything,' said Tess.

'Fanny was a mouse who was afraid of her own shadow, Mummy says, and everybody's scared of something, Tess.' Rosie started putting on mascara. 'Me, I'm terrified of snakes and spiders – tarantulas, my God, some people keep the things as pets, can you imagine? Fan has to be fairly nice to me, in any case. Mummy's put a lot of work her way, including all that competition stuff at Melbury Court.'

'Don't tell me, let me guess – your mother owns it?' Cat asked Rosie.

'No, she doesn't own it. But Daddy was related to the owner, that's before the house was a hotel. When Fan was looking for a country house to feature in her new wedding promotion, Mummy said, why don't you use Aunt Daisy's lovely place? The people who have it now could do with the publicity.'

Aunt Daisy – Daisy Denham, Rosie Denham – yes,

of course, thought Cat. 'Did you know Daisy Denham personally?' she enquired, now making the connections and realising that Rosie and the actress had to be related.

'Yes,' said Rosie. 'My granny and Aunt Daisy were great friends. I used to visit regularly when I was a little girl.'

'You sat on a famous film star's knee?'

'I can't remember doing that,' Rosie said. 'But I expect I did. Aunt Daisy didn't have children of her own, but she was very fond of Granny's four, especially Aunt Lily and my dad.'

'What are you two going on about?' demanded Tess.

'I'll tell you later,' Cat replied.

'Yes, we ought to go and see what Fanny thinks,' said Rosie.

'Why should it matter what Fanny thinks?' Tess frowned. 'We all look gorgeous, don't we?'

'You still don't get it, do you?' Rosie shook her head. 'You think she's dressed us up because she wants us to prettify her party? We're promoting Lulu's dresses, Tess. So if Fanny says we need to change, we come back up and change.'

'Come on, Tess,' said Cat, as Tess looked mutinous. 'It's flattering to be allowed to model Lulu's gowns. Fanny could have said you had to be a maid instead.'

'Yeah, right,' muttered Tess, 'and she'd have got the maid from hell. You could have bet your Birkin fake and every other bag you own on that.'

As Cat and Tess and Rosie trooped downstairs to be inspected and – Cat hoped – passed fit by Fanny Gregory, three dumpy little women in black dresses and low heels came bustling in and started sorting out the food and wine.

The doorbell rang and soon the atrium was filling up.

Apart from Rosie, who was clearly working, who was meeting, greeting and doing her assistant thing, Cat could see that only she and Tess were under thirty-five.

But this was fine, because the men all looked at them appreciatively, they all had lovely manners, and they said nice things to both of them but didn't pinch their bums.

The women were so rich, so beautiful and so well-dressed themselves that they didn't seem to mind that these two interlopers in their borrowed frocks were ten years younger and quite attractive, too.

'A lovely party, Fanny, darling.'

Cat heard this repeated again, again, again as Fanny circulated, as she played the gracious hostess. She looked divine in soft black velvet with a huge amount of powdered cleavage on display.

Caspar was the height of canine beauty, glossy, black and gorgeous, with a jewelled collar around his velvet neck.

'What about this painting, then?' said Tess, as she and Cat watched Fanny and her greyhound work the room.

'It starts tomorrow, I expect,' said Cat. 'These people wouldn't want to get magnolia emulsion on their gowns from still-damp walls.'

'Your Fanny's up to something. I don't know why she got you to come here. But I'm sure as hell no painting's in her cunning plan.'

'You may be right.'

'So what happens next?'

'God only knows,' said Cat. 'You look great in blue,' she added, trying to change the subject. She didn't want to think about what Fanny might have planned for later.

'You look ace in green. I'm going to pinch these babies,' Tess continued, glancing at her shoes. Then, when Cat looked horrified, she grinned. 'I was only joking, don't give birth.'

'I hope you're having lots of fun, my darlings, among us geriatrics?' Silent as a serpent, Fanny had come up behind them and had put her arms around their shoulders, leaning on them for support.

She was clearly sloshed, but Cat was certain – sloshed or sober – Fanny never, ever dropped her guard. She hoped Fan hadn't heard what Tess had said about stealing the shoes.

'Yes, it's great.' Cat nodded vehemently. 'We were just saying about the frocks and shoes, they're wonderful.'

'Yes, of course they're wonderful, my darling – everything's couture. I think we're ready for some music,' she continued, or rather she announced. She snapped her fingers and, as if by magic, two young men in black – one tall and handsome, one shorter and more ordinary-looking – appeared as if from nowhere, trundling speakers and a deck. 'Okay, people, party, party, party!'

'Yeah, and about time, too,' said Tess.

As music started pulsing through the barn Tess kicked off her shoes. Then she was dancing, and very soon a dozen of the men were jigging up and down looking like they'd been electrocuted, trying to out-peacock one another, obviously anxious to impress.

Cat was being talked at by a fifty-something woman in a dress made out of scarlet feathers who was also wearing lots of diamonds when Fanny sidled up to them and whispered someone lovely had arrived. Someone she knew Cat would like to meet because they had an awful lot in common.

'Oh, who's that?' asked Cat, who had been knocking back the champagne cocktails, and whose other self knew she was drunk, even though the first self wasn't going to admit it.

'Just you wait and see!' Fanny grinned, and Cat resigned herself to being lectured by some bloke who had a private gallery in Soho or Mayfair. Or by some old geezer who would spend a full ten minutes staring-but-not-staring at her chest, but who probably didn't want to hear about a salvage yard in Walthamstow. Or by a woman who wanted some authentic Jacobean panelling, or perhaps Victorian garden art …

'Come along, my angel.'

Fanny led her from the atrium and out into the hallway. The front door was open, letting in the gentle summer breeze and making Cat feel suddenly stone cold sober. 'Fanny,' she began, 'I don't know what you're playing at, but I—'

'Off you go,' said Fanny, giving Cat a gentle but insistent little shove, then skittering back inside to join the party.

Cat felt Caspar rub his face against her hand and she was momentarily reassured.

But then she felt sick, because at last she realised what this charade, this pantomime, this farce was all about. She'd seen the man in the black dinner jacket standing on the drive, his back towards the house.

As he turned around, she backed away.

'I'm sorry,' she began. 'I can see all this has been set up at huge expense, and Fanny must have taken endless trouble. But I still don't want to talk to you.'

Adam went on checking through the final set of drawings.

Next year, he decided, the Scottish castle would look really good. It would look more than good, in fact. It would look fantastic. He'd be inundated with commissions. He'd be working for the sort of people who had bank accounts the size of Russia.

They might even be Russian – or Chinese or Canadian or South American. They might live in Moscow or Toronto or Beijing or Buenos Aires – in fact, they could live anywhere, because he could go anywhere. He could do anything. He would be an international player and he'd be winning this particular game.

Although his personal life was a disaster – Cat hadn't come to meet him at the Lion that Wednesday afternoon, and he'd been almost certain she'd turn up. But, as was usual when it came to women, he'd been wrong, wrong, wrong – his professional life was looking set to work out fine.

At nine o'clock he closed his laptop, shoved some stuff into a holdall, left the flat and started walking, heading for Euston station where he'd catch the train to Aberdeen.

There was a lot of traffic, and so he didn't know his phone was grumbling in his pocket until the caller had got bored and given up on him.

He fished it out, he crossed his fingers and he prayed it had been Cat.

Fanny Gregory, it said.

He sighed and shook his head. My God, she was persistent. Some people, did they never take a break? She must know today was Saturday?

What did she want now?

The Tudor sundial she'd decided she must have, like the one she'd seen at Hampton Court?

The Italian marble nymph he had assured her he could almost definitely source, but she might have to wait a month or two – she couldn't have it tonight?

He was regretting ever giving her his business card, ever getting involved with finding stuff for that old barn in Surrey which she was determined to restore, revamp, refurbish in record-breaking time.

As for the other stuff – she could forget it all.

She could forget he had agreed to meet her for a drink to talk about some work which he might do on her old barn. She could forget she'd somehow got him to confess that yes, he liked the girl from Chapman's yard. She hadn't been mistaken when she'd seen him look at Cat like that at Melbury Court.

Yes, he'd seen her since, because he'd done more business with the yard. Yes, she was sweet and smart and pretty. Yes, she definitely knew her way around the architectural salvage trade. Yes, her boss was lucky to have an office manager like Cat.

But no, it wasn't going anywhere. No, he didn't care if she had finished with her fiancé. What did that have to do with him, and no he didn't do parties. He couldn't dance, and he didn't like talking nonsense to a lot of suits. It wasn't him at all.

So no, he wasn't going to her party, even though she'd said he must, even though she'd told him she was desperate for handsome men to make the whole thing look a bit more glamorous, my sweet, and he was the sexiest and most gorgeous man she knew, my angel, darling heart.

Flatter, flatter, flatter – she was so transparent that he couldn't help but laugh, and she was so vain she thought that when he laughed she'd won him over.

'So you will try to make it, sweetheart, won't you?' she'd concluded, with a winning flutter of the lashes and a charming widening of the eyes.

'No,' he'd said. 'I'm busy.'

'What are you doing, then?'

'I'm going to Aberdeen.'

'But it will be a lovely opportunity for you! I could introduce you to some influential people who have country houses, and who could put a lot of work your way, make you recession-proof.'

'Fanny, what bit of no, I'm busy, don't you understand?'

'You can go to Scotland some other time, my angel. I want you at my barn on Saturday.'

The phone began to jig around again.

'Yes?' he said resignedly, aware that if he didn't talk to Fanny Gregory now, she would go on pestering him all night.

He listened patiently to what she had to say.

Or was trying to say.

He had to make allowances because she was so drunk she couldn't seem to get her words out right.

'I can't come to your party,' he repeated. 'I'm going to catch a train to Aberdeen. Fanny, it's my work – my livelihood. I can't just not turn up. I can't tell my client I'll try to fit him in some other time.'

'Your livelihood, you say,' slurred Fanny, hiccupping. 'Darling Adam, sometimes you're so stupid.'

'What's that supposed to mean?'

'This is about your life.'

'Babe, the feeling's mutual,' drawled Jack, as Cat insisted she didn't want to talk to him.

'So why did Fanny tell me to come out here and see you?'

'God alone knows, honeybee. What is it with that bloody dog?' he muttered. 'Why is it always hanging round the place like a bad smell?'

He turned away again. 'Annabelle?' he called. 'You coming to this party, then? Or have you changed your mind?'

'Sorry, darling – shoes.'

As Cat stood there flummoxed, feeling stupid, a bony woman in a near-transparent orange dress and glitter-speckled Perspex platform heels came tottering into view.

She stared at Cat with bloodshot, pink-rimmed eyes. 'Who's this?' she asked and blinked her gunked-up lashes.

'Nobody,' said Jack, and ushered Annabelle inside.

The woman should sit down again, thought Cat, before she crumples like a broken marionette. She's clearly stoned out of her mind.

As Cat stood there by herself in the soft summer darkness, she felt the night air kiss her face and cool it down. Then she felt Caspar rub his head against her hand again and felt a little better.

But what the hell was Fanny playing at?

If she was trying to stage a grand reunion between Cat and Jack, and force them to get married after all, she had no business.

Cat was never going to marry Jack. She'd sooner chop her fingers off than wear his wedding ring. So all this was a total waste of everybody's time.

Jack was a guest, or that was what it looked like. He was all dressed up, in any case. He couldn't have been told to come and paint the barn, so was he a member of the inner circle now? What had Fanny said – that Jack was busy, that he had auditions? So was Fanny now his agent, had she started representing him?

Or more than representing?

Cat wouldn't put it past her, or past him.

But, if Jack and Fanny were a couple, who was that toothpick Annabelle, and where did she fit in? She wasn't some young bimbo, even though she dressed like one. She was fifty, if she was a day. She had a turkey neck, gaunt, stick-like arms which had no flesh on them and deeply-hollowed shoulders, and in that horrid frock she was a sagging cleavage tragedy.

Maybe Jack was renting himself out, providing personal services to desperate old women?

Or maybe Fanny had branched out into the escort business, and Jack was her first escort, and she was taking twenty, fifty, seventy-five per cent?

Cat thought – I'll go up to my room. I'll have a little bit of peace and quiet, chill out for half an hour. I'll drink a litre of water, several litres, and then I might stop feeling quite so weird.

Maybe it was all those champagne cocktails? Or maybe she'd been right about the coma theory?

Oh, I know, she thought, it's like that Julia Roberts movie, Erin Brocko-whatsitsname. There's something in the water.

Someone's putting mercury or arsenic – or those things Homer Simpson makes, isotopes, or whatnot – in the tank back at my flat.

Someone's out to get me.

So I'll need to work out what to do.

But now, she thought, I need to have a little break from party, party, party.

She went upstairs and Caspar followed, keeping close.

'Where are you now?' hissed Fanny into her mobile phone.

'I'm on my way,' said Adam. 'I'm driving past Heathrow. I'll be there in – half an hour, forty minutes, right?'

'It shouldn't take you that long,' Fanny told him. 'What are you driving, darling – a tractor or a hearse?'

'I can't afford to lose my licence, Fanny.' Adam overtook a Tesco lorry which flashed its lights at him as if to warn him that it would get its own back very soon. 'What's the tearing hurry, anyway?'

'I didn't tell you when I called you earlier this evening, but I've mucked it up, and I need you here to sort it out.'

'What do you mean, you've mucked it up?'

'I thought it was you arriving, sweetheart. Three hours late, of course, but looking like you'd made some sort of effort. I was most impressed. It was someone else, though, and now the girl's gone to her room, where she's no doubt sobbing fit to break her little heart.'

'I'm sorry she's upset, but what's it got to do with me?'

'You like her, Adam,' Fanny snapped. 'You damn well know you do.'

'You're making wild assumptions, Fanny.'

'Why are you coming, then?'

'You nagged me into it.'

'I never nag, my angel, I persuade. Why are you driving past Heathrow? Your GPS not working?'

'I haven't got a GPS. I'm an old-fashioned guy and I use Ordnance Survey maps. Fan, I'm going now. Otherwise I'm going to get pulled over by the motorway police for talking on a mobile.'

'You haven't got a hands-free?'

'No, I've never felt I needed one.'

'Of course you need a hands-free, sweetheart, everybody does. I couldn't run my business if I didn't have one. So I don't know how on earth you manage to run yours. I hope you're wearing something smart, my darling?'

'I'm in jeans and trainers.'

'Tell me that's a joke, my love?'

'You didn't say there was a dress code.'

'If I had, would you have taken any bloody notice?'

'Probably not,' said Adam.

'You have to be the most contrary man I've ever met.'

'You're the most contrary woman.' Adam saw the flashing lights of a police patrol car in his rear-view mirror. 'Fanny, do you want me there or not?'

'I want you here, and I want you to hurry.'

As the police drew level, Adam threw his phone down. They clocked him driving sensibly, and passed.

Fanny was still squawking something, but he couldn't be bothered to listen to Fanny any more.

He should be on his way to Aberdeen.

But if Cat would see him, talk to him, just for half an hour, for half a minute, he could still get to Aberdeen in time, if he drove through the night.

'Jesus, what a riot,' said Tess, who had come upstairs to fix her make-up and who now decided she would have a little break from party, party, party. 'Shove up, Cat and dog.'

So Cat and Caspar obligingly shoved up, allowing Tess to flop down on the beautiful French bed where Cat and the greyhound were relaxing, chilling to the muffled sounds of party, party, party coming from below.

They stared up at the ceiling, Caspar deep in canine contemplation, Cat and Tess zonked out.

'Those old timers, mate, they're just amazing,' Tess told Cat in tones of shock and awe. 'How can they drink so much and still stand up? Champagne cocktail after champagne cocktail – that woman in the scarlet feathers must have drunk a dozen. I'd be in a coma.'

'I would, too,' said Cat. 'But they've had years of practice. They probably go to parties awash with fizz and brandy all the time.'

'Yes, they must,' said Tess, and now she raised herself up on one elbow, scrutinising Cat. 'Hey, have you been crying?'

'No.' Cat turned to look at Tess. 'See – mascara still intact, lipstick not chewed off, all right? I needed to take five.'

'Only I saw the scumbag and some hideous bottle blonde downstairs, and she was chewing off his face.'

'It's okay,' said Cat. 'I saw him too, and honestly it's no big deal.'

'But why's he here?'

'Fan must have invited him.' Cat shrugged. 'Do you know something?'

'What?'

'I am so over him!'

'About time too, my friend.' Tess held up her hand and Cat high-fived it. 'We'd better go back down,' she said. 'Fanny's going to wonder where we've gone. She told me we're both doing a fantastic job tonight. Showing off Lulu's gorgeous frocks, I mean. Actually, Cat, she said we ought—'

'We ought to watch it, mate,' said Cat.

'What do you mean?'

'She's up to something, I can tell.'

'You're paranoid,' said Tess.

'I'm not,' retorted Cat. 'I still can't work out what she's playing at tonight. But I know she didn't invite us here and dress us up in Lulu's frocks out of the kindness of her heart. Or even to promote the frocks themselves, although that's obviously part of it. We're here to serve some purpose, and I wish to God I knew what her ladyship is plotting now.'

'I told you, you're the human sacrifice in the black mass.' Tess grinned. 'It must be nearly midnight, so you can't have long to wait before you meet your doom.'

Adam parked the Volvo next to a brand new silver Jaguar which he could have sworn shrank back in horror.

He wondered if he had some decent shoes and smartish trousers somewhere in the compost in the boot? Perhaps he ought to have a look?

But then he thought – no, sod it. Fan insisted I should come. So she'll have to take me as she finds me. Let me in, or tell her staff – she's bound to have some staff, a housekeeper, a butler, maybe both – to throw me out.

When she had told him Cat was crying, it had stabbed him through the heart, to think she might be crying and he might be the cause of it. Or was he deluded, and was he – not Fanny – making wild assumptions and behaving like an idiot again?

There was only one way to find out. He got out of the Volvo and crunched across the gravel, heading for the barn.

The front door was open and, as he walked in, he met three women in black waitress dresses and white frilly aprons coming out.

He passed a door that opened into an enormous kitchen which was silent except for the soft humming of a dishwasher and freezer.

Then he almost fell into a couple of gorgeous apparitions which had floated down the spiral staircase on his right with a sleek black greyhound following them.

The apparitions stared at him with round, astonished eyes, like princesses encountering a churl – if he meant a churl?

He blinked and tried to focus.

'Cat?' he began and, as he realised he was right, he felt his face – no, make that his whole body – turn into one big smile.

'Adam?' Cat was frowning – in horror, disbelief?

'Yes, that's right, it's him!' cried Tess. 'It's the other scumbag, so now we have the pair.'

'What are you doing here?' asked Cat.

'Fan invited me.'

'You know Fanny Gregory?'

'Yes, of course,' said Adam. 'We met at Melbury Court, don't you remember?'

'Oh, yes – she took your shirt off.'

'What?'

'I'm sorry, Adam.' Cat began to giggle. 'You're looking very scruffy, so are you sure you're coming to the party? It's all designer frocks and dinner jackets back through there, and you'll look very out of place.'

It was obvious to Adam Cat had not been crying. Fanny had been lying or mistaken, for Cat's eyes were sparkling and her cheeks were glowing rosebud-pink. She looked amazing in that beaded dress. She looked like someone who belonged inside the pages of a fashion magazine.

But – oh, the relief – she didn't look angry. The last time he had seen her, she had been so angry that she had made him flinch. But this evening she looked curious – just curious, and perplexed.

'Do you want to talk to him?' asked Tess.

'I suppose I could,' said Cat. 'After all, he's driven all this way, unless he flew here on a magic carpet.'

'I'll see you later, then.' Tess turned to go back to the party. 'Come on, Caspar love,' she said. 'We need to go and sort those sound men out. They can't go on playing bloody Abba all the bloody night, even ironically. Yell if this guy tries anything,' she added. 'I'll come back and black his eyes for you.'

'Come into the kitchen, Cat?' said Adam.

'Oh my goodness, there's an invitation, how can I resist?' Cat shook her head at him, but followed all the same. 'I'm very drunk, you know,' she added. 'I don't know what I'm saying.'

'I do know what I'm saying.'

'Go on – say it, then?'

'I'm sorry I didn't tell you about Mads.' Adam took Cat's hands in his and gazed into her eyes. 'She and I split up before I met you, and that's the honest truth. I did ask her to marry me. I thought I was in love. But when I met you, I realised Mads and I were just a fantasy – a dream of love. You were the real thing. Oh, Cat, my darling – I've missed you so much!'

'I've missed you, too,' said Cat. She bit her lip, as if to punish it for letting those few dangerous words slip out. 'Mind you, like I said, I'm very drunk. You can't believe a single word I say.'

'I thought it was *in vino veritas*?'

'You what?' frowned Cat.

'It doesn't matter.'

'It sounds like something on a sundial.'

'It means there's truth in wine.'

'So I'm telling you the truth?' Cat put her arms around his neck. 'Okay, more truth – I think I'd like to kiss you.'

So Adam closed the door behind them and took her deep

into the dark recesses of the softly-humming kitchen. Then he kissed her, and she kissed him back with such enthusiasm that he never wanted her to stop.

He found the zip on Lulu Minto's beautiful green gown.

She found the buttons on his shirt and started to undo them one by one.

'Adam, we shouldn't be doing this,' she whispered, but she didn't stop undoing buttons.

'Why?' he asked as he kissed her some more, as he kissed her mouth, her face, her neck.

'I'm sure it's not respectable, snogging in somebody else's kitchen.'

'Maybe not,' said Adam, but he didn't stop snogging anyway. 'Do you happen to have a bedroom, Cat?'

'I believe I do.'

'Any chance of finding it, do you think?'

'Yes, perhaps,' said Cat. 'We could start by going up the stairs.'

Sunday, 3 July

This must be love?

Adam rolled over on his side and realised with a surge of happiness that he had not been dreaming.

Cat was there beside him, her hair a tumbled, glorious dark blonde mass across her pillow, her long, dark lashes lying like feathers on her creamy cheeks, and she looked good enough to eat. Or at least to kiss awake, and kiss and kiss again.

So that was what he did.

'Where's Tess?' she asked, when she had finished being woken.

'Tess?' repeated Adam, looking blank.

'Tess, my friend, this is her room, where is she?'

'I don't know.'

'Jesus.' Cat jumped up and ran into the little single bedroom which was off the master suite.

But to her relief the room was empty, and the duvet on the bed was still immaculate, so no one could have slept there.

She got back into bed. 'Adam,' she said nervously, 'I seem to have mislaid a very expensive cocktail dress.'

'Green with lots of beading round the neckline?'

'That's the one.'

'It's in your wardrobe.'

'But how did it get into my wardrobe?'

'I put it there,' said Adam.

'How, when I was wearing it?' Cat frowned.

'You took it off.'

'What exactly did we do last night?'

'You don't remember?'

'I remember some of it.' Cat blushed. 'You told me about

Maddy and we went into to the kitchen and we kissed and then we came up here. But there are gaps.'

'Let me refresh your memory.'

'Cat, I want to marry you,' said Adam, when Cat's memory had been sorted out.

'Oh, don't let's start that again,' said Cat. 'It only leads to trouble and confusion, doesn't it?'

'It doesn't have to lead to trouble. I ask you to marry me – you say yes – it's sorted. Cat, don't spoil my plans, especially when I've got ulterior motives.'

'What ulterior motives?'

'I'm hoping to inherit all your worldly goods.'

'They amount to twenty pairs of shoes, a few designer fakes, a beaten-up old Honda that's not fit for the road, one sofa I don't even own – and my enormous debts.'

'What debts?' Adam kissed her cheek and wound a lock of hair around one finger. 'You mean you have a serious shopping habit? You have credit cards and stuff?'

Cat shook her head and sighed. 'I wish it was that simple.'

'We'll sort it out,' said Adam. 'It will be all right.'

'You sound very sure.'

'It's going to be fine, you'll see. But now, shall we get up? We're Fanny's guests, remember? So we ought to go and have some breakfast and say thank you for a lovely party.'

'You didn't go to a party, Adam.'

'Yes I did.'

'But you didn't have a single drink. You didn't meet any of the other guests. You didn't dance.'

'I had a party of my own in Fanny's kitchen, then up here.'

'Fanny,' Cat said wryly. 'She does love manipulating people and playing games with them. I still don't know what game she's playing with me.'

'We'll sort Fanny out,' said Adam as his phone began to jingle-jangle.

'Perhaps you ought to answer that,' said Cat.

So Adam did, thinking it's unlikely to be Fanny, anyway.

The screen said Malcolm Portland.

'God,' said Adam, grimacing.

'God what?' asked Cat.

'I should have been in Aberdeen a couple of hours ago.' Adam pressed the button. 'Hello, Mr Portland,' he began. 'Yes, I know,' he said. 'Yes, I'm very sorry, but I was held up. Yes, it was an emergency. So I can't be up there until Monday morning now.'

Then Malcolm Portland did a lot of shouting and used a very Anglo-Saxon swear word several times, rather creatively.

Adam let Mr Portland finish ranting. 'I don't work for people who speak to me like that,' he said, and then he disconnected.

'Who on earth?' asked Cat.

'The man who bought the Scottish castle.'

'The one who wanted you to do it up, and who was going to pay you so much money that you would be able to rent a yard and start employing other people?'

'Yes.'

'Oh, Adam, I've spoiled everything!'

'There'll be other castles.' Adam tossed his phone on to a chair. 'I didn't want his business, anyway.'

'You did.'

'I didn't, Cat. I was almost ready to tell him I was getting out. All he did was make me do it now.'

Twenty minutes later Cat and Adam went downstairs.

It was a lovely morning and the kitchen doors were open wide onto the terrace.

'A vast improvement, darling,' whispered Fanny, materialising from behind a variegated fig tree.

'Fanny, don't creep up on me!' cried Cat. 'You'll end up giving me a heart attack.'

'I'm sorry, sweetie pie.' Fanny lit a cigarette and blew a perfect smoke ring. 'It's good to see your tastes have changed, and for the better, too. As I think Tess and Rosie would agree.'

She glanced through the glass doors into the kitchen where Adam, Tess and Rosie were at breakfast. They were now the best of friends, or so it seemed to Cat. Adam was not a scumbag anyway, for he was being smiled at, flirted with and asked to pass the marmalade with much eyelash fluttering and accidental cleavage revelation.

Caspar had his head on Adam's lap and was gazing up at him with adoration in his amber eyes, probably because he fancied some of Adam's toast and marmalade, decided Cat.

She hadn't felt like eating. Out here in the garden, she could breathe in the fresh air and try to get her champagne cocktail headache under some sort of control.

'What do you mean, a vast improvement?' she demanded, as Fanny went on puffing like a steam engine and blowing out more smoke rings into the summer sky.

'What do you think I mean?'

'I couldn't begin to guess,' said Cat. 'You shouldn't smoke,' she added. 'It's very bad for you.'

'It's my little sin,' said Fanny, sighing. Then she grinned suggestively. 'If I had to choose between them, it would be no contest. I can't say I took to Jack at all. But this one – he's delicious. I can't imagine any woman saying no to him.'

'Fanny, what exactly are you playing at?'

'I don't play at anything, my angel. I do everything for real. I'm sure you must have noticed?' Fanny tapped Cat's forearm with one crimson-taloned finger. 'Darling, about Lulu's lovely frock—'

'The frock is fine, don't worry. It's hanging in the wardrobe in my room.'

'I was going to say, before I was so rudely interrupted – really, you young people, you have such appalling manners, your mothers can't have taken any care of you at all – you looked very nice in it last night. So nice, in fact, that darling Lulu got eleven orders for that particular model, and she's so delighted she says you may keep the one you wore as your commission on the sales.'

'But Lulu's frocks are worth—'

'A cool two or three thousand, maybe more. You mustn't wear it when you go to get your groceries. You'll snag it on a trolley.' Fanny smiled her vixen's smile. 'You didn't do much magnolia-slapping, did you?'

'I haven't forgotten, Fanny,' Cat said sharply. 'I'll come back next weekend.'

'Excellent,' said Fanny. 'You could bring Adam, too. Oh look, here he comes. But what's the matter, darling? You were flirting very happily with the pretty ladies around the kitchen table just a minute or two ago. But now you look quite grim.'

'I lost him a job,' said Cat.

'What happened?' Fanny asked him, widening her eyes.

'I had a disagreement with a client who seemed to think he owned me.'

'Oh dear, we can't have that,' said Fanny, smirking. 'Goodness gracious me, fancy anybody having the enormous cheek to think they might own Mr Adam Lawley! So he's not your client any more?'

'No, he's not,' said Adam.

'Where was this client based?' asked Fanny.

'Scotland,' Cat replied.

'You mean the man in Aberdeen?'

'Yes,' said Cat and wondered if Fanny Gregory knew everything.

'Oh, don't go and work in Scotland, darling.' Fanny shuddered. 'It's a ghastly place. I went there once, when I was married to a millionaire. It was full of midges, drunks and stags.'

Adam and Tess and Cat went back to London, leaving Fanny on the phone, Caspar trying to extract a rabbit from its burrow by the boundary fence, and Rosie in the kitchen, supervising several cheerful ladies who'd turned up with vacuum cleaners, buckets, mops and dusters in a yellow minibus.

Tess drove back in the Peugeot, taking all the leftovers and the better-looking of the sound men, with whom Cat guessed Tess must have spent the night. He'd been in the garden smoking even more than Fanny, and looking worse for wear.

The other was left to follow in their van.

Cat had been so embarrassed when Tess had begged the tiny cakes and canapés and dinky little scones, even though this meant that Tess and Cat and Barry would have luxury coffee breaks the whole of the next week.

'But why shouldn't I have asked?' said Tess. 'She's never going to eat all this herself. She'll only chuck it in the bin. Anyway, my honey pie, as Fanny said herself – ask, and it shall be given.'

Cat could see that Tess had been bewitched. On Monday, it would be all Fanny this and Fanny that and when could they go back to Surrey? When could they start painting? They must get Bex to come along, as well.

Cat hoped Tess would not start all this angeling and darlinging and sweeting business, too.

Cat and Adam followed in the Volvo.

'I'm sorry about Scotland,' Cat told Adam.

'Oh, don't worry, Cat. It's like I told you – I didn't want that job in any case.'

'You did,' said Cat. 'You were going to earn a lot of money and invest it in your business.'

'There'll be other jobs. Tell me about this loan shark,' prompted Adam, as they turned out of the drive.

'What loan shark?'

'I mean whoever's chasing you for money.'

'Oh, it's not a loan shark.'

'It's a money-lender, then?'

'I don't want to talk about it now,' said Cat.

Then she walked the fingers of one hand down Adam's shoulder, down his arm, on to his lap and down his leg. 'Sorry,' she added, well aware that she was sounding anything but sorry. 'I know I shouldn't distract you when you're driving.'

'No, you shouldn't,' Adam said as he pulled off the road. 'What am I going to do with you?' he asked, then answered his own question at some length and very thoroughly.

'What's in that letter on the dashboard, Adam?' Cat asked half an hour later, pointing to a thick, cream envelope which had a shield or crest upon its flap.

'A cheque, drawn on some bank I've never come across before. At first, I thought it was a joke. But when I googled Mason Armstrong, I found it did exist. It's a private bank, apparently.'

'I didn't know there were such things.'

'You have to be quite rich to be a customer, or whatever they call you in these places – a client, an investor?'

'So who's the millionaire?'

'You remember that old guy whose tyre I changed when we were on our way to Wolverhampton?'

'Oh, him – yes, I do.' Cat felt her colour rise. It had been the day the git came back and she'd run out on Adam. What a fool. 'Did he send you what he owed you, then?'

'Yes, and a bit more.' Adam passed Cat the letter which accompanied the cheque.

My dear Mr Lawley

Do please forgive me for taking such a dreadfully long time to write to you. I have been unwell and have only recently recovered.

I am very embarrassed to have kept you waiting for repayment. But I now enclose a cheque to cover both the cost of taking Boudicca back to my house and to make some little recompense for the inconvenience caused to your good self and to the extremely kind young lady who was travelling with you.

I see from your card you are a freelance project manager, specialising in restoring English country houses. If you might like to do some work on mine, I would be very happy to discuss it.

But I understand you will be busy so I shall not importune you further. I shall wait for you to get in touch with me, which in due course I hope you will.

My most sincere regards and grateful thanks

Daniel Askew Moreley

Cat gave the letter back. 'He's sent you – what is it – another two, three hundred pounds?'

'Yes, give or take a couple of quid.'

'But Adam, he was poor!' cried Cat. 'He wore those awful clothes and drove that horrible old wreck.'

'It was a rather beautiful old wreck, as I recall. It must have been quite something when he had it first.'

'Well, he couldn't afford to be in the AA or RAC.'

'How do you know that?'

'I suppose I don't exactly know. I just assumed. Why are you grinning, Adam?'

'Mr Moreley's actually the fourteenth Baron Moreley. I looked him up on Google. I looked his house up, too.' Adam got out his phone, tapped a few keys, brought up an image. 'Just take a look at this.'

'My goodness, Adam, that's fantastic! It's Tudor, isn't it?'

'Possibly late Tudor, more likely Jacobean.'

'It's just your sort of thing,' said Cat.

'It might be, yes.'

'What do you mean, it might be?'

'It will depend what he wants doing.'

'But you'll go and see him?'

'I think so. You'll come, too?'

'Of course I will – and don't forget, if this guy's made of money, we want your hankies back.'

'We do indeed,' said Adam. 'Cotton's quite expensive nowadays. Cat, I've been thinking ...'

'What?'

'Do you—would you like—I need a partner. I mean in the business. I need someone to organise me, tell me where I need to be, stop me taking on too much and double-booking all the time. You're a brilliant organiser.'

'Do you think so?'

'Yes I do, and so does Barry Chapman, he told me so himself.'

'I see,' said Cat. 'When would all this happen?'

'As soon as you could leave your job with Barry and come to work with me.'

'I couldn't just leave Barry in the lurch. He'd need to

find another office manager, someone who could do the books and organise the place and knows about the salvage business, too. I'd have to train the newbie up. It would take two, three months.'

'But you'll think about it, will you?'

'Yes,' said Cat, and smiled a feline smile. 'You did say partner, didn't you? I'm not going to be your typist, secretary, glorified PA.'

'Of course you'll be my partner, but there's one condition.'

'What?'

'You have to make the coffee. I've never got the hang of making coffee and you do it very well indeed.' Adam turned the key in the ignition. 'Let's get going, shall we, and talk about it while we're on the road?'

'You did what?' demanded Bex, when Cat and Tess called round on Sunday evening to ask about her date with Mr Tesco and the tenpin bowling. 'You met Lulu Minto? You wore her frocks?'

'Yes,' said Tess, and smirked complacently. 'They were new designs as well. They're not yet in the shops. Maybe they won't ever be in shops. They'll be made to order for selected clients like A-listers and royalty. You haven't lived, you know, until you've worn a Lulu Minto dress. The cut, the quality, the finish—'

'Do you have any photographic evidence?' asked Bex.

'We didn't have time to mess around with photographic evidence,' said Tess. 'But there was some guy taking snaps, so we might eventually turn up in *Hello*. Oh, and Cat was given a Lulu Minto sample, weren't you, Cat?'

'I was indeed.'

'She's going to let us borrow it.'

'I'm not!'

'Of course you will,' said Tess. 'We're your best friends.'

'I thought you were going decorating,' Bex said, looking sick.

'We did, too,' said Cat.

'If I'd known you were going to a party—'

'Didn't Mr Tesco live up to expectations, then?'

'No,' said Bex and scowled. 'He was an hour late. He expected me to pay for him. He said he'd lost his wallet on the train. But he didn't seem very fussed about it. I'm sure it was a lie.' Bex looked mournfully at Cat and Tess. 'So you two scored?'

'We did.'

'What were they like?'

'They're meeting us in a pub at eight o'clock, so come and see,' invited Cat. 'Mine's the guy I met at Barry's yard.'

'Mine's a freelance sound man and he has a mate,' said Tess.

'So there's a spare for you.'

'You mean a reject, don't you?' muttered Bex. 'He'll be some mutant who has personal hygiene issues and psoriasis?'

'Bex, he's very nice,' insisted Cat. 'No scales, no fins, no horns, no tail, own teeth, nice eyes, own hair.'

'I bet he's short and fat.'

'He's a little on the chunky side,' admitted Tess.

'But he has a gorgeous smile and he looks as if he's got a lovely sense of humour,' added Cat. 'Please come and meet them, Bex – they're dying to meet you.'

'Listen, Bexy – you can come and help us paint the next time,' Tess continued generously.

Doesn't this woman ever take time out?

Fanny was on the phone to Cat at daybreak.

'I was about to call you,' Cat said as she rubbed the sleep out of her eyes. 'I was going to ring and thank you for a lovely party.'

'Yes, my party,' Fanny drawled. 'It was a huge success. My phone's red hot. My client list is growing by the hour. I'm going to let my barn out to a film production company. You wouldn't believe how much these guys will pay for beautiful locations so convenient for London. But anyway, my sweet, I have to see you now, if not before. We need to talk.'

'Fanny, I can't drop everything and come into your office, you know that. I have to go to work.'

'Oh yes, your work,' said Fanny, sighing. 'As if I could forget about your work and what a lot it means to you. Well, I'll be here all day, my love, and probably half the night. Call in after work, why don't you? We can get a takeaway or something and have a little natter. We can have a cosy, girly chat.'

'Yes, okay,' said Cat resignedly. A cosy, girly chat, she thought – as if. She really didn't want to talk to Fanny. But she knew she must. She had to get this business sorted, find out what she owed this bloody woman, start to pay her off at twenty, thirty quid a week.

She turned to look at Adam who was still fast asleep. She wondered if she ought to tell him what was going on?

Or should she keep it to herself?

She wished she knew.

'But why are you so keen to represent him?' Cat demanded as they ate their sushi from little lacquered bento boxes, and as Fanny explained to Cat how she was going make quite sure Jack's contract was completely watertight. In this business, it was so important everyone knew where they stood. 'You don't even like him.'

'Do I have to like him?' Fanny offered Caspar a little piece of California roll which he accepted graciously. She shrugged her shoulders and her cantilevered bosom rose in all its splendid majesty. 'Sweetheart, I know literary agents who have gangsters, paedophiles and murderers on their lists. People they wouldn't dream of taking home or even taking out to lunch but who can help them rake it in. I don't want to be Jack's friend, my darling. I'm just going to make him work for me.'

'Jack's not keen on work.'

'He's keen on money and on being a celebrity.' Fanny grinned. 'My princess, as our Jackie-boy gets richer, so shall I.'

'But Fanny, he's – well, I don't like to ask, but does he have the talent to succeed?'

'You don't need talent these days, only looks,' said Fanny as she hoovered up a slice of tuna. 'So it's just as well he has the looks. Anyway, my love – I took him for a drink one evening and I plumbed his shallows. He finally accepted he's never going to make it as a stand-up. He's not remotely funny, never has been, never will be – as I'm sure you know.'

'But he hasn't had the breaks, and he—'

'Oh, don't defend him, angel, he'd never dream of sticking up for you.' Fanny speared a prawn. 'He doesn't have a future as a comic, that's for sure. But he's very pretty so I'll get him work on cable. Jack will be the guy who's in the wet room as some famous actress soundalike talks up luxury fluffy towels in sixteen vibrant colours.'

'Oh,' said Cat.

'Then he'll be the grinning hunk who's clasping the faux gold and man-made-but-you'd-never-know-it emerald collar around the model's neck. He's got quite nice hands, so they could hold the limited edition silver tankards, royal wedding souvenirs and cartoon character boxer shorts that come in packs of ten.'

Fanny ate a piece of pickled ginger. 'He can be the borderline celebrity who is posing naked with a fish – my goodness, how amusing – in all the summer issues of those horrid magazines for girls with dirty minds.'

Cat thought, it gets worse and worse.

'When it's Christmas time he'll still be naked,' added Fanny. 'But he'll have some tinsel round his neck. Or maybe that would not be such a brilliant plan? Someone might decide to tighten it. But they could hang some baubles on him somewhere, couldn't they? He could be a sex god Christmas tree?'

'Someone has to do it, I suppose.'

'Of course they do, my darling.' Fanny grinned. 'I told him, once you're on their lists, my sweet, the people who cast that sort of stuff will find you irresistible.'

'They will?'

'They'll call me first, no question. Soon, the *Daily Mail* will start to follow him around. He'll be snapped with models and so-called actresses, falling into clubs and out of taxis. He'll be in *heat* and *Cosmopolitan* wearing just a spray-tan and a smirk.'

'Omigod,' choked Cat.

'I'll probably be able to get him work in pantomime in Hartlepool or Sheffield. He'd like that, wouldn't he? He wouldn't have to speak or act, or not much, anyway. My angel, he'll be famous, and that's what he's always wanted, after all.'

'Poor Jack,' said Cat. 'Fan, you're going to make him look ridiculous.'

'He's capable of managing that all by his little self. Just take a look at this.' Fanny pressed a key and then she turned her laptop round so Cat could see the screen.

Cat stared horrified at what was clearly the beginning of a movie made for lonely adults staying in disreputable hotels.

As the camera roamed around the set, picking out a jumbled mass of miscellaneous clutter including whips and chains, the contents of a sadist supermarket's bargain basement, Jack's face appeared in close-up. So did several other parts of him, together with some bits and pieces of two very large and very terrifying women in leopard-print high-heels and nothing else.

'I've never understood the dubious charm of S & M,' reflected Fanny. 'It puts you off your popcorn, doesn't it?'

'God, it's horrible.' Cat turned the screen away. 'Fan, he'll be a laughing stock when all his mates see this.'

'Quite possibly,' drawled Fanny. 'But angel, does it matter? Do you care?'

'Well, I suppose so, just a bit.'

'You're too soft, my darling. Listen, Cat – he treated you like gum, to be chewed up and then spat out. He called me a hideous old slapper with – what was it – plastic jugs and orange hair. The cheek of it, my stylist would be outraged, this is Sienna Gold. I'll have you know my boobs are all my own. He was mean to Caspar, too. He called my darling boy a bloody dog. Cat, my love, you've gone all red, why's that?'

'It's quite hot in here.'

'No it isn't, sweetheart – the temperature is absolutely perfect.' Fanny looked at Cat with narrowed eyes. 'You've been having very naughty thoughts.'

'I – yes, I have.' Cat had long since realised there was nothing she could hide from Fanny. 'I'm sorry, Fanny, but for a while I wondered if—if you and Jack—'

'My goodness, how disgusting.' Fanny shuddered. 'Cat,

my angel, you're like all the young. You see a man and woman talking and you think of just one thing.'

'I'm sorry, Fanny.'

'I should think so, too,' said Fanny. 'Darling, I'm attracted to very clever men – to men with power and money – to men who fascinate and mystify. As for Jack – well, it took me two seconds flat to work out Jackie-boy. He's very easy on the eye, I'll give him that. But he's very stupid and his looks will fade and then he will have nothing, so he's not my sort at all. Angel, have a petit four?'

'A what?'

'A petit four.' Fanny pushed a pretty little silver box at Cat. 'They're flower-scented fancies, lavender and violet and jasmine – interesting, eh? The woman who makes them wants me to promote them, to get them put in goodie bags at literary parties, dinners, lunches and the like. But they're rather horrid. When I tried one, I was almost sick. They taste of soap and smell like cheap deodorant. Caspar doesn't like them, do you, darling? When I gave him one, he spat it out, and usually his manners are exemplary, as you know.'

'I think I'll pass,' said Cat, now determined not to be deflected, charmed, or lulled into a false sense of security by clever, devious Fanny Gregory.

'Take the box then, angel. Do admit, my sweet, it's very lovely. All that silver foiling, swirly writing, rather classy, don't you think? A bit too classy, actually, for what are just pretentious little biscuits. It's rather like our Jack – an excellent example of ridiculous over-packaging, considering what's inside.'

'Yes, perhaps,' said Cat, still stony-faced.

'So go on, darling, put it in your bag. You could keep your buttons in it, couldn't you, or perhaps your earrings?'

'I don't want it, Fanny,' Cat insisted as she pushed her sushi box aside. 'What are you going to do about the money?'

'What money, darling heart?'

'The money you said I owed you when I broke it off with Jack.'

'Oh, forget it, sweetheart,' Fanny said. 'You don't owe me a thing.'

'I'm sorry?' Cat stared, open-mouthed. 'What did you say?'

'I think you heard me, angel.'

'But all this time I've worried and I've wondered and I've tossed and turned at night!' Cat jumped up and glared at Fanny, outraged. Caspar looked alarmed as well. 'You told me I'd signed a binding contract! You said I had agreed—'

'Cat, my love, stop hyperventilating.' Fanny stroked her greyhound's sleek, dark head and calmed him down again. 'Put yourself in my place for a moment. I was just a little bit annoyed with you and lovely Jack. I couldn't have you thinking it was perfectly okay to say you'd graciously accept the prize, but then five minutes later to say you'd changed your minds, and I'd just have to go along with it.'

'Fan, it wasn't like that at all, you damn well know it wasn't! You had me lying awake and fretting, thinking I would have to borrow money from a loan shark, at a huge rate of interest—'

'Darling, if you'd used your common sense and gone to a solicitor, he'd have charged you fifty quid and told you not to worry.'

'What?'

'Cat, I probably couldn't have touched you for a single penny, even if I'd been inclined to try. My time is precious, angel. It simply wouldn't have been worth my while.'

'So you played with me. You made me worry that I'd be in debt forever.' Cat slumped down into her chair again. 'Fanny, that was mean of you,' she said reproachfully.

'Yes – perhaps a teeny tiny bit.' Fanny had the grace

to look ashamed – for half a second, anyway. 'I'm sorry, sweetheart.'

'How much money did you lose?'

'Oh, I didn't spend a penny piece.'

'But Fan, you told me – what about that first time?'

'What do you mean, my angel?'

'When we went to Dorset and you showed me round and Rick took all those photographs?'

'I sold them to an agency, of course,' said Fanny, smiling sweetly. 'When someone googles images for pretty blonde and English country house, you ought to come up first.'

'Oh,' said Cat, then realised she was not at all surprised.

'But that's enough of talking about tedious little you,' continued Fanny merrily. 'Now I've got my runners-up in training, and I think they'll soon be sorted out. My flower, I must admit that I don't find them as attractive as you and lovely Jack. But, all things considered, they're turning out quite well.'

'Who are they, then?' asked Cat.

'Tony Smith and Brenda something unpronounceable. I think it must be Polish. Or Latvian, perhaps? Lots of consonants jammed up together, anyway.' Fanny Gregory sighed. 'Tone and Bren they call each other. Ghastly, isn't it? When we do the promotion, I think I'm going to call them Ant and Bee.'

'What are they like?'

'They're very sweet, my angel, but they're desperately dull. She works in a beauty salon in some boring suburb of – I think she said Northampton. Something hampton, anyway. She waxes women's whatsits all day long. I can't imagine anything more tedious and depressing. Tone's involved with sewers or drains, I can't remember which, but it's something sordid to do with pipes and smells.

'Cat, it's such a shame that you and Jackie-boy fell out.

You made a gorgeous couple. If you could have managed to get on for just a few more months – well, you would have been so perfect for the magazines.'

'We'd have been divorced within a year.'

'Oh, quite probably,' said Fanny, nodding. 'But you'd have had the loveliest of weddings, and I'd have made a mint.'

'Fan, how did you know about me and Adam?' Cat enquired casually.

'You and Adam, darling?'

'Fanny, please stop messing me about?'

'Honestly, my angel, I don't know what you mean. But it was obvious he liked you. I saw the way he looked at you when we met by accident in Dorset. When he came to Surrey to quote me for a little bit of work he might do on my barn – the stables round the back need sorting out, and sorting stables is his special subject, after all – I got him opening up.'

'You asked him about me?'

'It wasn't very difficult to get him to admit that if you weren't engaged he might be tempted. I can be very persuasive, as you know. You seemed so upset about your breaking up with Jack, and I thought you needed cheering up. But darling, are you saying there was something going on already?'

'You don't know we went to Italy?'

'No – I thought you said you went alone?' Then Fanny's sharp, blue eyes began to glitter, like they did when she was on to something, or she thought she might be. 'Come on, darling – tell?'

So Cat explained.

'Oh, I see,' said Fanny acidly. 'Well, you're a dark one, aren't you?'

'You really, truly didn't know?'

'My darling, how on earth could I have known?'

'You know everything,' said Cat.

'Well, perhaps I had a little inkling.' Fanny smiled her smuggest smile. 'I'm quite good at inklings. Anyway, my sweet, I need to see some other people now. You must get back to Adam.'

'Yes, I'm meeting him in half an hour,' said Cat, pushing back her chair and standing up.

'Before you go,' said Fanny, 'Rosie's had an offer of a PR job in Paris for a year. She says she'd like to take it. I can't blame the darling girl. She'll have such fun in France and she already speaks the language. Then, when her sister finishes at Oxford, they want to start a PR and promotions business of their own.'

'Yes, she mentioned that to me,' said Cat.

'Oh, did she really?' Fanny smiled a steely little smile. 'I'm going to have to watch my back with Rosie, I can see. She'll be after all my smaller clients, and she can't have the lot. So, anyway—'

'You'll want somebody else to boss around?'

'I'll need a new assistant, certainly. Angel, I was wondering if you'd like to work for me? It's forty thousand basic, lots of tips and bonuses and freebies and sweeteners and samples – adds up to quite a package, all in all.'

'No,' said Cat.

'At least consider it?'

'I don't need to consider it.'

'What if we said forty-five and private health insurance?'

'Fanny, I could never work with you,' said Cat, refusing to allow herself to realise this was twice what Barry paid and was probably more than Adam earned. She hadn't thought to ask what her new job with him would pay. 'I'd sooner sweep the streets.'

'I wondered if you might say that, my angel, but I thought I'd ask you, anyway.' Fanny stood up too and held out one red-taloned hand. 'I hope we can be friends?'

Cat stared for a moment, but then she started laughing, thinking that for sheer effrontery and blatant chutzpah Fanny Gregory could have no equal. She pitied Jack, but told herself it also served him right. So she shook Fanny's hand.

'We're friends,' she said.

'Excellent,' said Fanny. 'So I'll be in touch about the work.'

'What work?' demanded Cat. 'Fanny, I've already told you I could never work with you.'

'But you're going to change your mind, my angel.' Fanny allowed herself a little chuckle. 'People always do. You and darling Adam – let me help you make some serious money?'

'Fanny, I don't want anything to do with you and money.'

'We'll see, my love, we'll see.'

'Fanny says she didn't know that we met up in Italy,' said Cat, when she joined Adam later in a Starbucks close to Fanny's office.

'Why should she have known about us meeting up in Italy?'

'She's a witch, she's psychic, she knows everything,' said Cat. 'If she didn't know about us going to Italy, and if she didn't know we'd had a row, why did she invite you to her party? Why was she so keen to try to get you off with me?'

'She invited me because I'd sourced some garden stuff and it was her way of saying thank you. I expect you were some sort of present, Cat, gift-wrapped in a Lulu Minto frock.'

'Yeah, right.'

'Oh, and because she thinks I'm the most gorgeous, sexiest man she's ever met – she told me so herself.'

'She must need contacts, then.'

'Yes,' said Adam, laughing. 'Yes, she must.'

'That's not all she needs.'

Then Cat told Adam everything, and he frowned and muttered, and finally he said he thought what Fanny bloody Gregory needed most was locking up.

'You can't lock up our fairy godmother,' objected Cat.

'She's not our fairy godmother,' growled Adam. 'As you said, the woman is a witch. But listen, when she said you owed her money, why didn't you ask how much?'

'I did,' said Cat. 'I tried to make her tell me. But she said she didn't have the paperwork to hand. Then, when I said I had no money anyway, she said I'd have to work, and—listen, Adam, I know I should have gone to a solicitor. I wasn't thinking straight. There was lots of other rubbish cluttering up my life. Jack and—'

'Me,' said Adam. 'I'm so sorry, Cat. That night we came home from Italy – if only we'd gone back to yours, not mine.'

'I should have listened to you properly, not got all angry, all upset. I ought to have believed you, not stormed off in a huff.'

'In your place, I'd have stormed off, too,' said Adam.

'But you don't seem the storming kind,' said Cat. 'You're always so composed, so calm.'

'Oh, I can storm,' said Adam. 'Or do things I never meant to do and wouldn't have done if I'd been thinking straight.'

'You mean like telling Mr Portland you wouldn't work for him?'

'No, as time goes by I realise it was a godsend, dumping him. He and that wife of his – between them, they'd have driven me mad.'

'We can't have you going mad, it isn't in the schedule.'

'You're absolutely right.'

Cat looked at him and was reminded of Mr Rochester and Mr Darcy and Mr Jackson Brodie all blended into one.

She thought it must be time to get his shirt off.

'Adam, let's go back to mine,' she said.

'We messed up big time, didn't we?' said Cat, as she and Adam lay in bed together in her flat. 'I mean, before we met each other, before we got it right?'

'We did,' said Adam. 'I thought I knew Maddy through and through, but I didn't know anything at all. I had this image in my mind, of Maddy in some country cottage, making jam and growing vegetables and keeping chickens, going on family holidays in Tuscany with half a dozen children. But the woman in the country cottage wasn't Maddy, and it was never going to be like that.'

'I was on a mission to rescue Jack,' said Cat, and sighed. 'He always said he didn't have a family, that he'd never had a real home. So I decided I would give him both. Of course, he always was a dreamer, fantasist and liar. I didn't know the real Jack. I only knew a phantom. I knew the tortured genius I'd created for myself.'

'He's history now,' said Adam. 'What about the future, you and me?'

'The future, that's a big and rather terrifying prospect.' Cat looked hard at Adam. 'I didn't know Jack at all. Do I know you?'

'I think you know too much,' said Adam, laughing. 'You know about my moodiness, my awkwardness, my total inability to learn a foreign language—'

'Your kindness, generosity, honesty—'

'Stop it, Cat, I'm blushing, and it doesn't suit me. But anyway, you wanted to get married. You dreamed about it, planned it. I'm offering you the chance to live your dream.'

'You're asking me to marry you – again?'

'It seems a shame to waste a wedding opportunity and deny our mothers their chance to wear some really horrid hats.'

'Well, if you feel we should.'

'So that's a yes?'

'I think it must be,' Cat replied.

'I hear that note of hesitancy in your voice again. It's always there when I ask you to marry me.'

'Well, obviously there are terms, conditions.'

'What are they?'

'We have to get married at the Melbury Court Hotel.'

'Where else would we get married?'

'You agree?'

'Of course I do,' said Adam.

'We'll have to tell her ladyship, you know.'

'You mean Fanny Gregory, I suppose,' said Adam, shrugging. 'Why do we have to tell her anything? She'll only interfere.'

'If we don't let her know, and do it now, she'll very soon find out.'

'How will she do that?'

'She'll get out her cauldron, drop in bits of frog and newt, brew up a magic spell.'

'Magic, huh,' said Adam. 'I wouldn't put it past the bloody woman to have had us bugged. Perhaps we'd better get new mobiles? You ought to check the lining in your bag.'

'Yes, perhaps I should. God, I'm so tired,' Cat said, yawning. 'It must be all that partying.'

'The private party isn't over yet,' said Adam, turning out the light.

Tuesday, 5 July

Do we let her interfere?

When Cat told Fanny she and Adam were going to get married, she said they had to come into her office straight away.

When they called in that evening, she told them she'd decided she didn't want Ant and Bee to do a thing for the promotion, except of course the getting married bit.

'You're so much more attractive, much more charismatic, darlings,' she said wistfully. 'If you'd do a tiny little bit of work for me in lead-up to your wedding, I could make it really worth your while. I'm assuming it will be just months?' she added, frowning. 'You're not thinking of a long engagement stretching into years?'

'No, we're not,' said Cat. 'But those two other people, won't they want to do promotions, and won't they want to be in magazines?'

'I'll think of things for Ant and Bee to do to keep the sponsors sweet,' said Fanny. 'You don't need to worry about them.'

She went on to explain that Cat and Adam's schtick would be two lovely, smart but ordinary people – I'm so sorry, darlings, but you're very ordinary, you know – getting married on a shoestring in these very difficult, recession-burdened times.

'*Amor vincit omnia* and all that jazz,' she added, tapping like a woodpecker with OCD, already busy roughing out their schedule.

'God, more stuff from sundials,' muttered Cat.

'I beg your pardon, angel?'

'I dare say that was Latin, wasn't it? You and Adam here,

275

you're such a pair of intellectuals. He's always quoting Latin at me, too. What does that bit mean?'

'Love conquers everything,' said Fanny airily. 'Didn't you go to school at all, my princess?'

'Yes, but I didn't learn any Latin. I did Business Studies and IT, which are very much more useful in the modern world.'

'On the contrary, my love, you can't get anywhere in life without A-level Latin. I'm living proof of it.'

'You might have a point,' conceded Cat.

'Of course I do. So – are you going to help me out, my angels? Listen, I'm going to get you on the telly. You'll be famous, you'll be huge on YouTube, a thousand hits a minute, and I'll share the advertising revenue with you.'

'What percentage?' Adam asked.

'Eighty–twenty, in my favour, obviously,' Fanny told him, as she twinkled at him merrily.

'Come on, Cat, we're leaving.'

'Just hang on a moment, sweetheart. Let me have a little think. Shall we say sixty–forty?'

'Fifty–fifty.'

'Fifty-five to forty-five,' said Fanny.

'Yes, all right,' said Cat.

'Adam, darling?' wheedled Fanny.

'I suppose so.'

'Excellent,' said Fanny, and once again she smiled her vixen's smile.

'But there'll be no formal contracts tying us to Supadoop,' said Adam. 'We're not signing anything that isn't in our favour.'

'Of course you're not,' said Fanny. 'This will be an equal partnership, and anyway I trust you absolutely. Cat, will you be able to get some time off work at Microsoft?'

'Barry will probably let me work part time while this is going on.' Cat crossed her fingers, hoping Barry might.

She'd have to tell him that she would be leaving to go and work with Adam, anyway. So if he got another office manager fairly soon, perhaps the two of them could work in tandem, Cat training up the newbie and the newbie taking over while Cat was busy doing stuff for Fanny?

Yes, it should all work out.

Here, there and everywhere, will it ever stop?

Fanny milked every cash cow dry, exploited every opportunity. She made them keep a video diary which she flogged to cable. She had them blogging, Facebooking and Tweeting dawn to dusk.

Although she had accepted they ought to keep their day jobs – it makes you seem more real, my angels, shows that you're a-man-and-woman-of-the-people, it's the Susan Boyle effect – she still sent them travelling miles and miles around the country to be interviewed by local radio stations, local newspapers and to pose for photographs for regional and national magazines.

People came to stare at them because they were that couple off the telly. Phones and cameras clicked, and cyber-images of Cat and Adam sprang up everywhere, like cyber-mushrooms, overnight.

Who would design Cat's wedding dress? Fanny ran a competition in a magazine. Of course, it had an entry fee. She wasn't doing this for nothing, darlings. She had overheads.

Much to Cat's astonishment, eight thousand people entered, sending in a sketch or jpeg of the perfect gown. 'When you were a little girl, didn't you love drawing brides?' asked Fanny as she and Cat and Rosie sat sorting through the entries, many of which looked like they were the work of five-year-olds.

Fanny had been schmoozing with a host of possible designers, mostly young and hungry ones, but Lulu Minto loved one sketch enough to make the gown. Cat found she loved it too, and agreed the sketcher must be invited to the wedding. 'So everybody wins,' said Fanny smugly, sweeping a great pile of cheques into a dark green Harrods carrier bag.

'Especially you,' said Rosie as she picked up the bag.

'Well, of course,' said Fanny. 'Especially lovely me. Get those to the bank today, my darling. Cat, you're the sort of person who mixes with the common herd, so tell me, why do people still use cheques when God has given us Paypal?'

She got them an audition for a television commercial advertising laxatives, which meant they would be dressing up as constipated monkeys, man and wife, and which she said would be a lot of fun, and tremendous tie-in for their wedding, if they could square it with those spoilsports from the actors' union who wanted real performers to play any speaking parts.

But Adam put his foot down. 'I'm not having anything to do with it,' he said. 'I'm not a chimpanzee or a baboon.'

Fanny darlinged him and angeled him, but even she had realised when he meant it, when his dark eyes narrowed, flashing warning fire.

Cat was both astonished and amazed to find that anybody could refuse to do what Fanny wanted and not be blasted by a thunderbolt.

The only dampers on her happiness were Adam's absences on projects up and down the country. She couldn't shake the feeling that each time he went he might decide he wasn't coming back.

'Of course I'm coming back,' he said, when he finally got her to admit she was afraid the pressure would begin to get to him, that he'd do a Jack and disappear.

'Where are you going this week?'

'Wolverhampton, Middlesex and Dorset.'

'Melbury Court, you mean?' she asked. 'You're still working on the stables, are you?'

'Yes, that's right.' Adam found some photographs and got them up on screen. 'Look, here's the sauna and the plunge pool and a couple of the treatment rooms.'

'Scroll back a bit,' said Cat. 'Oh – isn't that the fountain? Why is everything wrapped up in sacking and blue plastic?'

'That's to protect its pipe work from the elements while we're trying to get its rubbish plumbing sorted out.'

So Cat relaxed a bit, because when Adam went away at least he kept his phone on all the time, and he called home often.

Their reunions were wonderful – and partly filmed, of course. Carrying their camcorders around became an automatic reflex, and Fanny was delighted with the footage they produced.

She said they'd have some lovely moments they could show their children. That sequence where they had a fight with shaving foam, when they'd squirted it all round the bathroom – darlings, so hilarious, Fanny told them. 'I laughed until I cried,' she said. 'It's already had a couple of thousand hits on YouTube, and the advertising revenue is pouring in. You're a pair of naturals, Cat and Adam. You've missed your vocations as a double act of circus clowns.'

'When all this is over, that bloody camera's going in the landfill,' muttered Adam, who hadn't even known the bloody camera was recording. Cat had put it on the bathroom windowsill, and she'd accidentally left it running. She'd handed in the footage without checking.

So Adam saw himself on television streaked from head to foot with shaving foam, and his friends went on and on about it, having a laugh at his expense for weeks and weeks and weeks.

Adam's friends – Cat found she liked them all, almost as much as she liked him. Jules and Gwennie turned out to be lovely. A heavy but attractive man of Adam's age and a dark-haired girl, when they met Cat they gave her a big hug and said they were delighted that Adam had at last found somebody to take him off their hands.

'We're so looking forward to the wedding,' Gwennie told them when they met up for dinner at a restaurant in town.

'I'd love to be a bridesmaid,' added Jules, and then he glared at Adam, mock-offended. 'Lawley, don't you look at me like that! I'll get my hair done, and I promise to shave my legs.'

'Sorry, all the bridesmaids must be girls,' said Adam firmly.

'I play the piano,' Gwennie told Cat later in the evening, when they'd had a lot to drink and were feeling like they'd known each other all their lives. 'I've been taking some refresher lessons recently. I'd love to play for you. As you're coming in, I mean, and going out again.'

'Thank you, Gwennie,' Cat replied. 'That would be really kind.'

Cat had never known a man could be so good at presents.

Lovely things and silly things, unusual things, all tiny but desirable, found their way into her washbag, handbag, got underneath her pillow, were slipped into the pockets of her coats.

A Japanese ivory netsuke of a little bride and bridegroom, a Victorian silver locket to go on her silver chain, and of course a ring, a band of gold with amethysts, carnelians, tourmalines – she didn't know where he'd got it, and of course he wouldn't say, but she was sure it had to be unique.

Adam often had to go to Melbury Court to check up on the progress of the work for which he'd been commissioned, the rebuilding and conversion of the Georgian stables.

Cat always asked about the fountain in the forecourt – was he doing any work on it right now, and did he think she'd ever see it play?

'It's a major project,' Adam said. 'We're gradually sorting out the plumbing, but it will take months – or maybe even years – of restoration before we can try it out again. It'll also be quite difficult to find exactly the right shade of marble to replace the bits that have been lost.'

'One day, maybe, Adam?' Cat asked him wistfully.

'Maybe,' Adam said. 'On our golden wedding anniversary, perhaps, when you and I have lost our marbles, too.'

Saturday, 12 November

Happy ever after?

It could not have been a lovelier day.

The last few golden, russet, purple leaves were falling softly from the trees. The sky was a deep, fathomless cerulean. The sun was almost hot. Melbury Court itself looked glorious, an enchanted castle in a children's fairy tale.

After an early morning frost, the air was crisp and energising, and the ground was steaming as the autumn sun beat down.

At noon, thought Adam, it should be more than warm enough for photographs outside. The wedding was being filmed, of course, for the final episode of the television series. But he wanted all the aunts and uncles to get their snaps as well.

Gwennie's phone was working overtime. She was frantically tweeting all her movie star-struck mates.

I'm in Daisy Denham's lovely house!
I've had a tinkle in her bathroom!
I'm in her garden and I'm walking in her honeysuckle bower!
I've seen the studio pix of her and Ewan Fraser – wow – totally last word in gorge and glam!
I've died and gone to heaven!

Adam hoped she wouldn't try to steal a souvenir, but was afraid she might, if she could prise a little something small and inconspicuous loose and slip it in her clutch.

He got quite anxious when he saw her sidle slowly up the Grinling Gibbons staircase. He was terrified she'd try to break a bit of carving off and get them all arrested or at least thrown out.

'Damn, forgot the cuffs,' said Jules, grinning like a gargoyle as he read Adam's mind.

'She's late,' said Gwennie, fussing with Adam's tie again and clucking like an anxious mother hen who's lost one of her chicks.

'No, she's not,' said Jules, whose hired trousers were that bit too tight and who was tugging crossly at his crotch. In the course of helping Adam celebrate his last weekend of freedom – a weekend which spilled over into the following week and made for perfect daytime television – he'd put on lots of weight. 'Anyway, she can't be late, you muppet, not when she's already here. Omigod, look out, here's Grendel's mother, and she's bearing down on you.'

Adam turned and there were Fanny and her greyhound stalking through the crowd of wedding guests, Fanny being charming as she parted wives from husbands, being beyond gracious as she waited for a couple in her way to realise this and stand aside.

She smiled and nodded, her antennae picking up a mass of fascinating signals, sharp ears listening hard, blue eyes darting here and there – looking for her next exciting project, probably.

One thing was certain – she wouldn't miss a thing.

'Hello, Fanny.' Adam bent to kiss her on the cheek. 'You and Caspar look – what can I say – astonishing.'

'Thank you, darling, so we should. It's all Balenciaga, even Caspar's collar. You don't look too bad yourself, considering your clothes are hired.' She flicked a piece of non-existent lint off Adam's shoulder. 'Your lovely little bride's a lucky girl.'

'When did you last see Cat?'

'Only a minute or two ago, so don't you fret, my angel, she hasn't run away. Rosie's lacing her into her gown – I must say Lulu has excelled herself – and Tex and Bess are busy doing something with her veil. She would insist on having real white roses in her hair, instead of a tiara, but the roses haven't been wired, and so we had to ask the hotel housekeeper for pins.'

'It's Bex and Tess,' said Adam.

'Whatever.' Fanny waved one white, bejewelled hand. 'The bridesmaids are in green, you know. I wouldn't have chosen green for bridesmaids. I think green's unlucky. But in a way it suits them, I suppose. They look like fairies in a forest glade.'

Bex shook out the wedding veil and Tess fixed it on Cat's head.

'I can't believe we're here at last,' said Cat, as she gazed into the huge gilt mirror which adorned the bridal suite.

'Yeah, it's been a long, hard slog,' said Tess.

'She certainly made sure that you and Adam earned your money,' added Rosie.

'You two must feel like you've run a marathon,' said Bex.

'More like half a dozen of them,' said Cat, because the past few months had been a nightmare of fatigue, confusion and bewilderment while they'd done promotion stuff for Fanny, earning the deposit on a house and trying to do their real jobs as well. It had been exhausting, and Cat knew she would never criticise a hunted, harassed, put-upon celebrity again.

She couldn't wait to have her real life back.

It had taken Bex and Tess a while to come to terms with all the luxury and splendour of the Melbury Court Hotel.

On the night they'd first arrived, they'd both run round

it squealing like a couple of excited piglets, exploring and exclaiming and experimenting, anxious to leave nothing out.

They were both delighted by the hotel's harem-style health club, which came complete with houris in white tunics, ready to do their bidding, and grant their every health and beauty wish.

But there were no eunuchs. It was health and safety, Cat supposed – no one was prepared to risk the dangerous operation just to get an industry award.

They booked themselves a range of treatments, and by the actual wedding day all three of them had been so waxed and groomed, so peeled and buffed, so tanned and glossed that they looked like goddesses, my loves, as Fanny Gregory put it when she saw them, but with a sarcastic little twinkle in her eyes.

When she had arrived at Melbury Court, Cat had been sad to see the marble fountain in the forecourt was still swathed in sacking and blue plastic and girded with a mile or two of tape.

But the house itself was perfect and the health club was fantastic.

The housekeeper and staff were warm and welcoming and couldn't do enough for them.

The food was wonderful.

She was content.

'She's coming,' someone whispered.

'God, she looks ace – fantastic,' murmured Jules, who'd sneaked a glance behind him. 'Mate, you're a lucky man.'

'I know,' said Adam, thinking with a little shudder how he'd nearly blown it, how his male ineptitude had almost lost him Cat, who he knew he loved more than his life – who made his life complete.

It was very strange how fate and destiny worked out, how

people you'd have crossed a continent – or at least a country – to avoid were the ones who made your dreams come true.

If it hadn't been for Fanny Gregory, who he admitted to himself he'd sometimes – no, come on, be honest, make that often – like to strangle, this would not be happening.

As he stood there waiting for his bride, he heard a little chuckle on his right. He knew it must be Fanny. He wondered what she'd planned today, if she was going to conjure up a pumpkin, wave her magic wand and turn the pumpkin into a golden carriage, in which they could go off on honeymoon.

The cable people would love that.

As Cat arrived at Adam's side, he smiled. She saw the pride and happiness in his eyes and almost started crying.

'No, don't you dare, you numpty,' muttered Tess, when she saw Cat's shoulders start to shake. 'You're on television and you'll ruin your mascara.'

The music died away. Amy Winehouse, Lady Gaga, Coldplay wouldn't have been right, thought Cat, as Gwennie finished playing something lovely and romantic on the grand piano and everybody sighed contentedly.

The registrar picked up her book and welcomed everybody to the wedding. The mothers started sniffing and the ceremony began.

Then everything went sort of blurred. Adam and Cat got married. Or Cat was almost sure they did. She couldn't remember making any vows. Rick the boy photographer took a hundred thousand snaps. Tess caught the bride's bouquet, neatly fouling Bex, who lunged for it and missed.

So it all went well, decided Cat, even though she couldn't have told a judge and jury very much about it. Bits came back to her in trailers, flashes, little windows of acute perception followed by great blanks. But the guests and television people had all been filming hard, and she was prepared to bet nothing had been left out.

The mothers wore revolting hats and comfortable shoes and lots of polyester and – as mothers were supposed to do – they sobbed and sobbed and sobbed.

Cat's father looked relieved, and Cat supposed it was because his only daughter hadn't married the scoundrel, after all?

Fanny had got sponsors to cover lots of costs, but he had paid the rest without complaining. Or without too much complaining, even though he'd wondered several times why bridal flowers cost so much. They could have had chrysanthemums from his greenhouse. 'You'd have only had to ask,' he said. 'Mrs Fink next door would have been pleased to bunch them up for you.'

Cat couldn't take her eyes off Adam, couldn't quite believe she'd married such a lovely man. Or that she'd met him by the purest chance. What if she hadn't been in Barry's yard that afternoon? What if she hadn't come to Dorset back in May? What if he hadn't needed any chimneys, spindles?

Fanny had organised the wedding banquet, from the wild mushroom, pecorino and sweet chilli starter to the last artisan and fairly-traded chocolate heart. Cat had to admit she'd done it well. After the final speeches, she had gone to find her fairy godmother, to give her a big hug.

But, as she went to look for Fanny, who she thought was probably the centre of attention among that crowd of husbands, upsetting all their wives, Adam caught her hand and told her Fan would have to wait.

'Come outside,' he whispered.

'But it's dark and cold,' she whispered back.

'You'd better wrap up warm, then.'

'Adam, are we going somewhere?' she asked softly as he

draped the lovely emerald velvet cloak which had been one of Fanny's wedding gifts around her shoulders.

'It's just a little way.'

'But what—'

'Come on,' he added urgently. 'I don't want those television people following us.'

Soon they were in the hotel lobby, and a moment later they were both outside.

'My wedding present to you,' said Adam.

'But where is it?'

Adam glanced behind him and nodded to a man who Cat had noticed lurking in the lobby. She had assumed he was a hotel porter. Why did she need a porter?

She peered into the murk.

When they'd first come outside, the forecourt had been dark as pitch.

But suddenly it was illuminated.

It became as bright as day.

There was an almighty whoosh, and then a thunder of cascading water, as jets and columns of it shot into the air and rained down on the mermaids, gods and goddesses below.

'Oh, Adam, it's amazing!'

Cat gazed enraptured as the fountain played and as the perfectly restored white Venus in its marble heart smiled her wedding blessing down on them.

About the Author

Margaret James was born and brought up in Hereford. She studied English at London University, and has written many short stories, articles and serials for magazines. She is the author of sixteen published novels.

Margaret is a long-standing contributor to *Writing Magazine* for which she writes the Fiction Focus column and an author interview for each issue. She's also a creative writing tutor for the London School of Journalism and wrote two of its distance-learning courses. She is the co-author with Cathie Hartigan of *The Creative Writing Student's Handbook*.

An active member of the Romantic Novelists' Association, she contributed to the 50th anniversary anthology *Loves Me, Loves Me Not*.

For more information on Margaret visit:
www.margaretjamesblog.blogspot.com
www.twitter.com/majanovelist
and www.facebook.com/margaret.james.5268

More Choc Lit

From Margaret James

The Silver Locket

Winner of 2010 Reviewers' Choice Award for Single Titles

If life is cheap, how much is love worth?

It's 1914 and young Rose Courtenay has a decision to make. Please her wealthy parents by marrying the man of their choice – or play her part in the war effort?

The chance to escape proves irresistible and Rose becomes a nurse. Working in France, she meets Lieutenant Alex Denham, a dark figure from her past. He's the last man in the world she'd get involved with – especially now he's married.

But in wartime nothing is as it seems. Alex's marriage is a sham and Rose is the only woman he's ever wanted. As he recovers from his wounds, he sets out to win her trust. His gift of a silver locket is a far cry from the luxuries she's left behind.

What value will she put on his love?

First novel in the trilogy.

Visit www.choc-lit.com for more details including the first two chapters and reviews, or simply scan barcode using your mobile phone QR reader.

The Golden Chain

Can first love last forever?

1931 is the year that changes everything for Daisy Denham. Her family has not long swapped life in India for Dorset, England when she uncovers an old secret.

At the same time, she meets Ewan Fraser – a handsome dreamer who wants nothing more than to entertain the world and for Daisy to play his leading lady.

Ewan offers love and a chance to escape with a touring theatre company. As they grow closer, he gives her a golden chain and Daisy gives him a promise – that she will always keep him in her heart.

But life on tour is not as they'd hoped. Ewan is tempted away by his career and Daisy is dazzled by the older, charismatic figure of Jesse Trent. She breaks Ewan's heart and sets off for a life in London with Jesse.

Only time will tell whether some promises are easier to make than keep …

Second novel in the trilogy.

Visit www.choc-lit.com for more details including the first two chapters and reviews, or simply scan barcode using your mobile phone QR reader.

The Penny Bangle

When should you trust your heart?

It's 1942 when Cassie Taylor reluctantly leaves Birmingham to become a land girl on a farm in Dorset.

There she meets Robert and Stephen Denham, twins recovering from injuries sustained at Dunkirk. Cassie is instantly drawn to Stephen, but is wary of the more complex Robert – who doesn't seem to like Cassie one little bit.

At first, Robert wants to sack the inexperienced city girl. But Cassie soon learns, and Robert comes to admire her courage, finding himself deeply attracted to Cassie. Just as their romance blossoms, he's called back into active service.

Anxious to have adventures herself, Cassie joins the ATS. In Egypt, she meets up with Robert, and they become engaged. However, war separates them again as Robert is sent to Italy and Cassie back to the UK.

Robert is reported missing, presumed dead. Stephen wants to take Robert's place in Cassie's heart. But will Cassie stay true to the memory of her first love, and will Robert come home again?

Third novel in the trilogy.

Visit www.choc-lit.com for more details including the first two chapters and reviews, or simply scan barcode using your mobile phone QR reader.

More from Choc Lit

*If you loved Margaret's story, you'll enjoy
the rest of our selection.
Here's a sample:*

Please don't stop the music

Jane Lovering

***Winner of the 2012 Best
Romantic Comedy Novel
of the year***

***Winner of the 2012 Romantic
Novel of the year***

How much can you hide?

Jemima Hutton is determined
to build a successful new
life and keep her past a dark
secret. Trouble is, her jewellery business looks set to fail – until
enigmatic Ben Davies offers to stock her handmade belt buckles
in his guitar shop and things start looking up, on all fronts.

But Ben has secrets too. When Jemima finds out he used
to be the front man of hugely successful Indie rock band
Willow Down, she wants to know more. Why did he desert
the band on their US tour? Why is he now a semi-recluse?

And the curiosity is mutual – which means that her own
secret is no longer safe …

Visit www.choc-lit.com for more details
including the first two chapters and
reviews, or simply scan barcode using
your mobile phone QR reader.

Never Coming Home

Evonne Wareham

Winner of the Joan Hessayon New Writers' Award

All she has left is hope.

When Kaz Elmore is told her five-year-old daughter Jamie has died in a car crash, she struggles to accept that she'll never see her little girl again. Then a stranger comes into her life offering the most dangerous substance in the world: hope.

Devlin, a security consultant and witness to the terrible accident scene, inadvertently reveals that Kaz's daughter might not have been the girl in the car after all.

What if Jamie is still alive? With no evidence, the police aren't interested, so Devlin and Kaz have little choice but to investigate themselves.

Devlin never gets involved with a client. Never. But the more time he spends with Kaz, the more he desires her – and the more his carefully constructed ice-man persona starts to unravel.

The desperate search for Jamie leads down dangerous paths – to a murderous acquaintance from Devlin's dark past, and all across Europe, to Italy, where deadly secrets await. But as long as Kaz has hope, she can't stop looking …

Visit www.choc-lit.com for more details including the first two chapters and reviews, or simply scan barcode using your mobile phone QR reader.

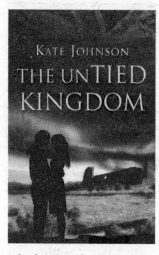

The UnTied Kingdom
Kate Johnson

Shortlisted for the 2012 RoNA Contemporary Romantic Novel Category Award

The portal to an alternate world was the start of all her troubles – or was it?

When Eve Carpenter lands with a splash in the Thames, it's not the London or England she's used to. No one has a telephone or knows what a computer is. England's a third-world country and Princess Di is still alive. But worst of all, everyone thinks Eve's a spy.

Including Major Harker who has his own problems. His sworn enemy is looking for a promotion. The General wants him to undertake some ridiculous mission to capture a computer, which Harker vaguely envisions running wild somewhere in Yorkshire. Turns out the best person to help him is Eve.

She claims to be a popstar. Harker doesn't know what a popstar is, although he suspects it's a fancy foreign word for 'spy'. Eve knows all about computers, and electricity. Eve is dangerous. There's every possibility she's mad.

And Harker is falling in love with her.

Visit www.choc-lit.com for more details including the first two chapters and reviews, or simply scan barcode using your mobile phone QR reader.

CLAIM YOUR FREE EBOOK

of

The Wedding Diary

You may wish to have a choice of how you read *The Wedding Diary*. Perhaps you'd like a digital version for when you're out and about, so that you can read it on your ereader or anywhere that you can access iTunes – your computer, iPhone, iPad or a Smartphone. For a limited period, we're including a **FREE** ebook version along with this paperback.

To claim, simply visit ebooks.choc-lit.com
or scan the QR Code.

You'll need to enter the following code:

Q181302

Introducing Choc Lit

We're an independent publisher creating
a delicious selection of fiction.
Where heroes are like chocolate – irresistible!
Quality stories with a romance at the heart.

Choc Lit novels are selected by genuine readers like yourself.
We only publish stories our Choc Lit Tasting Panel want to
see in print. Our reviews and awards speak for themselves.

Come and support our authors and join them in our
Author's Corner, read their interviews and see their latest
events, reviews and gossip.

Visit: www.choc-lit.com for more details.

Available in paperback and as ebooks from most stores.

We'd also love to hear how you enjoyed *The Wedding
Diary*. Just visit www.choc-lit.com and give your feedback.
Describe Adam in terms of chocolate
and you could win a Choc Lit novel in our
Flavour of the Month competition.

 Follow us on twitter: www.twitter.com/
ChocLituk, or simply scan barcode using
your mobile phone QR reader.